Forever Friends

Forever Friends

SARAH MACKENZIE

FOREVER

New York   Boston

Copyright © 2019 by Hachette Book Group, Inc.

Cover illustration and design by Elizabeth Turner Stokes
Cover copyright © 2019 by Hachette Book Group, Inc.

Forever
Hachette Book Group
1290 Avenue of the Americas, New York, NY 10104
read-forever.com
twitter.com/readforeverpub

First edition: December 2019

Forever is an imprint of Grand Central Publishing. The Forever name and logo are trademarks of Hachette Book Group, Inc.

The publisher is not responsible for websites (or their content) that are not owned by the publisher.

The Hachette Speakers Bureau provides a wide range of authors for speaking events. To find out more, go to www.hachettespeakersbureau.com or call (866) 376-6591.

Library of Congress Control Number: 2019948229

ISBNs: 978-1-5387-5112-1 (trade paperback), 978-1-5387-5109-1 (ebook)

Printed in the United States of America

LSC-C

10   9   8   7   6   5   4   3   2   1

Forever Friends

Chapter One

Sadie Landry sliced a handful of strawberries to stir into her toddler's Greek yogurt cup, absently humming along to the Pop 4 Kids playlist on the iPhone she'd propped against a stack of picture books. As she peeled back the foil top, the scent of sour dairy roiled her stomach, and she lurched with a gag. Good lord, had it gone bad? She checked the expiration date. Two weeks away.

Weird. Since when had the scent of yogurt become so nasty? Lincoln wolfed it down for breakfast every morning and she loved adding it to her strawberry-banana smoothies.

"Mommy! I make the pee-pee!" Lincoln had started stringing sentences together a few weeks ago. His adorable squeak still came as such a surprise that it took an extra second to register that these particular words were the polar opposite of delightful.

She glanced at the "Keep Calm and Carry On" print hanging on the kitchen wall. Was momsanity a diagnosable condition? *Hmmmm.* Something to research during naptime. Right now it was time to refocus on her nearly two-year-old, nearly potty-trained son, tugging at the waistband of her leggings, his hazel eyes a dead ringer for Ethan's, constantly shifting from green to brown to gold.

"Mommy? You hear me right now?"

It'd be great if her husband was here and not down in Boston, two hundred miles away.

She tossed the yogurt in the trash, just in case it *was* rancid. "You made a pee-pee?"

"Yep!" Then he hunched, crestfallen. "But not in potty."

"Oh." *Shit.* She tried channeling her inner Mary Poppins, despite the headache that had been nagging her since she woke up. "Um, well…mistakes allow thinking to happen."

He wrinkled his nose. "What you say?"

"Never mind." So much for staying up last night studying *Communicating Positively with Your Toddler.* The tips that seemed so practical on the page at ten thirty felt ridiculous in practice today.

"Come see. Come see. Dis way." He bolted from the kitchen.

She shoved her iPhone into her demi-cup bra—thank God she was wearing one—and gave chase. *Please not the sofa. Anywhere but the sofa.* While the midcentury loveseat complemented the cottage's nautical theme, it turned out that white wool wasn't exactly a toddler-friendly choice.

Mom fail.

Or maybe it was karma being a bitch. After all, scrolling through her former design firm's Instagram feed a few minutes ago was in clear violation of her New Year's resolution to live more in the present. But after noticing the foyer's dust bunnies had not only colonized, but were enjoying a population explosion under the shoe storage bench, she'd found herself escaping through the personal account of her replacement at Urban Interior Studios.

In hindsight, a mistake in more ways than one. Emma Finley wasn't just leggy and platinum, but she'd also nabbed a coveted design award for a hot new sushi restaurant concept in Providence. And had that been Emma's Seaport townhome with the wrought-iron fireplace and a Jo Malone candle burning in the background? Good grief—how much was the firm paying her? When Sadie had worked for the group, she'd felt fortunate to afford the rent on a poky South Boston studio.

Her lips crooked up at the memory of her old place with its claw-foot tub and creaky floors. Even after a long day, Sadie would always stroll the three blocks down to M Street Beach to read a few chapters on a park bench.

Ethan had asked her to marry him in that apartment, her back pressed against the Formica countertop while he kneeled on the kitchen rug.

She furrowed her brows.

If Ethan had proposed two and a half years ago, that meant she'd been gone from the firm for how long now? Two years?

Yep. Almost to the day.

Just then, her boob buzzed. Tugging her phone back out, Ethan's name appeared on her screen.

"Honey. Hi." Sadie instinctively smoothed a hand over her messy bun. Down the hall, Lincoln hopped from foot to foot, motioning for her to join him. Was it worth telling her husband that his first-floor office might have sprung a leak? A Lincoln-sized leak.

"How'd your meeting go?"

"Mommy! I say come see this silly pee-pee!" Lincoln called. "I still get M&M?"

She'd gobbled the last of the potty-training treats for breakfast. *Oops.*

3

"Sore subject," Ethan groaned. "The meeting was a bust."

Her husband was currently splitting time between his remote home office in Maine and his company's corporate headquarters in Boston. The fall and holidays had gone fine with Ethan only making the trip a handful of times. Unfortunately, with January's arrival came a slew of reasons for Ethan to be on-site. At this point he was traveling to Boston every week, often for days at a time. Not the plan they'd made when deciding to relocate.

"What a bummer. You were so excited about the presentation." Sadie racked her brain, unable to recall exactly what he'd been working on this month. He was a hustler, eternally developing new products for his tech company, his can-do attitude the reason why he'd scrambled up the corporate ladder, impressing managers at every level.

That was, until his recent boss.

"Marlow stood me up."

She could hear the exasperation in his voice and clearly pictured the hand he must be raking through his wavy brown hair. "Turns out the bastard ditched our one-on-one to take a client to Palm Beach on the company jet."

Sadie had a mental flash about being whisked away on a Gulfsteam, sipping a mimosa and nibbling a cheese plate, before blinking back to reality.

"That sucks. But he probably acts like this because he's threatened by your talent."

"You think?" Ethan didn't sound so sure.

"I know." She frowned at her Fitbit watch. Ten fifteen already? Seriously? Where had the morning gone? "Look, it's either that, or he has an asshole gene. His ancestors probably burned witches or took part in the Spanish Inquisition."

Ethan chuckled, and Sadie smiled at the receiver. She hadn't made her husband laugh much lately and the infectious rumble swelled her heart.

Unfortunately, they'd have to reconnect tonight. She still had to uncover Lincoln's pee and hightail him to his two-year checkup that was in fifteen minutes at the Coastal Kids Medical Group.

"Hey, tell you what. Let's pick this back up when you get home," she said in her most soothing tone, just as Lincoln crashed into her knees. "Whoa, bud! Crap, that hurt!"

She yanked her toddler back with a gasp. He'd been out of her sight for what? Three minutes? And in that time, he'd managed to unearth her favorite lipstick and cover his chest in red streaks. He'd even pulled off a Jackson Pollock–inspired art scene over the foyer's creamy damask wallpaper.

That's it. They might as well move to a barn.

"Lincoln, no! Bad! Bad, bad, bad!" Her low-grade headache ratcheted up a notch. "Seriously what the f-f-frog."

Her last-minute save didn't stop her son from bursting into startled sobs.

It wasn't an official f-bomb, but it came close. The last thing she needed was Lincoln roaming the playground while swearing like a sailor.

"No, no. I'm sorry. I didn't mean you are bad. You're a good boy. The best boy ever. But that's Mommy's nice wall. Drawing is for paper. Drawing on a wall is bad."

"Sade? You two okay over there? Is Lincoln hurt?"

"He's fine. We're fine." She engulfed Lincoln in a hug, pressing her cheek to his soft chestnut curls, willing him to calm down.

"Cool. Cool. So I've gotta jet, but remember what my mom says—they call it the terrible twos for a reason, right?"

Sadie tried to laugh. It came out like a donkey's death rattle.

5

"Hey, why don't you give her a call? She'd love to give you some advice."

Oh, wouldn't she?

Sadie would rather cannonball butt naked into the frigid ocean out her bay window than discuss parenting strategies with her mother-in-law. Yes, Annette Landry had raised three healthy, successful adults, and she'd enjoyed doing it, too. No, she had *loved* it. Staying at home was "such a precious gift." Something she "never dared to take for granted."

She probably mopped up potty accidents in her signature twin-set, too, complete with the pearl earrings and perfectly applied mascara.

Sadie, on the other hand, had found her yoga pants and sweat-shirt so comfy yesterday that she'd slept in them…and was still wearing them today.

Underwear included.

A fact that would make Annette's sculpted bob stand on end.

But while Annette might get on her nerves, her mother-in-law had raised the man of her dreams. And that had to count for something.

"Your mother will be here in the morning for Lincoln's party. I'll borrow her ear then." She prayed she sounded halfway chipper. "Drive safe, honey. I'll see you tonight."

They hung up, an absentminded "love you" on both ends.

*   *   *

Fortunately, the misaimed pee-pee had ended up in the bathtub.

Unfortunately, removing the lipstick from a squirming child's torso was going to have to count as her day's cardio. There really should be an energy drink named "Toddler." In the end, she resorted to pouring makeup remover over a hand towel and rubbing it against Lincoln's baby-soft skin.

As for the wallpaper, well…she'd figure that out when she got back home.

Tugging a superhero shirt over his head, she gave both his dimples a noisy smooch that sent him giggling. "Next time you're curious about one of Mommy's things, you need to come and ask my permission to play with it. Okay, bud?"

He nodded shyly. "Kay."

She helped him into his parka before deciding her hoodie could ward off the spring chill just fine. So much for waltzing into the doctor's office with an insulated mug of coffee and perfectly flat-ironed hair. Popping two ibuprofens and smearing on some deodorant would have to count as a win.

As the idyllic, seaside cottages blurred past her minivan window, she tried to practice gratitude. Cranberry Cove wasn't just a postcard-perfect Maine village, but her hometown. When Ethan had bought the Brewer place—formerly her beloved grandma's home—as a surprise wedding gift, she'd blamed her tears on the fact that she was eight and a half months pregnant and busting out of her bridal gown. She knew she was lucky to raise her son in a place right down the block from where she'd grown up and where he could enjoy some of her happiest childhood memories, like collecting seashells and licking butter off her fingertips during summer lobster bakes.

She glanced at Lincoln in the rearview mirror. He had a cardboard book about monkeys propped open in his lap and was examining the pages with such focus, she almost believed he could read the words. Like Ethan, he was an overachiever, already learning his ABCs and counting to twenty. He was cranky if he missed a nap, and certainly a handful at times, but what toddler wasn't? He also gave smiles, giggles, and generous hugs.

And sure, maybe he was a budding graffiti artist (he'd really gone wild with that lipstick) and the root cause of her perpetual exhaustion, but he was also the reason she climbed out of bed each morning. She loved him beyond the power of words.

Was she happy? Grateful? Fulfilled?

Of course.

She was beyond lucky. She had everything a person could ever want.

She nabbed the last spot in the town's municipal parking lot. Okay, she had everything except time. Still, she stole a few more seconds to wipe the sleep crusties from the corners of her eyes and apply a quick coat of Burt's Bees lip gloss. No need to tell the world that her last bath was with a handful of baby wipes.

Where was that woman who used to strut into client meetings wearing four-inch, cherry-red heels and deliver design pitches like it was what she'd been born to do?

Stay-at-home motherhood hadn't just knocked her down a peg; it had dumped her off the stool and doused her in finger paint.

As long as she could remember, she'd dreamed of being a mom. She'd fantasized about cute names, nursery decor, and tiny outfits. She'd dreamed about how the baby's hair would smell after a bath or how they would cling to her pinkie finger while napping on her chest.

Turned out that she'd fallen in love with a Pottery Barn version of parenthood.

The reality was that her pelvic floor had been destroyed by a thirty-six-hour labor of a nine-pound-ten-ounce baby, postpartum depression had hit her like a Mack truck, and she still tinkled when she sneezed. She'd been puked on, pooped on, and every night when her head hit the pillow she'd wonder how the heck she'd crossed only a few to-do items off her list.

Parenting wasn't just work—that she could handle—it was how it was a mirror reflecting all her shortcomings: impatience, selfishness, vanity, and anxiety.

But she'd turn this ship around. She *had* to. Failure wasn't an option. So she straightened her slouch and pasted on a determined smile, ignoring the part of her that screamed, "I don't know what the hell I'm doing and the idea of screwing up terrifies me."

"Okay, lady, get it together."

Who'd gotten accepted into the New York School of Design? Who'd been a successful professional? This was just wrangling one kid—not rocket science, for Pete's sake. Mothers have mothered for millennia. She'd done her fair share of babysitting as a teen. Time to quit worrying and get it together.

"Whaddya say to hitting the 'restart' button?" she said to Lincoln, unclipping him from his car seat. He relaxed in her arms and she touched the tip of her nose to his, relieved he didn't seem scarred from her earlier freak-out. "Onward and upward, right, love bug?"

Propping Lincoln on her hip, she made her way toward the Coastal Kids Medical Group.

Until Dot Turner stepped into her path after a scant ten feet.

"Sadie, darlin'. How's it going?" she drawled in her thick Maine accent, punctuating each word with a thrust of her five-pound hand weights. Dot was in her seventies now and had been Sadie's middle-school gym teacher. She still wore her signature neon-pink tracksuit and was probably in even better shape than she'd been fifteen years ago. "Heya, Link."

Sadie hid her wince. The nickname always made her think of

breakfast sausage. And just now the idea of processed meat made her want to barf.

"Hi, Ms. Turner." Sadie smiled weakly, pretending that her stomach hadn't just randomly decided to exit through her mouth. Had she undercooked the chicken last night? "I know, I know…I should call you Dot. But old habits die hard. How are you?" Running into old teachers was one of the weird but enjoyable side effects of moving back to Cranberry Cove.

"I'm grand," Dot panted. "Just grand. Training to solo hike the Appalachian Trail this June. Ain't that something?"

"Wow," Sadie said breathlessly. "Impressive."

"Ayuh, another one for the bucket list. Say, you should join me for a jog sometime." Dot winked. "Everyone with a pulse should be able to run three miles. Use it or lose it, kiddo."

Sadie gaped—Dot wasn't insinuating that she was overweight, was she? Sadie had worked hard to shed the baby weight, although she'd slacked in the last few months. She needed twenty-eight hours in a day to fit in all her jobs: nurse, short-order cook, playmate, teacher, housekeeper, babysitter.

Who knows where the hours went. It was like living life stuck on fast-forward.

"Okay, gotta go, kiddo." Dot forever called her students "kiddo." "Need to keep the old ticker over one twenty! See ya around."

Sadie sucked in her stomach and continued her walk. Wave caps broke in the distance and the air had a salty tang. Lincoln closed his eyes and smiled, the breeze tickling his cheeks.

Just as they passed the Cranberry Cove Bank with its emerald-green shutters and orange brick, a police cruiser rolled to a stop.

"Morning, Sadie. Lincoln." Officer Tyler Cox tipped his hat like a movie star from an old western movie. He looked like one, too, with his eternal five-o'clock shadow and whiskey-colored eyes. "You two holding up okay?"

Everyone knew Ethan commuted and the citizens of Cranberry Cove, especially the town's small-but-mighty police force, were constantly checking in on Sadie as if they knew she was barely treading water.

"We are, thanks." *Fake it until you make it.*

"I pee-pee!" Lincoln announced. "I make the silly pee-pee go in the tub!"

Sadie wrinkled her nose. "Not our preferred location obviously, but we'll take what we can get."

"You?" Lincoln pointed to Tyler. "You make the pee-pee, too?"

Tyler cleared his throat and Sadie was willing to bet that her cheeks matched the Lobster Shack sign swinging over her head. "Okay then. Well, on that note, we're really running late to see Dr. Hanlon. See you around."

At this rate, they were going to be twenty minutes past their appointment time. It would take a miracle for Dr. Hanlon to still see them, but rescheduling would be yet another item on her ever-growing to-do list.

She only made it a few more steps before another interruption.

"Where's the fire?" Essie Park called from a bistro table in front of Morning Joe's Coffee Shop, the *Cove Herald* opened next to her delicious-looking latte. Even though Essie was forty-something, she looked a decade younger with her light peach skin, jet-black hair, and chocolate-brown eyes. While the town's number-one real estate agent always attributed her good looks to her Korean genes, Sadie couldn't help but wonder if Botox played a helping hand.

"Can't chat." Sadie refused to stop a third time. "We're so freaking late."

"Well don't slow down my account. I only wanted to pass along the latest bit of real estate news—the Old Red Mill finally sold. Isn't that something?"

"For sure!" *Why in the world would that interest me?* The question vanished as she *finally* barged through the front door of the Coastal Kids Medical Group. The walls were a calming shade of marine blue, and a saltwater fish tank lined an entire wall. Two children were standing in front of it, their breath fogging the glass while they inspected the clown fish and anemones.

As usual, Renee Rhodes was perched at the reception desk in her high-backed ergonomic chair and she smiled brightly in greeting.

"Hey, neighbor." Sadie straightened her posture. "I know being fashionably late doesn't apply to doctor visits, but it's been a morning. Is there any chance we can still be seen?"

Her next-door neighbor, Renee, would never be late to an appointment. Sadie used to babysit her daughter, Tansy, and she'd always arrived to an impeccably clean home that smelled of peonies and fresh-baked snickerdoodles. Renee would leave something delicious for dinner and have checked out the latest cartoon from the library for the girls to watch. The perfect mother. The kind of "together" woman Sadie had always imagined that she'd be

"It's late," Renee admitted, after a glance at the clock. "But don't worry, I'm sure Dr. Hanlon can squeeze you—"

Before Renee could finish her sentence, another wave of nausea hit. This one meant serious business.

"I'm sorry, can you take him for a sec? Please?" Sadie shoved Lincoln at Renee, bolting to the restroom.

Before the door latched shut, she fell to her knees, vomited into the toilet, then slumped against the tile wall. Pressing a clammy, cold hand against her forehead, she gasped. "Stupid chicken thighs."

It was last night's chicken, right? Yes, of course. It had to be. Because the alternative was simply too terrifying.

Chapter Two

"Can you spy the orange-and-white fishy?" Renee Rhodes asked Lincoln, pointing to the saltwater tank. "You have to look hard because he swims fast!"

The toddler nodded, fixing his gaze on the clown fish with nose-scrunched determination.

"Great! Now see if you can spot the crab."

He clapped his hands and wiggled his little butt.

God, kids were so sweet at this age.

After ensuring Lincoln was hypnotized by the underwater world, Renee made her way to the watercooler to fetch his poor mama a drink. Sadie looked rotten, her freckled cheeks sallow and dark circles bruising the skin beneath her eyes. A far cry from the perky babysitter who would bring her daughter *Baby-Sitters Club* books and Popsicle-stick craft projects.

She smiled as she held the glass under the tap. For nearly eighteen years, Renee's calendar had been scribbled with bake sale reminders, PTA meeting times, and school performance dates. Her nights had been spent sneaking veggies into sauces, helping

Tansy with homework assignments, and reading *In the Night Kitchen* a hundred times.

Some might find it boring, but she had loved every second.

Sadie was just starting that journey; a notion Renee sheepishly admitted made her a little green with envy.

The Landrys had bought the one-hundred-year-old cottage next to her two years ago, when the Brewers relocated to North Carolina. Prior to the Brewers, Sadie's grandparents had lived in the home. While the Brewers had been great neighbors, Renee loved the fact that the cottage was back with the original family.

Before moving in, Sadie had had the house renovated. And, as an interior designer, she'd done an exceptional job. From the refinished hardwood floors to the recycled glass kitchen countertops and curated New England artwork, the Landrys' cottage looked like something out of the pages of a home design magazine.

And in addition to their gorgeous home, they had the best gift of all: little Lincoln, so curious and sweet. The early years weren't easy, of course, but the happy memories eventually won out: watching your child take their first steps on the beach or getting a lick of ice cream.

Her gaze strayed to the framed photo of Tansy on her desk. It was from her graduation last June. Her smile was big (and straight, thanks to a small fortune spent on braces) but her eyes were narrowed, the sun shining in her face. Her yellow National Honors Society cords hung around her neck and Renee's mother's diamond studs glinted from her ears.

My beautiful, smart girl.

Tansy was a freshman at the University of Southern California, worlds away from their little New England town.

"I'm telling you, Mom, I love it here," she'd declared only two weeks into the term, a time when most students struggle with the first pangs of homesickness. "I never want to leave. It's like I was always meant to be in SoCal."

"Yeah? That must feel so...exciting," Renee had said, trying to force a smile into her voice. "I guess California *is* the perfect place for the next Nora Ephron."

"Uh-huh. Sure, Mom." Tansy had sounded strangely self-conscious at the comment.

"What?" The two of them had swooned over Nora Ephron films for years, gushing over favorites like *When Harry Met Sally*. Tansy was an aspiring screenwriter, and they loved to dream she would be the next queen of romantic comedies.

Tansy sighed. "I've gotta run to class. Chat tomorrow?"

Except they never did. Not the next day, or the day after that. It was left to Renee to reach out and more often than not, her calls were sent to voicemail. Texting had become Tansy's preferred method of communication and Renee was eternally trying to decipher the subtext of animated gifs.

Sadie stumbled out of the bathroom and Lincoln ran toward her, nestling his head against her thighs as if he couldn't get close enough.

"Here you go." Renee handed her the glass. "Sip this. It should help."

"Thanks." Sadie's eyes didn't match her smile. "Sorry about that whole production. I probably undercooked dinner. Or maybe I'm coming down with some spring flu...?"

She stared at Renee for some sort of answer, like she was the designated adult in the room.

"Also I've been having these crappy headaches. And mood swings. Crazy mood swings. And on top of that? I'm so wiped out all the time. Like I could pass out by two in the afternoon. Is that normal? You know, for life with a toddler? I mean I sound like I'm falling apart, don't I?"

There was no polite way to ask the obvious question, so Renee blazed ahead.

"Is there any chance you could be pregnant?"

The frazzled young mom shook her head with such force that she risked giving herself whiplash.

"Oh, God, no. Not a chance." She tried to laugh, though what came out sounded like a gasp or sob. "That's impossible."

"Okay." Renee nodded, understanding this was not a path she wished to travel down. "I'm sure it's just a little virus then."

"Well if it isn't Lincoln Landry!" Renee's boss, Dr. Dan Hanlon, called, entering the waiting room, ending the awkward moment. He held up one of his big hands and Lincoln high-fived it with gusto. "Whoa there. You've gotten stronger since I last saw you! What's your favorite green vegetable?"

Lincoln clapped a hand over his mouth and giggled. "Broccoli."

"Sorry we're so late," Sadie apologized, her cheeks splotchy. "I don't want to mess up your schedule, and completely understand if you don't have time to—"

"It's no worry at all. Life with a toddler is the definition of 'unpredictable.'" Dr. Dan smiled kindly. "Why don't you and Lincoln head back to room three?"

Sadie nodded gratefully, tucking a stray lock of brown hair behind her ear before marching off. Dr. Dan's arm grazed Renee's as he walked by, shooting her a conspiratorial "what can you do" shrug before following the pair down the hall.

Her arm tingled from the contact and Renee bit her lower lip as she contemplated yet again just how well Dr. Dan's ocean-blue eyes matched his tie, a tie she'd given him last Christmas.

Not that it meant anything. It was just a tie. A tie she'd researched during a three-hour online shopping mission and a gift she'd wrapped three times before she got the bow exactly perfect.

A simple tie. A boss gift. No big deal.

Nothing to see here.

Every morning, Dr. Dan passed along the tear-off from his word-of-the-day desk calendar. Today's word? "Chary," which meant careful, cautious. How appropriate. Best to be *chary* in this situation. She had no business crushing on her boss or his dead-sexy baby blues.

Intensely private in some ways yet incredibly warm in others, Dr. Dan was a widower who knew his way around his forty-foot sloop moored down at the harbor. And lord, did he have the tan, craggy good looks to prove it—not to mention a darn near perfect shoulder-to-hip ratio.

"I wanted to see all the fall foliage," Dr. Dan had once given as a vague explanation for his move. "Not to mention a low cost of living and high quality of life." Though according to Essie Park, who had sold him his log cabin out in the willy wacks, he'd come from away, seeking a change of scenery following the death of his wife.

"Sounds like Sam Baldwin to me," she could hear Tansy saying with her impish grin, referencing her favorite movie, *Sleepless in Seattle*. "Maybe he's ready to find his Annie Reed?"

Renee cleared her throat and her mind.

Though Essie was well intentioned, she never met a story that she didn't embellish. For all Renee knew, Dr. Dan had been a widower for years and was no stranger to the dating scene. He probably had a new fascinating woman on his boat each weekend.

All that added up to mean that Dr. Dan's bare left hand was a whole lot of none of her business.

And even if he *was* available, he was her employer—a no-go zone, venture into that territory and there be dragons. Besides, why would he ever look twice at her, a homebody receptionist who hadn't gotten any in a decade? If he wanted a catch there were plenty of fish with perkier boobs and sexier underwear.

* * *

At five fifteen, Renee checked out the final patient of the day, Eloise Collins with a double ear infection. The little girl clutched a stuffed rabbit to her chest, sucking her thumb.

"Thanks again for squeezing us in." Jack Collins signed his credit card receipt with a flourish. "I know the office closes at four thirty, but I've never seen Ellie like this."

"Don't give it a second thought." Renee smiled in understanding. "We couldn't have Miss Eloise going all night in pain. The prescription Dr. Hanlon gave you will kick the infection fast. It always worked for my daughter. She was on the swim team, and if there was a single germ in the pool, I swear it found its way into her ear canal."

Jack nodded absently, helping his daughter into her bright pink jacket and waving goodbye. Renee watched them go, thinking of all the times she had to give Tansy eardrops. Tansy hated the sensation, so she'd always pop on the Disney Channel as her daughter relaxed her head into her lap. Working quickly and humming softly, Renee would drip in the antifungal medication, massaging her tiny earlobes after each dosage.

She gave a wistful smile as she locked the front door and slid into her windbreaker.

Kids—the reason parents lost it, *and* the reason they kept it together.

Just then, a hand clasped her shoulder, the touch so unexpected and unfamiliar that she yelped.

"Shoot! Didn't mean to scare you." Dr. Dan flashed an apologetic grin and took three brisk steps back, leaving ample personal space. "I just came out to say thanks for sticking around late. I'd have hated to send the Collinses to urgent care."

Renee nodded, barely able to process his words. How could she think of anything else when the warm sensation of his palm remained branded on her skin? "Thirty miles would feel like three hundred to a sick kid."

"You've got such a good heart." He looked down at her with such intensity that it was either transfer her gaze to the carpeted floor or combust into flames.

"You can count on me," she muttered lamely, repeating the silly line her entire drive home.

You can count on me?

What was she, a loyal golden retriever?

Renee parked her silver sedan on Seashell Lane and clicked the automatic lock button—always twice for extra measure, despite the fact that Cranberry Cove must be the safest town in America—before opening the gate to her picket fence. A cobblestone path led to her gray-shingled cottage. This house, her home for the past twenty years, was the second-best treasure from her marriage to Russell Rhodes, the first being Tansy, of course.

Oh, Russ. They'd moved here at twenty-two—such babies!

Did her ex ever think about their days here in the cottage? Did he ever regret the life he tossed away like a used tissue?

When they first moved in here, she'd had a perfect picture of how her married life would turn out. Long walks together on the beach at dusk, skipping stones into the water. Four to six noisy kids. A house filled with love and laughter.

Renee's sigh felt loud in the silence. It wasn't all doom and gloom. She had Tansy. And her garden: the phlox, forsythia, and lilacs, the blueberries and sweet fern—everything slowly waking from a long winter's nap. She hugged herself close. The world was coming alive. It seemed so monumentally unfair to feel this empty inside.

"Hey there, mister!" Sadie was laughing next door. Renee could see them across the fence in their little kitchen, the window above the sink propped open. Lincoln was setting dish soap bubbles on his mother's nose and cheeks, finding the effect hilarious. "What is Daddy going to say when he gets home? Think he'll recognize me?"

Lincoln broke into helpless giggles. "Mommy! Mommy! You look like Santy Claus!"

"Ho! Ho! Ho!"

Tears welled up in Renee's eyes as she plopped on the wooden bench in her side yard and picked up a tiny stone bridge from the ground. It was part of Tansy's childhood fairy garden, which Renee still tended to with such devotion, one would have thought she was caring for Versailles.

She fished around in her purse until she located her cellphone.

The phone rang four times before Tansy picked up with a breathless "Hey." Music thumped in the background.

"What's up?" Tansy shouted. "Whatcha need?"

"Hello to you, too." Renee arched a brow. "I was just checking to see what you were up to." Clearly not hitting the books.

"It's the Final Four tonight!" Tansy's voice muffled as she pressed her lips too close to the mic. "Um, sorry it's sort of loud! We're getting ready to watch the game."

Renee flipped through her limited sports knowledge. Final Four, so that meant…

"Basketball?"

"Ding! Ding! Ding!"

Renee bit her thumbnail, an awful habit she'd carried all the way from girlhood into middle age. "Since when are you into basketball?"

"Whatever. It's fun." Tansy sounded a little loopy, a little too carefree. A distinctly male voice murmured in the background, right as her daughter gave a coy giggle. "Hey look, I've gotta run! Doing anything fun tonight?"

"You bet," Renee lied. "Off to Bree's. We're...um, making Italian. Lasagna, in fact. And we're going to check out that new Rebel Wilson movie."

"Oh, haven't heard of it, but sounds awesome!" Tansy accepted the fib easily, readily. "Give Aunt B a squeeze for me!"

The subsequent silence was somehow even worse than before. A caterpillar crawled near the toe of her shoe. She watched its painstaking journey with a small frown. What would it be like to encase herself in a cocoon and emerge as a beautiful, bold butterfly?

She lingered on the bench long after the caterpillar disappeared into the undergrowth, not quite sure what to do with herself. She didn't even jump when a clap of thunder erupted in the sky. Not until the first raindrops started to hit her cheeks did she finally stir, gathering her purse to head inside her empty house, where she would eat leftover chicken pot pie and binge Netflix until it was late enough for bed.

Tansy was off tailgating. Sadie was soon to be snuggled up with her handsome husband and sweet toddler as they read one final bedtime story. Bree was undoubtedly knitting while gossiping with her bestie, Jill. And Dr. Dan was definitely sharing a bottle of red with a gorgeous, fascinating woman.

God she was lonely.

Chapter Three

Sadie sat on the edge of the bathtub and slow blinked at the double pink lines.

But...how? She was on birth control, took her pill religiously as soon as she woke up. She'd sit up in bed, set the tiny pill on her tongue, and wash it down with an entire glass of water.

Wait, had she missed one? Maybe when Lincoln had that upper respiratory infection? His little nose had been running nonstop and his barking cough was painful just to listen to. She'd crawled into bed with him a few nights, holding him close and stroking his back, doing whatever she could to help him sleep away the sickness.

Come to think of it, maybe she'd missed two pills.

So that was the punishment for missing two pills then—two pink lines.

Two children.

She tapped her bare foot against the black-and-white floor tiles. She hadn't had a pedicure since last summer, and you could tell. How was a woman who couldn't take care of her own two feet supposed to raise two whole children?

When Sadie got pregnant with Lincoln, it was also a surprise. She'd been pitching a design concept for a hybrid floral and dessert shop when the first wave of nausea hit. Her mentor, Erin Bellman, had held the trash can for her while she puked.

"Too much fun last night?" Erin murmured, eyebrows raised.

Sadie paled. "We stayed in and watched a movie. I must have a bug."

Erin sent her home and when Sadie stopped at the pharmacy for Sprite and saltines, she hastily grabbed a pregnancy test, as well.

Those two lines, the ones from two years ago, were somehow not as scary as these.

How ridiculous is that?

She and Ethan weren't married then. In fact, they'd only been dating for six months. Six months! They'd been still very much in the honeymoon phase.

"I don't want you to freak out," she'd told him calmly, pushing the positive pregnancy test across her coffee table. "I'm pregnant. *We're* pregnant. But I can handle this."

She had a good job at Urban Design Studios, a job she was lucky enough to love. While no Suze Orman, she was (mostly) practical with her money. And with twelve weeks of fully paid maternity leave and coworkers happy to share nanny recommendations, Sadie felt as prepared as she'd ever be.

Little did she know parenthood would be like jumping out of a plane without a parachute, occasionally exhilarating, and always terrifying.

Ethan had reacted well, though. Sadie had braced herself for the worst and had instead gotten the best. Ethan had engulfed her in his arms and held her tight. "I love you," he'd whispered. "We'll make this work together."

And true to his word, Ethan had proposed there in her studio apartment the very next evening, presenting her with a diamond engagement ring stunning in its simplicity.

What was Ethan going to say to this news? Would he be excited? Scared? Worried? Hell, maybe she'd get a pair of diamond studs this go-around.

Sadie giggled, half delirious.

Just when she had hoped to soon see the light at the end of the toddler tunnel, she would be plunged back into darkness. Middle of the night feedings? Colic? Endless diapers? Of course she knew all the perks of parenting, but right now that joy seemed out of reach.

Instead she was going to be trapped in her house trying and failing over and over and over...forever. It wasn't just the mental and physical exhaustion; it was the pressure to be the *best* mom with Pinterest-perfect lunches, curated wooden toys, and a flawless bikini body.

Stop!

She didn't have the energy reserves to mom shame herself. Instead, she shoved the pregnancy test toward the back of the top vanity drawer, splashed cold water across her face, and tried to focus. Ethan had arrived home from Boston an hour earlier, and then ducked into his home office for one final phone meeting. That left the remainder of the party chores to Sadie, and considering Ethan would have to drive down to Portland to pick up Annette at the airport early tomorrow morning, time was not on her side.

She kneaded her temples, willing the headache to go into remission. She could brew a pot of coffee and power through the exhaustion, but a pregnancy headache? That was an entirely different beast.

Those things had teeth.

Annette would no doubt arrive at the cottage looking as if she'd been at the day spa rather than on a cramped prop plane, and waste no time at all handing out the little gifts she'd packed.

"Can you believe this? Mom brought me Skyline!" Ethan would exclaim, proudly holding up the blue cans of chili, as though Annette didn't do this every, single time. "And Montgomery Inn sauce? You shouldn't have!"

Sadie was shocked Annette didn't check a personal cooler on her Delta flight so she could bring her son a few pints of Graeter's ice cream, as well. She was like some strange female version of Santa Claus, except she came bearing gifts from Southwest Ohio.

During her grumpier moods, Sadie couldn't help but suspect Annette's ulterior motive was to make Ethan homesick. His two siblings, Stephen and Kelly, both lived in Cincinnati with their respective families, and it killed Annette that Ethan had chosen to establish his family in Maine and not the Midwest.

"Lincoln will want to know all his cousins." Annette loved to pout.

"And he will," Sadie had replied confidently. "We visit every summer and Thanksgiving, remember? And everyone is always welcome here."

Unfortunately, they hadn't been great about their end of this promise. With Ethan's crazy work schedule, it had been almost a year since they'd last visited Ohio. Annette likely knew how long it had been, down to the number of seconds.

And now the idea of herding *two* kids on a plane…she'd rather take a bath with a man-eating shark.

She pulled out her phone and reviewed her party checklist in her notes. Despite the fact that she'd been dashing around like a chicken with her head cut off, the list didn't feel any shorter. No, it only seemed to multiply and grow. How did that math work out?

Next she needed to pick up one of those classic number birthday candles from Shopper's Corner. Lincoln blowing out a flame atop a large number two was a perfect photo op—plus, she and Ethan would be able to look at the photos later and immediately know which birthday he'd been celebrating.

And there was still more cleaning to do. The bathrooms needed a scrub, and the living room windows could stand to be sprayed with vinegar. At least the sheets in the guest room were fresh, and she'd been careful to wash them with Dreft per Annette's instructions: "Anything stronger than baby detergent makes me break out in hives!" followed by "You did remember to stock Benadryl, didn't you, dear?"

Sadie had picked up the chicken tenders and croissant sandwiches earlier that afternoon, so lunch was all set. The refrigerator was wiped down and stocked with nutritious and kid-friendly snacks. And the kitchen was so clean, you could eat off its newly refinished floors.

Beep! Beep! Beep!

Sadie's stomach plunged—the smoke alarm? What the what? Oh…God…no…

Shit. The freaking cupcakes! She'd put them in the oven nearly forty-five minutes ago! But somehow finding out she was expecting a new life made them slip her mind.

Sprinting toward the kitchen, Sadie stepped on one of Lincoln's Duplo blocks and howled. What were his toys doing flung down the hall? He stuck his head out of his doorway, his eyes huge and scared.

She smothered a string of swear words, bent down and scooped him up.

"Shhhh. Shhhh. Don't worry. Everything is going to be okay! Mommy just burnt something."

She continued toward the kitchen, only to collide with a headset-wearing Ethan who impatiently gestured toward his office. His brows furrowed the way they always did when he got peeved.

"Conference call, remember," he stage-whispered, gesturing for them to keep it down.

She noticed the can of soda on his desk beside an open bag of corn chips and a salsa jar. He had ESPN muted on the television set, and the *Boston Globe* flung open on the arm of his Lazy Boy.

Home office or man cave?

"Sorry." She wove around him and into her beautiful, clean kitchen now filled with acrid smoke. She set Lincoln on the ground before rummaging around for oven mitts. "Sweetie, stand back while Mommy gets the cupcakes out, okay?"

"Kay," Lincoln agreed.

Except when Sadie pulled the charred dessert from the oven and set them on the stovetop, she was surprised to be hit with a sudden gush of cold water.

Huh?

She whirled around, only to get sprayed right in the face.

"Lincoln! What are you doing?" she sputtered. "That went up my nose!"

"Putting fire out! Like fireman!" he said proudly, having scrambled on top of the kitchen counter and grabbed the spray nozzle from the sink. He squirted more water at both Sadie and the cupcakes, proving that contrary to this morning's pee-pee debacle, he possessed remarkable aim.

Sadie shook her head, at a complete loss as to where she should begin with this one. Honestly, she was impressed with Lincoln's reasoning skills, unsure whether to howl with laughter or break into hysterical tears.

"What's going on?" Ethan appeared in the doorway, gaping between Sadie and Lincoln. "Little man, you shouldn't be up there. You could fall and get hurt."

Sadie snorted at his judgment-laden tone, her temper joining the inferno. "Well since I no longer have time to shower, I figured I'd multitask and have Lincoln hose me down."

Ethan stared, completely missing the joke, which only annoyed her more. "Listen. I can't work with all of this noise. I'm going to my car to finish this call." He started for the front door.

"Are you serious right now?" Sadie scooped Lincoln off the counter and stalked after him. "That's the best you can offer the situation?"

He doubled his pace. "You need to calm down."

Jesus take the wheel.

"You're really not going to even offer to help me? Stop! Do not run away from this!"

"You think I have time to stand around and listen to you act like a toddler, too?"

Oh, no he didn't.

As he slipped into his car, Sadie erupted from the porch. "You make me feel like a single mom! I never signed up to do this all alone!"

He turned the keys in the ignition and gunned off down Seashell Lane.

Sadie stared after his sporty Audi, her breathing heavy and unshed tears burning in her eyes. They never used to fight. Now it seemed like there were land mines hidden in every day. What was Ethan going to say when she told him about the second baby? Clearly, he couldn't even handle a little smoke and water. How was he going to survive another round of 2:00 a.m. feedings, teething tears, and diaper blowouts?

She buried her face in Lincoln's hair, letting the soft ringlets tickle her cheeks as she tried to calm down. Hopefully seeing fights like this weren't going to mess him up for life. Her own parents never argued in front of her. The worst she'd seen was them exchange stern looks.

Sadie could see it now, Lincoln at twenty sitting on a trendy sofa in some psychiatrist's office as he sighed, "I think all of my problems started the night my mom burned the birthday cupcakes."

Whirling around on her bare feet, she was startled to see Renee Rhodes frowning from across the picket fence.

Oh, perfect.

Not only had her next-door neighbor witnessed her poor excuse for time management at the doctor's office this morning, she'd nabbed front-row seats to an ugly argument.

Renee cleared her throat. "Everything okay?"

Sadie swallowed hard and forced a brittle smile. "I'm fine, honestly. We're just, uh, gearing up for Lincoln's birthday party tomorrow, and things have gotten hectic."

Oh, God. Had Renee heard the single-mom comment? How rude. She'd almost certainly offended her.

"Why are you wet?" Renee asked.

Sadie glanced down at her soaked yoga pants and sweatshirt. "The cupcakes were burning, and Lincoln tried to extinguish them. And me."

"Is dessert as soaked as you?"

"You bet. We may have a future Cranberry Cove firefighter on our hands."

"Yeah! Fireman!" Lincoln cheered, pumping his little fist into the air. "Me!"

Renee tucked her gardening gloves inside her back pocket. "Do you have a backup dessert?"

"Yeah right." Sadie shook her head. "I can't even seem to pull off plan A."

Renee opened the gate, walking toward her front door. "No use crying over burned baked goods. It happens to the best of us." Her voice was calm and take-charge. Renee's soothing tone reminded Sadie of the way her Grandma Hester used to console her, her serene words healing every disappointment, from a bad test score to being excluded from a classmate's birthday party.

Plus? The smile tugging at the corners of Renee's lips was helping Sadie see the humor in the mishap.

"You know what? I've got a few pounds of frozen blueberries leftover from last summer. And I've been looking for an excuse to bake a pie—or five." Renee smiled.

"That's sweet, but please don't feel like you have to. This isn't your circus," Sadie protested weakly.

"I know. I want to." She gave a reassuring wink. "This is what neighbors do in Cranberry Cove."

Chapter Four

Unlike Renee's pantry, Sadie's wasn't filled with a mishmash of five kinds of flour, confectioners' sugar, cornstarch, baking powder, baking soda, chocolate chips, dried fruit, and who knows what else. Instead, hidden behind a Shaker door were rows of neatly labeled Mason jars.

"Wow, are you organized or what?" Renee blinked. "No surprise from the babysitter who used to arrive complete with craft kits."

"Huh?" Sadie glanced up from the ruined cupcakes she was tossing into the trash, cocking her head with a sparrowlike movement. "Oh those? Ha, honestly, half of that stuff is probably expired, and the worst part is that I'll never know because I pitched all the bags." Her wan smile grew wistful. "You remember my crafts?"

Renee nodded. "Tansy still hangs the felt snowman you made with her on the tree every Christmas."

Sadie seemed to almost flinch, turning to face the window. A strange melancholy seemed to settle into the room. Down the hill, the waves were ebbing. The outgoing tide revealed exposed rocks, splinters of wood, and wild mussel beds. "God, I used to be so organized. But when it comes to dealing with my own kid—it's a whole different story."

"Okay, time to make a plan." Renee clapped her hands, an inexplicable feeling of fullness rising in her chest, in sharp contrast to the hollow emptiness that seemed to cling to Sadie. "I'm going to run back to my house and grab those blueberries. Can you pop a large metal mixing bowl in the freezer?"

Sadie blinked, turning from the window and refocusing. "Bowl. Freezer. Got it."

"Here's how the evening is going to go. I'm going to whip up a few pies and muffins to serve at the birthday party tomorrow, and you're going to put your feet up and relax. And Lincoln can watch a show or two."

"I don't know. He's already had his thirty minutes of screen time," Sadie began to protest.

"Sadie, let me be real. Desperate times call for desperate measures. I once set Tansy in front of *Barney* for an entire weekend when I had the flu," Renee said. "I promise you it won't rot his brain."

"No, of course not." Sadie exhaled in relief and nodded. "You're right. And thanks. I really do need a break."

With a sudden purpose in her step, Renee bustled back to her own quiet cottage where the vacuum cleaner marks still looked pristine three days later and only a single water glass sat in the kitchen sink.

She reached toward the back of the freezer and retrieved the berries. After gathering two bottles of red and white wine, she was struck with a pang as she gave the feeling welling within her chest a name. While Sadie Landry was spiraling in full-on crisis mode, Renee was happy.

It felt good to be needed, she realized, staring at a framed photo of Tansy on the wall.

Her daughter was wearing braided pigtails and a dress that featured a red skirt and blue top with white stars. The sparkler in Tansy's little hand illuminated her face, and the gap where her front two teeth should have been made Renee's heart ache for that simpler time. Cranberry Cove's annual Fourth of July celebration featured a picnic, fireworks show, and an afternoon parade for the smaller children. How many times had she helped Tansy decorate her bike with streamers and pinwheels and cheered as her daughter pedaled down the town's main drag?

It wasn't that she took pleasure in Sadie's ill luck; it was more that it felt so good to be useful again. To be able to feel less alone, even for a few hours.

When she returned to Sadie's cottage the young mother had turned on the *Wild Kratts* and was on her knees mopping up the water on the kitchen floor.

"Hey there," Renee said. "I don't know what kind of wine you like, so I brought choices. Pick your poison."

Sadie sat back on her heels and burst into tears.

"Oh crap. What did I say?" Renee dropped to the floor beside her, rubbing her back while making a reassuring crooning sound.

"I...I'm so sorry, you're going to think I'm a total basket case." Sadie wiped her nose with the back of her hand. "It's just that you were right, Renee, with what you said earlier at Dr. Hanlon's office. I'm...Oh, God, I'm pregnant."

"It's okay. Shhhh. It's okay." Renee engulfed her in a hug, which only made her cry harder. "So, this was a bit of a surprise?"

"Understatement of the decade."

"Ah, well. Some of life's greatest gifts are surprises," Renee replied awkwardly, stringing together a slew of idioms and hating how much she sounded like a Hallmark card. "But seriously, you're a wonderful mom, and Lincoln will be thrilled to have a little brother or sister."

"No need to sugarcoat it. Trust me, I know better than anyone how much I suck at motherhood."

"Suck?" Renee flinched. How could the world's most amazing high school babysitter and loveliest home maven think she sucked at motherhood? "How can you say that?"

"Easy. Look at the evidence." Sadie sniffed, trying to wipe away her tears with the sleeve of her shirt. "I can't ever get my son anywhere on time, and you saw for yourself that my husband thinks I'm a total flop. I know it sounds stupid, but I thought I'd be a great mom. Like the one in *The Parent Trap*."

Renee tried and failed to suppress a smile. "Natasha Richardson's character?"

"Yeah. She was a fashion designer—do you remember that?" Sadie rubbed her blotchy cheeks. "She was all chic and accomplished, yet somehow still kind and motherly. I thought I would be like that, keeping up with design and still being this kick-butt caregiver."

"She also agreed to split up her set of twins, potentially never seeing her other daughter again." Renee winked. "So, I wouldn't say she was perfect. Plus she's uh…you know…not real."

Sadie huffed a faint laugh.

"For the record, you are a fantastic mother. Think of the way your son watches you. Like you're the best person on the planet." Renee nodded toward Lincoln, who looked happy as a clam drinking from his sippy cup, a favorite blankie wrapped around his arm. "I don't think a sucky mom would spend an entire morning drawing elaborate chalk drawings on the driveway. Or bring home a bubble machine. I also don't think a sucky mom would need to take a wagon to the library each week, because a sucky mom would not check out dozens of books to read together."

Sadie nodded, tears filling her eyes all over again but a small smile finally spreading across her face.

"Everyone has a hard day here and there. And you can't beat yourself up for those. They happen to all of us. I promise." Renee stood, walking toward the fridge decorated with finger paintings. "Now, how does a mocktail sound?"

"Blissful," Sadie murmured, rising herself and dusting off her pants.

Renee retrieved a cocktail glass from the cabinet and filled it with ice, sparkling water, a splash of grapefruit juice, and even a sprig of mint. She gave it a good stir and handed the cool drink to Sadie.

"I tried to have a second child." The words tumbled out of Renee and it was hard to tell who was more surprised, Sadie or herself. Her younger sister, Bree, was the only person she'd ever admitted this to, but she felt compelled to share it now. Maybe, *hopefully*, it would help. "After Tansy and before the divorce. Ever since I was a little girl, I'd imagined having a house full of children—four, five…maybe even six."

When Tansy turned one, Renee and Russ had started trying again. She'd gotten pregnant with Tansy so quickly into their marriage that she qualified as a honeymoon baby. But months and then years went by without any luck. Renee and Russ tried to focus on Tansy, the beautiful blessing they'd already been given, but it was hard to ignore the growing sadness each month, the silent disappointment.

"I'm sorry." Sadie grimaced at the floor. "I know I must sound like a brat. I'm just daunted. First world problems and all that."

"You don't have anything to apologize for. That was my dream to have a bunch of kids. I didn't mean it should be yours." Renee shook her head, not quite sure where she had intended to take the conversation. She didn't mean to accidentally veer down a path that was all about her. Maybe this is what happened when you spent too much time alone. You lose people skills. "Less talk, more pies. Time to get to work."

Sadie slid onto a kitchen barstool and sipped her mocktail while Renee got to work, first combining the flour and salt and then cutting in the cold butter.

"Do you have a pastry blender?" Renee asked.

"Probably." Sadie gestured toward a deep drawer to the left of the kitchen sink. "Ethan's mother went through our entire wedding registry and then provided me with a list of essential items I simply *must* have forgotten."

Her lips curled in a mischievous grin. "Sounds like your mother-in-law has a strong personality?"

"Annette means well," Sadie ventured cautiously. "She'll actually be flying in tomorrow from Cincinnati for Lincoln's party."

"Big trip for a second birthday bash." Renee blended the butter into the flour mixture before adding a splash of ice water.

"Ethan's her youngest, and between you and me and the *Wild Kratts*? He's her favorite child." She rolled her eyes and Renee laughed. "I think that's part of why I have a panic attack whenever she comes. I stress that I'm not good enough for her darling."

"I highly doubt that." Renee dusted the countertop with flour before deftly rolling out the dough. "And not to brag, but these pies are going to knock her Cincinnati socks off. And you better take every ounce of credit for them."

After she'd flattened the dough to a perfect thickness and cut it into discs, Renee wrapped each piece with plastic and set them in the refrigerator.

"The dough needs to chill for an hour. I can come back later," she said awkwardly, forgetting this waiting period of the pie-making process. "Or I can take it to my house and finish the crusts there, of course."

"I hope you're kidding." Sadie wrinkled her nose. "Because one of us should enjoy that wine. Please pour a glass and hang out. It's so nice to catch up."

Renee agreed—it would be nice to truly catch up. The last time she'd talked to Sadie, really talked to her, had been shortly after Sadie's parents' big going-away party, and Sadie had still been in college then. Once Sadie's parents had moved to D.C., they'd lost touch until she and Ethan bought the cottage. They'd lived beside one another for two years now, and yet, all they'd exchanged were neighborly pleasantries, Christmas cookies, and mixed-up mail.

As she set the blueberry-and-sugar mixture to a simmer on the stovetop, Renee felt the wine's warm, happy buzz—or maybe it was simply the thrill of connecting with someone other than herself. When was the last time she'd shared such an open, honest conversation with someone? With her friends around town, she tended to keep things breezy and casual, only sharing the attractive parts of her life: Tansy's impressive scholarship or funny stories from work.

Now as Renee swept up crumbs and got started on the blueberry muffins, she got up to speed on Sadie's parents' life, how her father had been hired as a financial manager for the Department of Treasury, and they'd recently moved into their dream home: a Georgetown brownstone.

"Are they thrilled?" Renee asked.

Sadie gave a one-shouldered shrug. "Everything there is currently neat and in order, which means they must be positively ecstatic."

Renee didn't question the edge to Sadie's voice, and instead told her all about Tansy's new life in Los Angeles. Sadie said how fun and exciting that sounded, even though Renee swore she slightly hesitated over her word choices.

"How has working with Dr. Hanlon been?" Sadie asked while replacing the *Wild Kratts* with *Yo Gabba Gabba!* "I'm so glad there's finally a full-time pediatrician there instead of that revolving door of temporary docs."

Renee's cheeks flushed. Hopefully Sadie didn't notice that she suddenly resembled a tomato. "It's been a very smooth transition," she replied with professional blandness. "Lincoln's in fab hands. Um, can you preheat the oven for me, please? Four hundred degrees."

Her thoughts strayed to Dr. Dan's big strong hands, his bare left one in particular, and wondered how they'd feel sliding up the back of her arms. Were his fingertips callused from sailing? Rough and strong?

"Hey, um…can I ask a personal question?" Sadie asked right as the kitchen timer dinged.

"Of course," she replied, retrieving the discs of pie dough and ducking her head to hide her burning cheeks. Hopefully she wasn't about to ask if Renee was a secret horndog.

"Well, did you know your divorce was coming? Like…were there signs things were going wrong?"

"Oh." Renee paused from rolling the dough, momentarily frozen.

Sadie had never known Russell. She hadn't started to babysit for Tansy until a few months after he'd left, when Tansy was only five.

"Yes and no," Renee replied, spilling a little sugar. She wiped her trembling hands on her jeans as memories flooded in.

Those too-quiet family dinners, the only source of conversation a babbling Tansy, and the year Russ forgot her birthday. How he wanted to move to a ski town and how he accused Renee of being a prude on the nights she was just exhausted.

"I knew we had problems, but I never expected him to leave me for Tansy's kindergarten teacher."

Sadie whipped around from the oven. "Hold the phone. I'd heard my parents talking about Russell like he was a major jerk, but never got the whole story."

"It was a big scandal at the time. At least they waited until the end of the school year." Ms. Samantha had been a slightly younger, slightly thinner, and slightly more attractive version of Renee. She even had strawberry-blond hair. "They moved to Stowe, Vermont, and now have three children."

"No way. I didn't realize Tansy has half-siblings."

"She only sees them sporadically. Unfortunately, Russell never made much of an effort to integrate her into his new family." Renee cleared her throat, the lie heavy on her tongue as she tried to sound more upset about this injustice than she actually felt. The awful truth was that she was selfishly glad to have Tansy to herself. Russ had taken her self-esteem, belief in love, and trust. But her daughter was hers. "But why dredge up ancient history?"

Sadie sucked on her bottom lip. "Because I know you saw Ethan and me have that stupid shouting match. Things haven't been great here lately."

Renee stirred cornstarch into the sweet mixture warming on the stovetop before transferring it into the prepared pie shells. She slid four beautiful pies into the oven and quietly closed the door.

"We all lose our tempers sometimes, especially when small kids are thrown into the mix, and no one's getting anything close to eight hours of sleep," she said diplomatically. "Marriages are hard work. Do you know what my mother always told me? It's not fifty-fifty. It's a hundred-hundred."

"I think I've heard that somewhere, too. And yeah, you're right. I haven't slept a solid night in what feels like forever. Is it any wonder I feel like I'm turning into an emotional zombie?" Sadie gave a small laugh. "But…I mean, what's going to happen to us once we throw this second child into the mix? In some ways, I feel like we're doomed."

"You can't think like that," Renee said, crossing her toes that everything would work out. She might not believe in fairy tales anymore, but this sweet cottage felt like something out of a storybook…and Ethan was so earnest, Lincoln so lovable, and Sadie so sweet. She wanted so badly for them to have a long happily ever after.

"Who knows? Maybe the new baby is your family's missing puzzle piece."

"You think?" Sadie sounded puzzled herself but a little more hopeful.

The two women chatted a while longer, this time about easier, more mundane things, like the weather and Essie Park's new haircut, before Lincoln ran into the kitchen exclaiming, "Mommy! What dat smell? Is sugar?"

They both giggled at the hopeful note in his tiny voice.

"They're Renee's magical blueberry pies and muffins." Sadie scooped Lincoln into her arms while Renee removed the treats from the oven. "Did you know we live next door to a bona fide superhero?" She turned to Renee with a grateful smile. "I'm serious. You really did save the day."

"Aw, it was nothing. Really." Renee set one warm pie in the center of the kitchen island and handed Sadie a fork. "Here. This one is for now."

Sadie took a step back, "Please don't tempt me. I gained too much with Lincoln and I only just got rid of the baby weight. I'm not looking forward to ballooning up again."

"I'm going to stop you right there. Baked goods are food for your soul." Renee arched her brow, not lowering it a centimeter until Sadie gave in, begrudgingly accepting the fork.

"Fine, fine." Sadie delicately cut into the flaky crust. She blew on the steaming forkful for a few seconds before taking a nibble. Her eyes widened, and she quickly went for a second and then third bite. "Renee! Holy crap. This is the best thing I've ever tasted."

Renee was chewing a bite of her own. She smiled and nodded. The truth of the matter was she couldn't cook up romance if her life depended on it, but pie? She could bake a pie blindfolded and with one arm tied behind her back. From the time she was a girl, baking had made Renee feel happy and useful. It had given her a sort of power. She would never forget the first time she put a pie into the oven all by herself at the age of twelve, and the huge smile that had spread across her dad's face with that very first bite. "Now this is a treat!" he'd gushed.

Ever since that first pie, Renee had gone out of her way to bake for neighbors who were housebound or under the weather, friends with new babies. Whenever she got wind of someone feeling down or needing a bit of a pick-me-up, she was on their doorstep with a freshly baked pie. Her friend Myles "ordered" two pumpkin pies for his Friendsgiving feast every year. Bree often requested a peach pie for her knitting group. Even Essie sometimes dropped elaborate hints regarding cherries and her favorite flaky crust.

"No, I mean it. This is literally the most delicious thing I've ever tasted. Forget warm chocolate chip cookies. Forget maple-walnut ice cream. Forget Boston cream pies." Sadie's angular face grew serious yet excited. "Stop everything you're doing and open a pie shop. Like, yesterday."

Renee laughed. "Oh, come on. You're the one with baking in your blood."

Sadie grinned. "Because of Grandma Hester?"

Renee nodded.

"Unfortunately my gene pool didn't come with a talent for the kitchen. Still, some of my favorite childhood memories are spreading my coloring books across her kitchen table as she rolled out dough. She always explained everything as she went, almost as if she was on a cooking show. I loved it," she said with a laugh. Sadie handed Lincoln one of the cooling muffins and the toddler actually squealed. "Yummy! Yum, yum! More?"

"I'm serious," Sadie continued. "Why don't you sell these? The world deserves this pie, or at least Cranberry Cove does."

"Because I have a perfectly nice job at Dr. Hanlon's." Renee dabbed the corner of her mouth. "Thanks for the compliment, but I'm happy with my life, just as it is. I like to bake for my friends. That's enough."

Just then, the front door swung open and a deep male voice called, "Sade?"

Sadie and Renee exchanged a quick glance before a subdued Ethan entered the kitchen, carrying a bouquet of pink tulips.

"I'm— Oh! Renee," he murmured sheepishly, giving his neighbor an awkward half wave. "Hi. I didn't know you were over."

"She saved my sanity and the birthday party." Sadie gave the flowers a hesitant nod. "For me?"

"Sweets for the sweet." Ethan kissed Sadie's forehead and traded her the flowers for a squirming Lincoln. But not before whispering something into Sadie's ear that caused her lips to curl into a pleased smile. "It smells incredible in here."

"Renee just whipped up the best blueberry pies." Sadie gestured to the counter.

"It's no big deal. Seriously. But I should go." Now that domestic bliss seemed to have returned to the Landry household, Renee felt

42

like a third wheel. The evening had been a welcome surprise, but it was time for everyone to return to their real lives.

As she strolled back to her empty house, breathing in the cool, briny air, her own words echoed through her head.

I'm happy with my life, just as it is.

In her quiet kitchen, she made chia seed pudding for tomorrow morning's breakfast before taking a hot bubble bath upstairs. She flipped through the most recent issue of *Real Simple*, being careful to keep the magazine from falling into the tub while bookmarking a recipe for a Mediterranean couscous dish.

Dan likes Mediterranean food.

I wonder what he ate for dinner tonight.

Bree called as she dried off.

"Whatcha up to?" her sister asked. Renee could hear pots and pans clattering in the background.

"I'm more curious to know what you're up to."

"I got carried away at the shop again," Bree said. "I'm teaching that intro to knitting course, and I have three kids this session! Which is awesome, of course, but kids tend to get pretty distracted."

Renee laughed, thinking of the many times Bree tried teaching Tansy to knit, and her daughter ended up with a book in her hands instead.

"Anyways, I'm just making a late dinner now. Spaghetti care of Paul Newman."

"Gourmet."

"Shut up. I was actually calling to see if you wanted to go with me to that pinot-and-paint fund-raiser at Chickadee Studios," Bree said. "It's tomorrow night. Are you free?"

Of course Renee was free. And yet she faltered, just as she always did.

"Maybe," she said.

"Maybe?"

Renee shrugged, even though her sister couldn't see her. Ever since Tansy had gone away to college, she'd felt herself become more of a hermit than ever. What interesting things did she possibly have to share with the group? The word of the day she'd received from Dr. Dan? A synopsis of the umpteenth novel she'd read? A review of the mushroom stroganoff recipe she'd recently made?

Her life was so pathetically boring.

"I'll think about it, okay?" Renee said. "Promise."

"Mmmm-hmmm." Bree didn't sound convinced. "I'll drop you off some tickets. Try to do more than think. Do!"

After hanging up, Renee ran lavender-scented moisturizer over her arms and elbows, her legs and knees, before massaging a new night serum across her forehead and freckled cheeks. She brushed and flossed her teeth, swishing her mouth with minty mouthwash. She stood in front of the bedroom window for a few moments, always taking one last glance at quiet Seashell Lane below, as if she was head of some sort of neighborhood watch brigade. Then, finally, she slipped into her cotton pajamas, played Enya on her phone, and climbed into her sleigh bed.

This was good. She was lucky. Beyond fortunate. Her home was paid off thanks to a small inheritance from her parents. She had a job that connected her to children and families in the community. Her daughter earned a full ride to one of the most prestigious universities in the country. For the first time in her adult life, she had savings and no money stress. And tonight? Tonight, she'd been able to help a neighbor get through a stressful situation. Even better, she'd connected with Sadie Landry in a much deeper way than their previous babysitter-mother or cordial neighbor relationships had ever allowed. It had felt so satisfying, so freeing to talk to Sadie as openly as they had.

And yet, as Renee stared at the bedroom ceiling, she felt herself closing up as she always did, building the same safe walls around her inner self that she'd meticulously maintained for years now.

I'm happy. I'm happy. I'm happy…

But while white lies were easy to tell, you couldn't hide from yourself.

She might be fortunate, but she wasn't fulfilled.

And she didn't have the first clue what to do about it.

Chapter Five

Sadie handed the last of Lincoln's party guests a favor—a mini woven picnic basket, which included a bottle of bubbles, sidewalk chalk, and organic gummies—gently nudging her son forward.

"What do you say to Clementine?"

What a great name. Maybe if the baby is a girl, we can do something sweet and old-fashioned like that. Charlotte? Camilla?

"Tank you," Lincoln mumbled down at his tiny loafers.

"Aw, lovely manners." Daphne Stewart, Clementine's mother, smiled. "I don't know how you do it! This party was something pulled straight from Pinterest."

"It was nothing." Sadie waved her off airily even though she was ready to fall asleep in her Adidas. It had been great catching up with her high school friends who had stuck around the Cove and grown up to have children of their own. Daphne had once been the senior class wild child, notorious for streaking during football games. These days she owned Stripe—a boutique dress shop on Main Street that sold locally made frocks and delicate, handmade jewelry.

"Well I know it can take a ton of work for something to appear effortless."

"Don't make me blush. Anyway, you and Jacob have to come over soon. Maybe for a barbecue on the deck when the weather is a little more predictable."

"Predictable?" Daphne laughed. "This is still Maine we are talking about, right?"

"Hey now, the most predictable thing about this place is our unpredictable weather."

After giving Daphne a quick squeeze goodbye, she shut the front door. "We survived."

Ethan's arms slipped around her middle, his hands resting right where the baby hid. Was this the moment to break the news? She'd tried telling him last night, after he'd arrived home with the beautiful apology bouquet, after they'd shared a slice of Renee's pie and laughed over how ridiculous they must have sounded shouting in the front yard, but then? Annette had called in a tizzy. She couldn't find her birthday gift for Lincoln *anywhere*, and had she sent it to their house by mistake?

Naturally, Annette had found the gift fifteen frazzled minutes later (because apparently having Ethan "help" over one thousand miles away proved useful), and Sadie had taken deep, deep breaths and reminded herself to remain calm.

She means well. She means well. She means well.

"Mmmmm. Somebody smells berry-licious." Ethan nestled his bristly face in the crook between her cheek and shoulder and gave her a soft kiss in her favorite spot. She closed her eyes, enjoying his woodsy scent—the Ralph Lauren Polo cologne she'd gotten him for Christmas. "Nice job. Reminds me of the over-the-top themed parties you used to throw down in Boston."

"Really? A two-year-old birthday bash reminds you of *those* parties?" Green Jell-O shots came to mind from Sadie's very glittery and very green St. Patrick's Day get-together as well as the witches' brew she'd concocted for one Halloween, complete with a fog machine for an extra effect.

"You know what I mean," he said with a half smile. "Just that you think of every last detail."

"Well, thanks, honey," she said.

Ethan moved his mouth closer to her ear. "I plan on showing you my gratitude later."

"Oh yeah?" Sadie gave him a lazy grin, wiggling her bum against his belt buckle. Exhausted as she was, it had been a while. Come to think of it, she knew exactly how long. And wouldn't it be better to drop the pregnancy bomb after lovemaking? She gave a little shiver, imagining his big warm hands splayed over her naked belly as they spooned in bed. The soft protective kiss he'd plant on her shoulder. The happiness they'd share as they both imagined the new little life they'd created together.

Because he'd be thrilled, right?

Of course, he would.

So thrilled it's why she wanted to wait…to make it special.

Of course she wasn't procrastinating on telling him the truth because she was unsure of his reaction. He'd be over the moon. Probably make that one super excited face, the one he saved for when the Bengals made a touchdown or she bought a new little lacy something.

Ethan turned her around and planted a lingering kiss square on her mouth before pulling back and cupping her cheeks. "Hey. Where'd you just go?"

She huffed a laugh. "Hmm? Nowhere. I'm right here…with you."

The concerned look faded as his eyes crinkled. "You really did do a great job. Lincoln had a blast."

This time her smile was real.

Maybe Ethan was still sucking up after yesterday's fight, but even so—she'd take it. Because it felt freaking fantastic to pull something off—even if that something was a teddy bear picnic–themed birthday party—and be appreciated for the effort.

How was it possible to be this happy, this confident, following yesterday's drama?

Maybe she could pull of this whole mom of two thing. Let's see, if the baby was another boy, they were certainly set in terms of clothing. And if it was a girl? Sadie's mind filled with visions of smock dresses and spunky hair accessories. No matter the baby's gender, Lincoln would have a sibling, something Sadie herself had always wanted.

Yes. Everything was going to be perfect.

It had to be.

"Earth to Sadie—want to head upstairs?" Ethan teased.

She startled. "As exciting as a little afternoon delight sounds, well, your mom…" Sadie let her voice trail off.

"I'll ask her to take Lincoln for a walk on the beach to burn off the sugar." His phone beeped in his pocket and he withdrew it, frowning at the screen. "Damn. First I need to run upstairs and check on something. Hang tight." And he was off, taking the stairs two at a time.

Welp. She shrugged. Guess it was good she didn't just try to break the news.

Later. I'll tell him later when there are no distractions, she told herself, wandering back into the kitchen where Annette was elbows deep in a sink full of soapy water.

"Oh, no. Stop! You don't have to do that." She hurried to her mother-in-law's side. "Let me finish up."

Even though Annette Landry had only arrived in Cranberry

Cove that morning, she'd jumped in and helped with the party wherever she could. From refilling drinks and cleaning up toddler spills to entertaining the mothers with funny stories about her flight: "The woman sitting beside me ordered a Tanqueray and tonic at six o'clock in the morning! I mean, can you imagine? Then she slipped out of her shoes and propped her bare feet on the back of the seat in front of her."

Best of all? Not even a single passive-aggressive comment about Ethan, Sadie, and Lincoln moving to Cincinnati.

How silly that she'd wasted so much energy bracing for the worst, when Annette was being nothing but wonderful.

"Not a chance. You deserve a break." Annette rinsed a platter and set it on a double-folded dish towel to dry. "Those blueberry muffins were a creative choice, by the way. Everyone always does cupcakes, but that's just too much sugar for a little body, don't you agree?"

Maybe destroying dessert yesterday had been a blessing in disguise. "I'm glad they were a hit."

"And those pies were sensational. The entire party was," Annette said, and Sadie could tell she meant it. "Every detail was meticulous, from the gingham tablecloths to the sunflower arrangements. Oh, and the craft! Decorating little shirts for their new teddy bears! Just darling, and the children loved it."

"You think so?"

"I've already sent the girls photos." Annette pulled out her iPhone as if to show Sadie evidence. "The girls" were Annette's three sisters and passing along a glowing review to them was the highest form of flattery in Annette's world. "They were all impressed, of course, but I said what else would you expect from a former interior designer?"

Oof. Sadie watched a balloon waft listlessly around the living room. *Former* interior designer. The woman who had once submitted innovative design proposals to corporate executives—the same woman who had been called both a forerunner in ergonomics and a color maverick—was now the mastermind behind a teddy bear picnic–themed birthday party.

But the thing was? Sadie was damn proud of today, just as proud as she'd been of her chic design for a downtown champagne bar or when she'd mapped out an impressive open seating plan for a company of five hundred.

And judging by the amount of Pinterest posts, there was certainly a lot of interest and buzz around children's birthday parties. She would want to add a few more get-togethers to her portfolio first, but maybe she could open her own party-planning business? It was definitely an idea within the scope of possibility.

"Why don't you go take a hot shower and after I finish up here I'll play Hot Wheels with my favorite two-year-old?" Annette picked up Lincoln and held him close against her cashmere sweater. He played with the thick rope of pearls around her neck.

"That sounds amazing." She squeezed her mother-in-law's hand in appreciation and hurried up the stairs, before Annette could change her mind.

Except when she opened the door to their master bedroom suite, her husband was perched on the edge of their linen duvet, feverishly texting.

"Knock knock, Mister Love Man," she purred, cocking a hand on her hip, and sucking in her stomach. They hadn't gotten naked during daylight hours since Lincoln's birth.

Mister Love didn't even bother to look up.

Her shoulders caved a little. "What's going on? You look intense."

He started in surprise, darkening his phone and setting it—

facedown—on his walnut nightstand, right beside the sterling silver frame of their wedding portrait.

"Just…It's no one. Or, I mean…" Ethan paused. "Work stuff. I hate to do this, but I need to get back to Boston right away. I'm going to hop in the shower and hit the road."

"What? No! You literally just got back." She crossed her arms, meaning business. "Plus, it's Lincoln's birthday and your mother is here. Whatever it is can wait until Monday."

"Enough with the guilt trips." His voice was pained, exasperated. "I'm sorry, but if I say that I have to go. Seriously. I have to go." And with that he slammed the double doors to their bathroom behind him.

She glanced at his phone sitting innocently and unoccupied.

Something wasn't right.

She felt that truth all the way to her bones.

But Ethan also wasn't the cheating type. Of course, he had also been known as a bit of a player before she entered the picture. They had met while her company was redesigning Ethan's tech firm's space, and he had charmed her one morning near the coffeemaker with his knowledge of all things Frank Lloyd Wright and his slight twang she couldn't quite place.

"Careful around that one," one of his associates, a woman around Sadie's age, had said with a wink after Ethan had walked away. "He's a great guy, but with those bedroom eyes? He gets around."

"I was only being friendly," Sadie had laughed at the remark, swearing she wasn't interested.

But even if Ethan had a heartthrob past, he'd certainly never acted like it since falling for Sadie. From their earliest dates, Ethan had always been attentive and adoring. He worshipped her every feature, even her weird belly button and freckled forehead. He would accompany her on visits to the art museum and patiently read the *Globe* while she flipped through design books for hours on end. He got along well with her parents and knew her Starbucks order by heart.

So why hadn't he given her a straight answer about who he had been frantically texting?

A sinking sickness welled within her. What if he'd met another woman in Boston? She began to pace. Maybe that was why he'd surprised her with the Cranberry Cove cottage. It was genius, really. He could hide his wife and child up in Maine while sleeping his way through the city.

Her stomach was a knot as she remembered Renee's story about Russell and the kindergarten teacher. Breathing seemed impossible.

She could imagine it all too easily.

The other woman was blond and curvy, voluptuous, and definitely had an interesting career. An art collector perhaps? Her name was something sultry like Francesca or Alessandra, and she likely lived in a high-rise with a doorman who knew Ethan by name. Ethan and Francesca probably drank Veuve Clicquot before making love on a bear rug in front of a roaring fire while Kenny G played on the surround sound stereo.

The mental image was so ridiculous she should chuckle.

Instead…

She lunged for Ethan's phone, typing in his passcode, which had always been her birthday: 09-15-90

But this time his phone didn't unlock. Her lungs constricted. He'd changed his password.

It must be Francesca's (or Alessandra's) birthday now.

This was so freaking stupid. And insecure. And immature. And yet—

"What are you doing?" Ethan stood in the doorway of their bathroom, having already toweled off and changed into jeans and a crewneck. "Snooping?"

"I'm pregnant!" she blurted out, her heart racing. She hurled the word like a weapon or a talisman…she wasn't sure which.

The color drained from Ethan's face. He did not run to her side. He didn't try to embrace her. Nor did he appear in any way thrilled.

In fact, his eyes darkened with visible alarm. "You're joking."

She shook her head, praying he'd figure out a way to pull his head from his ass in the next two seconds.

"How are you going to manage?" The words came out in a strained whisper.

"*Me?*" Her bottom lip trembled, a dam about to break. Was he serious? "What about you? What about *us*?"

"No. Shit. I didn't mean it like that, Sade." He quickly back-tracked, though he still didn't move so much as a muscle. "It's just that every time I call you during the workday, you sound near tears. Sometimes I wonder if you're on the verge of some kind of breakdown."

She cradled her middle like she'd been sucker punched. It was one thing to feel the feelings. Another entirely for him to notice.

Notice and never check in.

"I mean, I know you've worked through the postpartum stuff, but you're still not yourself." Ethan was pacing now. "Two kids? I don't see how we'll cope without family help."

"Are you serious right now? First, it wasn't just postpartum *stuff*. It was horrible. I was on medication for over a year, remember? If anything I should be pissed as hell that you haven't done a dish in this house since I quit breastfeeding."

"Who puts the roof over our head?" He was shouting now.

"Don't act like I don't contribute. And I don't see why you don't make a schedule. Plan better so you don't get overwhelmed! You're drowning! And it sucks to watch."

"It's not as if you're tossing me a lifesaver. Do you know everyone in town pities me?" The words were thick with anger, resentment. "They think, 'Poor Sadie, trying to juggle everything on her own while her husband is off in Boston all the time. She's practically a single mother!'"

"Oh, give it up." He snorted. "Nobody says that."

"They do!"

"Fine then. Sorry for trying to financially support this family! And for buying you your grandma's house."

She forced herself to hold his gaze. If she closed her eyes she'd lose her nerve. She needed to get this conversation back on track. "You are more than a paycheck. Our son needs you. *I* need you."

A wail came from the doorway and the couple looked over to see Lincoln standing there, tears streaming down his face.

"Mommy!" He pressed his hands over his ears.

"Oh, baby." Sadie flew forward, shame heating her cheeks. "Shhhhh, it's all okay."

Annette rounded the corner a nanosecond faster, engulfing Lincoln in her arms and recoiling from Sadie as if she were a rabid raccoon.

"What on earth is going on?" Annette rubbed Lincoln's back, levelling a glare that could cut glass. "I could hear you two going at it from clear down in the kitchen."

Ethan turned two shades redder than he'd been just before and he hooked a hand around the back of his neck, clearly unsure who to console, who to appease.

Sadie crossed her arms, resisting the urge to point at her

husband and declare that *he* started it. "What's unacceptable is your son thinking he can treat me like a doormat," she declared, directing her words at Ethan. Anger was easier than dealing with his hurtful reaction.

Annette cocked her head. "You're a mother, so start acting like it. Do you think I ever shouted at Ethan's dad that way? Of course not. I was grateful for how hard he worked to provide for our family."

Saint Richard Landry had passed away five years ago, meaning Sadie had never known the man who was by all accounts a legendary husband—maybe too legendary according to Ethan—but Sadie would never venture into "besmirching" Richard's memory territory not even for the sake of a satisfying comeback.

But she couldn't stay in this bedroom, this house, a second longer. This space should be safe ground, a refuge, but right now it felt as treacherous as quicksand.

"Excuse me, I have to leave."

She flew past her mother-in-law, husband, and son, practically falling down the steep staircase and into the foyer.

"Hey! Where are you going?" Ethan called.

"I need air." She grabbed her keys and purse. She slid into the minivan and headed for town without any clear destination. She watched the cozy cottages pass by in a daze, their gardens backing up to the shores of the ocean. Did everyone assume the people who lived inside them had equally idyllic lives? Let her be the first to burst that bubble.

Chapter Six

Renee plopped the heavy bags of flour and sugar on the conveyor belt before searching through her crowded handbag for the brown leather wallet Tansy had given her last Christmas.

"Looks like you're baking for quite the crowd tonight." Renee's friend Myles Morrison grinned. Myles owned the downtown grocery store, Shopper's Corner, and swore knowing people's food purchases could provide the juiciest gossip of all. "Which makes me wonder—why wasn't I invited?"

"Oh, stop." Renee waved a hand at him. "You know if I was having people over, you'd be right near the top of the list."

"Speaking of the top of *your* list. You know, Dr. Hanlon was just in here."

"Oh?" Renee's heart fluttered. "That's, um, nice."

"How is that gorgeous hunka hunka man single?" Myles sighed dramatically, placing Renee's purchases inside the reusable tote that for once she'd actually remembered to bring along. "He comes in here every Saturday and buys the same things: lentils, salmon, apples, peanut butter, spinach, and a loaf of whole-grain bread."

"Yum." Choices that obviously did a body good.

"How old do you suppose he is? Late forties or early fifties?" Myles had stylishly rumpled sandy blond hair and deep smile lines etched around his bright brown eyes. He was a handsome, middle-aged man, yet still reminded Renee so much of the playful high school class clown she'd known so well. Ever since her divorce from Russell, Myles had been trying to set up Renee with various bachelors around town. "I'm already taken, of course, but you should go African savannah on that man, hunt him down like a gazelle at a watering hole."

"Uh-huh. I'm hardly a lioness. And stop it already, that's my boss you're talking about."

"You stop. Nathan and I have been bingeing old *Grey's Anatomy* and I am feeling this. Tell you what, I'm going to start calling him Dr. McSteamy."

Renee wanted to crawl under a rock. "Do so at your own peril. Remember I broke your nose in third grade."

Myles rubbed the bump. "Trust me, I remember. And I learned my lesson, too. Beware of the quiet ones, and never insult Renee's little sister."

Poor Bree had used a pair of scissors to cut her hair. And Myles had the nerve to make a joke about her crazy, choppy hairstyle, which meant Renee had no choice but to promptly bop him in the face.

The front door chime rang violently as Sadie Landry barreled in, eyes bloodshot and nose pink.

"Sadie?" Renee called, half relieved to get away from Myles and half concerned for Sadie's distraught state. "How did the party go?"

"Oh, Renee, hi." Sadie's voice came out an octave too high, as they both realized at the same instant that her jacket was on inside out. "Lincoln's party was awesome. So awesome. And everyone raved about your pies. As they should."

Renee nodded carefully, wondering if she should probe. "And your mother-in-law made it into town okay?"

"Yup. She's…at the house now. You know, just visiting." Sadie swallowed, before she let out a giant exhale. "I don't even know why I'm here. God knows we have enough juice boxes and macaroni-and-cheese packets to survive a hurricane."

"Sometimes it's just nice to get out."

"Yes. Yes, that's it exactly. I had to get out. I just don't know where to go." Her voice threatened to crack.

Renee glanced at her bags and considered the quiet evening she had planned. She was going to rewatch *Crazy Rich Asians* and try out a fig-raspberry-cardamom pie recipe she'd been inventing all day.

But now, seeing Sadie so completely unraveled, a different idea took hold.

"Wanna go with me to the pinot-and-paint fund-raiser? It's going on over at Chickadee Studios and proceeds benefit the summer youth art program."

Renee smiled as she thought of how surprised Bree would be to see her actually take her up on her invite.

"Weren't you supposed to buy tickets ahead of time?" Sadie asked quietly. "I mean, I love the summer art program. I always went when I was little. But I don't have a ticket."

Renee smiled. "Bree reserved two for me. I wasn't in the mood, but you know what, I need to get out more. And you look like you could use some fun, no offense."

Sadie trailed her out of Shopper's Corner and onto the sidewalk. Soon, all the window boxes that decorated Cranberry Cove's various businesses would be blooming, their flowers and vines vibrant and lush. Chickadee Studios, the town's popular gallery and gift shop, was just a few minutes' stroll from the grocery. The two women walked in silence, Sadie occasionally sniffling as Renee watched her with wary sideways glances.

She was dying to offer a hug or ask her some questions but just because they were neighbors didn't mean she had to be privy to every detail of Sadie's life.

Jill Kelly, the owner of Chickadee Studios, and Bree's best friend, greeted them.

"Sadie? Renee? What a fab surprise! Come on in. I've set everything up in the back. Pinot noir or pinot grigio?" Jill's hair always matched her glasses. It was her trademark. This evening her signature hue was violet. "I've also gathered a great cheese selection from Myles. There should be a few charcuterie boards floating around."

"Pinot grigio for me," Renee replied, while Sadie requested a water.

"La Croix or Spindrift? I'm becoming a sparkling water connoisseur." Jill's pale cheeks turned red. "I drink at least six different cans a day!"

"That's a lot of recycling!" Renee mock shuddered as Sadie laughed and said, "La Croix sounds great. Thank you."

Chickadee Studios had stark white walls and fairy lights hung across the ceiling, and Jill featured a different local artist's work every month. This month's choice was an artist who specialized in seashell murals. Distressed tables were covered with various pieces of jewelry, ceramics, and accessories.

"My mother-in-law would love this," Sadie mumbled to herself, examining a light blue merino scarf.

"Don't tell Bree. She'll get a big head," Renee fake-whispered. "But I'm so proud of her. Her stuff is incredible."

Renee and Bree's grandmother had taught both girls how to

knit, but it was Bree who had honed it into a true talent. When Renee was pregnant was Tansy, Bree had knitted the baby three blankets, four caps, and two dresses. She worked at the Castaway Yarn Shop, which was just a few doors down from Chickadee. The customers adored her, particularly since she was always happy to help repair a botched project, knitting and purling the way back to correctness.

Sadie bought the scarf while muttering something about a peace offering and slid the bag and receipt into her tote.

"I have you ladies set up here." Jill gestured toward two empty easels that were close to Dot, Essie, and Bree. The women were already a few glasses of wine deep and laughing hysterically.

"What's so funny?" Renee slipped an apron over her head. She squinted at the sample painting, which was of a lilac bush.

"Renee Rhodes? Is that you? In the flesh?" Bree joked, reaching over to squeeze her sister's hand. "My sister is out of the house! Is hell freezing over?"

"You ladies remember Sadie, right?" Renee set a protective hand on Sadie's shoulder, choosing to ignore Bree's teasing. She knew it came from a place of love, that and the fact that she often chose home over socializing, even after the excuse of being with Tansy was off the table. Sadie blushed and said a polite hello to the three women and Renee felt a rush of warmth at bringing people she enjoyed together.

"We were just dying over Dot's recent boyfriend," Bree volunteered, not even looking at Jill's lilac bush portrait as she splashed a generous daub of green across her canvas. "She invited him along on one of her power walks, and he couldn't keep up."

"So she kicked him to the curb three miles out of town." Essie gave an evil giggle. "He was panting and begging for Band-Aids, but Dot wouldn't slow down."

Dot Turner made a shooing gesture. "You all know how important fitness is to me! And of course, I wasn't about to blow my pace for some old duffer. Not when I've got the Appalachian Trail to bag!"

"Tell us what's new in your world, Sadie." Essie used the end of her paintbrush to push a strand of her jet-black hair behind her ear, showing off a giant diamond stud. "What are all the cool twenty-somethings doing these days?"

"Oh, yeah right. I'm living large. The craziest part of my week was pulling off a teddy bear picnic birthday party this afternoon," Sadie confessed, making the women cackle once more. "After I burned my original dessert last night, Renee came to the rescue and baked up four of her blueberry pies and as many muffins as all the two-year-olds could eat. Everything was a total hit." Renee pretended to be transfixed by her canvas as she felt Bree studying her thoughtfully.

"Renee's desserts are the best ever." Essie feigned orgasmic drooling. "A bite of her cherry pie is better than you-know-what."

The table dissolved into coy giggles.

"Her rhubarb is my favorite." Dot let out a wistful sigh. "Or maybe her chocolate salted caramel–pecan pie. An impossible choice."

"Jeez, thanks, guys. My ego has grown to the size of the North Atlantic. But there's no way that my pies are the best ever." Renee nodded toward Sadie. "That distinction goes to Sadie's grandma Hester. Gosh, remember her whoopie pies back when we were kids?"

"I heard she burnt the recipes on her deathbed," Essie hypothesized. "Lord knows that's what I'm doing with my diary before I croak."

"She always was the secretive type." Renee studied the sample portrait as if she were a student of Monet's. "She was quick to share a dessert but never a recipe. And lord knows I asked more than once."

"So true. Not that I can bake to save my life but I remember even I begged her once or twice for her vanilla-peach pie secrets," Dot admitted.

"I remember how she always arrived at the annual Fourth of July celebration with countless whoopie pies as well as seven different pies," Sadie said.

"Why was it always seven?" Renee asked.

"Her lucky number, I guess?" ventured Sadie. "My favorite was the cranberry-caramel. Yum!"

"Yes to that and all the other six, please!" Bree declared, making everyone laugh.

"What I remember most was the way she smelled." Sadie sighed. "Sugar and vanilla, all the time. I could use a little of that magic right now."

The women all grew quiet, not quite sure what to say.

Of course Essie broke the silence. "And how are your parents doing? Every time a new listing comes on the market, I send them a quick email. I always thought they'd be back in Cranberry Cove by now. I mean, D.C. is exciting and fast-paced if that's your scene, but few places are as special as the Cove."

"I thought so too," admitted Sadie, her voice small. "But my dad has his dream job, and now they have their dream house. No, I don't suspect they'll be back anytime soon. Maybe never. But, um, they visit, of course."

"Of course," Renee replied.

Sadie's parents had been high school sweethearts and homecoming king and queen. They had married right after college, settling in their hometown. Christopher had been a financial adviser with kind eyes and a broad smile, both of which Sadie had inherited. Melissa had worked in his office, always sporting the impossibly neat good looks of a Stepford wife.

Her parents had led a polished, practical life and they'd expected nothing less from Sadie. They'd kept an immaculate home and yard. They'd made an appearance at every important fund-raiser, always donating the perfect amount of money— not so little as to look stingy, but not so much as to look ostentatious. And the family had never missed a Sunday service at the local Episcopal church, wearing freshly ironed clothes, of course.

To Renee's knowledge, they now visited Cranberry Cove once each year—usually in the summertime—while the Landrys made the trip down to D.C. when they could.

It wasn't enough time, not in Renee's opinion.

When Tansy was two, Renee called her mother approximately twelve times a day. Plus, her mom lived just down the road and would stop by at least a few times each week, always with a casserole, fresh flowers, or an interesting article she'd cut out of a magazine. And she'd also had Bree and a husband who didn't spend half the week in Boston.

Renee studied her young neighbor, noticing how shy, almost crestfallen, she now seemed.

What a legacy to carry on between her legendary grandma and perfectly poised and astonishingly capable mother. It must be overwhelming being back here at times.

"Can I give you a lift home?" Renee asked Sadie when the fund-raiser started winding down.

"Oh, I drove. I'll be fine getting back. Thank you, though. Do you need a lift?" she lowered her voice. "Because I'm officially on designated-driver duty for the next nine months."

"I'll head home a little later, but let me at least walk you out," Renee insisted.

Sadie gave hugs all around before she and Renee walked out into the brisk night. "Thanks again for including me tonight," she said. "It's always fun getting to hear stories about my grandma."

"She was a special person, just like you."

As Sadie nodded, Renee noted the circles under her sad eyes.

"Are you sure you're okay?"

"No," Sadie admitted. "But I will be."

Renee squeezed Sadie's hand, hoping to offer her some small comfort. "Call me if you need anything. Okay?"

She regretted it as soon as it came out of her mouth—surely, her neighbor would find her suffocating, just as Tansy likely did off in California—but instead, Sadie hugged her tighter, whispering, "Promise."

Renee walked back into Chickadee Studios and returned to her seat.

"Hey lady." Essie raised her perfectly arched eyebrows in Renee's direction. "I have a proposition to make."

Renee arched a brow in return, as this was classic Essie Park. She was always coming up with big ideas, like the time she ran for class president and promised the school soda pop from the drinking fountains and dance parties every Friday afternoon. "And what's that?"

"I don't want to give too much away now, but how about you meet me at my office tomorrow morning for coffee?"

Chapter Seven

Sadie slumped in the front seat of the minivan, hands still gripping the steering wheel at ten and two, and studied her cottage—her grandma's home, the place where she was building her own family. Hearing the stories about Grandma Hester had opened up a vein of bittersweet nostalgia.

She thought of the way her mom used to drop her off, and as soon as her feet hit the pavement, Grandma would be pushing open that front door and ambling down the path to meet her.

"Ready to bake?" she'd always call out.

Her grandma's ramshackle style was a welcome haven from her more orderly, quiet home. She missed her so much even though she'd died right after Sadie had started high school. It made her happy to think that so many other people had joyful memories of her grandma and her cooking too.

Sighing, she surveyed the yard. Ethan had surprised her with two big hydrangea bushes for her last birthday, but they looked dejected and twiggy now. They wouldn't bloom until midsummer.

Taking a deep breath, Sadie dropped her keys into her purse, exited the car, and approached the alcove doorway like it was a medieval gallows. Ethan's car was still parked in the other spot, despite the fact that he'd been determined to floor it to Boston only a few hours ago. Was she relieved? Anxious? Disappointed?

The furtive texting had been strange earlier, but she didn't really think he was having an affair; he couldn't even cheat in cards without confessing his guilt. But something wasn't right, and hadn't been right for a while.

Sadie gently pushed the front door open, trying to be quiet. Lincoln went to bed at eight, and the last thing she wanted was to cause a scene by waking him. And yet, she pursed her lips, she'd had no trouble leaving him with his dad and grandma earlier.

God, how could she have just flown out of here like that? Her heart suddenly ached for her little guy. She wanted to rest her head on his curls and just let the world slip away. She loved him so much. The first floor was dark and still, the only light coming from the pendants that hung over the kitchen island. A piece of notebook paper, embossed with the name of her former design firm, was sitting out.

Sadie,

I've gone to stay at the bed-and-breakfast as I no longer feel welcome in your home. I also don't believe my doctor would want me to be in such a stressful environment. It isn't good for my blood pressure.

Have you considered anger management or perhaps counseling of some sort?

Annette

"Good lord," Sadie crumpled the note and threw it in the recycling bin. Looks like she wouldn't be winning daughter-in-law of the year. Leave it to Annette to insert herself in an argument that in no way involved her. Did she leave a nasty note for Ethan too? Doubtful.

Her own mother would have never done anything like this. No, even when Sadie herself did something upsetting as a child, like the time she'd glued various pieces of her mother's costume jewelry to a dress while playing "fashion designer." Melissa would simply sigh, "I'm disappointed in you. Now please go to your room and contemplate what you've done."

Yep. That was as emotional and angry as her mother would get. But somehow that wasn't comforting right now.

She turned up the dimmer light and gasped.

An empty macaroni-and-cheese box sat on the countertop beside a forgotten carton of milk. The sink was full of dirty dishes. How the heck had Ethan trashed the entire kitchen preparing such a simple meal? And who did he think was going to clean this all up? Some sort of house elf? She dumped the warm milk down the sink, tossed the carton into the recycling bin, and soaked the dirty dishes in the sink.

The house elf wouldn't be back on the job until morning.

Sadie crept up the stairs. Lincoln's bedroom door was closed, so quietly as she could, she nudged it open to peek inside. Her toddler was sound asleep, his mouth slightly ajar and his favorite stuffed animal, a velvet rabbit, tucked under his arm.

Lincoln's bedroom had been her favorite to decorate. She'd gone with a travel theme of sorts. The walls were a calming shade of blue and she'd hung framed whimsical prints of various cities on one wall: London, Paris, New York. Lincoln had shelves overflowing with books and a giant beanbag chair to snuggle up in. It was a cozy and happy space. It was also gender neutral, meaning they could use the nursery for the next baby and move Lincoln to the guest room.

Sadie whispered, "Love you" before pulling the door closed. The door to her and Ethan's room was ajar. She could see him sitting up in bed wearing his thick-rimmed Persols that had always turned her on, especially paired with his bare chest and plaid pajama pants. He glared at his phone with worried concentration, his brows furrowed and his lower teeth latched on to his top lip.

She stepped into the lamplight. "No Boston?"

"No." He didn't look up. "Mom got worked up after all the commotion, so I put her up in a B&B. And since our two-year-old can't stay home alone…"

"Yeah, he'd throw a rager. Goldfish crackers everywhere and a keg full of juice."

Her husband took off his glasses and polished the lenses with the sheet. "You can't just take off like that."

"A little hypocritical coming from the guy who drove off leaving me to deal with burnt cupcakes, a soaked kitchen, and a toddler," she said. "And if you were so concerned, why didn't you come after me?"

Ethan shook his head. "I didn't want to get into it again."

Nice. So his fear of arguing outweighed his concern for her well-being or safety. Real heartwarming.

"I ended up at a fund-raiser with Renee, for the summer arts program."

"Oh."

"And now I'm going to bed," she said flatly, disappearing into the master bathroom.

She brushed her teeth and then scrubbed her face with a makeup-removing facial wipe before slipping into a pair of silk pajamas. The floral-printed set was quite the upgrade compared to the sweatpants and oversized T-shirt she usually wore to bed.

She studied her reflection in the mirror. At first glance, she looked like a pretty young mother. But when she really examined herself, there were bags beneath her eyes and her skin looked dry and sallow.

Worst of all, she looked sad.

"You haven't worn that in a while," Ethan said when she scooted into the bed beside him.

She didn't know what to say, so she just nodded, plumping her pillow.

"I shouldn't have said what I did before," he said, turning to face her.

"Which part?"

"Any of it. Listen. I'm excited about this baby. I really am." He took her cold hands in his warm ones and squeezed. "I love being a father, and I can't wait to see Lincoln be an older brother."

Sadie sniffed, her throat getting tight. "I'm excited, too, but I'm also really scared, Ethan. It's like you said, I'm overwhelmed as it is. And it was really hard recovering from birth the last time."

He gathered her close and she relaxed into his gentle strength. This, *this*, was her Ethan. Not the guy she screamed at from the front porch. But this man who made her feel protected and loved.

"I know it gets stressful. Maybe sometimes I idealize it in my head, you know? When I'm down in Boston, I think of you and Lincoln, all cozy in our cottage, and I think how amazing that sounds, how much I want to be here with you both."

She liked the thought of that, of Ethan down in the city day-dreaming about her and Lincoln and their little home.

"You're a wonderful mom. Our child adores you. I do too. I'm sorry for not helping out more around here. Work is insane right now, Marlow is up my ass, and I've unloaded some of that on you. That isn't fair."

"No." Sadie nodded, and thought about asking why he changed his cellphone code but she didn't want to pop open a fresh can of worms, especially when they'd finally reached a fragile peace. "And I know I've been taking a lot of my stress out on you. I'm sorry too."

"Work is killing me right now, but it won't be forever."

"Do you think it'll get easier? This whole parenting thing?" Sadie touched her stomach. "Maybe we'll do better on our second try?"

Ethan tapped the light out and settled into his sleeping position. "It's all going to be okay."

She wanted to believe him, even more than that…she wanted to be sure of him. That he had her back. That she had his. Some days might feel like trench warfare, but they were fighting on the same side.

"Do you think you'll get in trouble?" she asked. "For not going down to Boston tonight?"

"I'll survive," he murmured.

She tapped her foot to his, their old signal, a sign that she was in the mood. Sex wasn't a Band-Aid, but she craved closeness. Maybe with Ethan inside her, they'd feel whole again.

But he didn't reply—he'd already fallen asleep, officially ending the conversation.

This was one of his dubious superhero skills. No doubt a coping mechanism to end conflict. Or maybe he really was just that exhausted.

She rolled over and pulled the sheet up around her neck. They'd said all the right things, apologized for the ugly words, and yet the entire interaction hadn't quite closed the gulf.

Sadie stared at the framed prints above the dresser, lit in the moonlight.

NEVER GO TO BED ANGRY

ALWAYS KISS ME GOODNIGHT

They were wedding gifts from her college friends and not exactly her taste. Especially in a moment such as this one, when they felt mocking. She wasn't mad. Not anymore. But she wanted everything to feel like it used to, back when they first fell in love and everything seemed perfect. Those days were over, but perhaps there could be a new kind of perfect ahead.

She closed her eyes, but tired as she was, couldn't drift off.

What if all that waited for them was a slow coast downhill until one day they hit the cliff of no return?

With Ethan snoring quietly, she slid out of bed and crept downstairs. It was only ten. She made herself a mug of chamomile tea, and after grabbing a chenille blanket, curled up on the sofa. She turned on the TV and scanned through the Netflix homepage, clicking by various shows and movies.

Nothing seemed like it could hold back her anxiety. Not even *Queer Eye*.

In a sudden rush of loneliness, she dialed her parents.

"Sweetheart," her mother answered on the second ring, "everything okay?" They had already talked earlier on FaceTime when both her mom and dad had called to wish Lincoln a happy birthday.

"Everything's okay but is now a good time to chat?"

"Your father's already in bed. We had dinner tonight with the ambassador of France, remember? A little too much burgundy may have been served. We opened the 2003 Domaine Denis Mortet."

"Bringing out the big guns," Sadie quipped, realizing that she had completely forgotten to eat any sort of dinner herself. She wandered into the kitchen and pulled a bag of baby carrots and a tub of hummus from the refrigerator.

"I'm just wrapping up some paperwork I wasn't able to get to earlier," her mom offered. "What about you? Spending time with the mother-in-law from Ohio?"

Even though she knew her parents wouldn't make the trip for their only grandkid's birthday party, Sadie had made a point to invite them. One of the little tests she found herself doing now and again. *Do you love me? If so, how much?*

And the fact that her parents hadn't taken her request seriously at all was a sprinkle of salt to an old wound. One where she felt like she cramped their style, unless she did something extraordinary that let them brag to their friends.

"Not really, she can be tricky." Understatement. "But the party went really well. I did a teddy bear picnic theme and put together these little picnic basket favors." Sadie swallowed hard before she continued. "I was actually calling to tell you some pretty exciting news on our end."

"Oh?" Her mother's voice lifted and Sadie could just picture her plucked eyebrow lifting too.

"Actually, I'm, um, Ethan and I are expecting again."

There was stunned silence before her mother leapt into action. "Another baby, how wonderful darling. May I offer my congratulations to Ethan?"

Sadie shook her head, even though her mother couldn't see. "He's already out for the night as well."

"Tomorrow then, and I'm sure your father will be thrilled with the news."

Fighting back tears, Sadie gave in to the real reason for the call. "I was actually wondering if you and Dad could come and stay with us when the baby comes? I should be due right after

Halloween. Maybe you guys could stay through Christmas? We'd really appreciate the extra help."

There was an uncomfortable silence on the other end of the phone.

Her mother cleared her throat. "Oh, honey. Maybe we can come up for a weekend or two, but you know how serious your father is about his job. Especially now that he's nearing sixty, he doesn't want the boss to think they can survive without him. And I have my own duties, of course."

Melissa's words stung, especially considering she herself hadn't worked since their move to D.C., though she did keep very busy serving on committees and volunteering.

"Oh." Sadie closed her eyes and wished she could pour herself a drink. "Well, of course. I understand."

She'd always considered her parents an emergency backup. Not people to call upon except in great need. And here she was and the answer was no.

"We'll work something out though. My friends tell me their kids are hiring night nurses or doulas or whatever they call them these days to help out. Maybe we could pitch in for something like that?"

"No. No, it's fine. We'll be fine."

But as they said their goodbyes, she wanted to throw a tantrum of her own. Beg to be taken care of. While her parents had always provided a roof over her head, nutritious meals on the table, and stylish clothes in her closet, they hadn't been the types to stay up late reading her bedtime stories or spend entire weekends camped out at the beach together.

No, it hadn't been until Sadie met Ethan that she felt truly and completely taken care of by another person.

But what if she ended up not being enough and pushing that person away?

Outside the window, a foghorn sounded, long and lonely.

Chapter Eight

W hat's this?" Dr. Dan smiled, as Renee set a masterpiece of a pie in front of him.

"Just a little something to get the week off to a sweet start." Renee had spent her entire Sunday cleaning, watching old home videos of Tansy, and baking pies. This raspberry pie had been her most beautiful one of all, and she'd known there was only one recipient deserving of its perfection.

"Would you judge me if I had a piece for breakfast?" he asked in great seriousness. "I don't want my street cred as a medical care provider to be tarnished."

"I promise your secret is safe with me."

"Wow, wow, wow," he moaned with his mouth full. Renee hated when people talked while chewing, but when Dr. Dan did it? Well, she didn't seem to mind at all. "This is incredible, Renee."

It was satisfying to watch anyone enjoy her pies, but to see Dr. Dan take such obvious pleasure? That had left her a little dizzy.

"Breakfast will never be the same," he declared practically

licking the plate. "I'll keep the rest of this pie hidden in my office, not to be greedy."

"Don't worry, there's more where that came from," Renee said, before she realized how that sounded and blushed.

Luckily she heard the sound of the door opening. "It's Declan Shroeder," she reported. "Another Lego stuck in nostril emergency."

They both laughed. The five-year-old had been in just last week with the same predicament.

"Renee, wait." Dr. Dan reached out, gently touching her shoulder. "I forgot our last word of the day. Here it is."

Ebullient: cheerful and energized.

"Here's to an ebullient week," he said.

"I'll toast to that," she whispered, raising a mason jar half-filled with chamomile tea.

She stared at the fish tank, tapping a pen on her cheek as she played the image of Dr. Dan taking a bite of her pie over and over again.

Poor Kristen Shroeder had to rap on the front desk twice to get her attention following Declan's appointment.

"I'm so embarrassed this happened again." She sighed, signing the credit card receipt with one hand while holding her boy's hand in the other. Her dirty blond hair looked like it hadn't been washed in days, and there were smudges of mascara beneath her eyes. "I don't know why this is a thing for him. It can't feel good cramming plastic up there."

"Stuff happens. My daughter once swallowed a button, and it scared me half to death." There she went, interjecting Tansy anecdotes at the first chance. "Anyway. As much as we love seeing Mr. Declan, hopefully you won't have to visit us again so soon."

Kristen laughed and thanked her, zipping up their jackets. As Kristen and Declan exited the doctor's office, Essie Park strolled in.

What is she doing here? Oh, no! The meeting!

They were supposed to meet for coffee yesterday morning, and Renee had just plain forgot, so caught up in her usual quiet routine. She was completely embarrassed. Though she had a bad habit of canceling plans, she always had the decency to call first.

"Essie! Hey," Renee said, standing up to greet her. Essie was wearing that amazing trench coat she'd gotten while visiting her relatives in South Korea last winter, and her black hair was pulled into a sleek bun. "I am so sorry about yesterday! I got carried away baking and I completely forgot about our meeting. And, um, we've been so busy here today. I guess it slipped my mind to shoot you a text this morning."

Essie did a dramatic once-over of the empty waiting room, the only movement being the pages of an old issue of *O* magazine fluttering in the breeze of a ceiling fan. Even the fish seemed quieter, more still than usual.

"Oh, hello Essie." Dr. Dan slipped in behind Renee. She loved the way he stood beside her chair. It made her feel cared for, protected. He set today's word-of-the-day tear-out on her desk. *Moxie.* "What brings you in?"

"Hello you," Essie almost purred. "I'm trying to twist your receptionist's arm to get her to join me for a lunch meeting."

He glanced at his watch, a classic, analog model and not one of those trendy smart watches. "We aren't expecting any patients for at least an hour. Why don't you take a break now?"

Renee looked out the front doors. It was a gorgeous April day, the sort where there's a blissful mix of a cool breeze and warm sunshine. And she would like to spend some time properly catching up with her friend, no matter what this "proposition" of hers might be.

"You know what? You're right," she said with a smile.

Essie clapped her hands together. "Let's go to the Perfect Pair."

Five minutes later they were walking into the Cove's popular café. The Perfect Pair had once been a greenhouse and was one of the more magical spots in town. Ferns hung from the ceiling and bistro tables were nestled among green, leafy plants and colorful flowers.

"Just two?" The college-aged hostess had auburn hair with bleached ends. Renee immediately thought of Tansy and wondered if she'd done anything dramatic with her hair. They hadn't FaceTimed in forever.

"Yes. Can we sit near the jasmine? That smell is just the best," Essie replied.

"Sure. Follow me."

The two women sat, spread their napkins across their laps, and ordered iced tea. They chatted about Essie's current remodeling project (she'd hired a cute handyman to refinish her laundry room and was considering wallpaper in her upstairs bathroom) before their brunch arrived.

"So, my proposition," Essie began carefully. "Have you ever been inside the Old Red Mill?"

Renee nodded. "We used to hang out on the grounds in the summer, bonfires and stuff."

"Renee Rhodes, trespasser and rule breaker. I'm impressed. Well, it's finally been sold and there are five leases inside. It needs work to get it up to snuff, but once it's there...Oh, I just know it's going to be the new hub for the town. So much potential. It's mind-boggling. I want you to consider opening the anchor store—a pie shop."

"Me?" Renee nearly dropped her fork. "But what about Castaway Yarn? Bree keeps saying that they're outgrowing their current space. Or what about Chickadee? Jill could host more art classes if she had the room."

"I love both those shops as much as anyone, but the first lease needs to be something universal." Essie pushed her food to the side, having only eaten a few bites. "Everyone loves your pies. Children, teenagers, women, men. There isn't one target group. It's the sort of spot that everybody in town could and would appreciate."

"But I'm a hobbyist. It's not as though I've ever been to business school or even had any professional training."

"So? You have raw talent. The rest you can learn."

Renee took another bite of quiche and mulled. On the one hand, thanks to Tansy's USC scholarship, she had the startup funds. Ever since her divorce, she'd squirreled away money for college. She'd hoped Russ would contribute when the time came around, but knew she couldn't rely on him. But as it turned out, Tansy's full ride left Renee with quite an impressive savings account.

Still, what if she funneled her nest egg into the pie shop and it went bust? The thought of flushing so many years of hard-earned money down the drain made her queasy.

"I'll think about it," she promised Essie. "I mean it. I'll consider your proposition, but I don't make snap decisions. You know me, I'm a ponderer." She needed to soak in her bath, the place where she did all her deep thinking.

Essie looked appeased. "That's all I could ask for! Ponder away."

Later that day, while she was powering down her computer and placing all of her paperwork into neat stacks, Dr. Dan stopped by her desk to say goodnight. It was something he did every evening and a bittersweet moment. She appreciated the gesture but hated that it meant them going their separate ways. It was nice to have someone to talk to throughout the day. It was nice to have *him* to talk to.

He propped himself up on her desk, his long legs dangling down. She noticed his socks were mismatched. "Everything okay? You seem distracted."

"What was the tip-off?"

"Maybe it was when you tried to apply a removable tattoo to Mrs. Smith's hand rather than Ellie's. I'm not so sure Elsa has the same broad appeal for thirty-somethings as she does for three-year-olds."

"Guilty as charged." She smoothed a hand over her red hair. "The Old Red Mill has sold and Essie is looking to lease out spaces. She wants me to open a pie shop there, to be an anchor store of sorts."

It felt strange to say the words aloud, like she was trying out a foreign language.

He shook his head, so excited he popped off the desk and started pacing. "It's brilliant."

"Really?" Renee stood so she could pull on her jacket. They were only a few inches apart, and she imagined she could smell the lemon tang of his soap. "Do you think people would pay for my pies? I know everyone seems to enjoy them, but it's not as though I've ever sold any before."

"One hundred percent," he replied, so confidently, Renee felt tingles. He nodded toward her desk. "What was our word of the day? 'Moxie'? I think it will just take a bunch of that."

Our word of the day.

Our. Our. Our.

It felt like her smile could light up the eastern seaboard. "Thank you, Dr. Hanlon."

"Dan, please. And I'm always here, if you ever need an ear," he said, before quickly adding, "I mean, I know you have Tansy, and your sister, of course I just meant—"

"No, thank you." Was he flirting? He was, wasn't he? Absolutely. Or maybe not. Gah, she was out of practice. She settled on, "I appreciate that."

She just wondered if he knew how much.

* * *

When she got home from work, she heated up a piece of rotisserie chicken and tossed herself a kale salad with hazelnuts and a tart vinaigrette. She ate her dinner with a glass of iced tea while perusing her favorite cooking blogs. But through it all, she daydreamed about the pie shop, the gingham curtains she'd hang in the windows and the mismatched plates she'd use to serve the warm, flaky slices.

What would Tansy say? She reached for her phone, eager to share the idea.

The phone rang four times before her daughter answered, breathless and distracted, as usual.

"Hi honey. Did you have a nice day?"

"Nice as a Monday can be." Her tone was flat, impatient.

"Right. I get that," Renee said awkwardly. "What are you up to tonight? Homework and studying?"

Tansy had always been a dedicated student, spending hours on her homework each evening, especially by the time her junior and senior years came around. Most weeknights, Renee would set a warm plate of supper on the edge of Tansy's antique desk and gently close the door behind her.

"I'm wading through this brutal philosophy paper on Nietzsche."

"Babe, I'm out. Same time tomorrow?" a male voice said in the background. Though the sound was muffled, his words were clear.

"Let me guess." Renee cleared her throat. "A study buddy?" Although Tansy had a few boyfriends through high school, none of them had been very serious, and she certainly hadn't distracted herself by having them over while doing schoolwork.

"Mom." Tansy's voice went from moody to straight-up cold. "School isn't just books."

Renee didn't have it in her to spar with her daughter, especially not over the phone and thousands of miles apart.

"Well, I'll let you go then," she said curtly.

Tansy either didn't recognize the hurt in her mother's voice or simply didn't care. Almost relieved, she replied, "Yep. Bye."

Click.

Renee took three deep breaths, the kind she practiced in yoga, to steady herself. Where had her sweet daughter gone and who was this stranger who had replaced her?

If Tansy wasn't going to be a good sounding board, that meant a bike ride to Bree's place on the hill was in order. The exercise would be good, and her sister was the best listener. She'd have things to say.

Renee pulled her vintage beach cruiser out of the shed and started off for Bree's. Sadie and Lincoln were in their driveway tossing a colorful bouncy ball back and forth as she rode by. Looks like peace had been restored at the Landry household. Should she ask or let it be?

She slowed down to say hi, to check in. "Hey Sadie, hey Lincoln."

"Hey Renee, thanks again for everything. I love your bike. I wish I had one."

Was it Renee's imagination or did Sadie still look a little wistful.

"Why don't you borrow Tansy's some time, and we can go for a ride?" she replied. "Catch up?"

"I'd love that!"

"Mama play!" Lincoln demanded, grabbing the ball out of Sadie's hands.

"Okay, I am seriously going to take you up on that," Renee said as she took off down the quiet street toward Bree's grand Victorian. Her sister had inherited the home from their parents following their mother's death from breast cancer. Renee pressed the doorbell to the side of the ornate glass front door and waited. The front mat had an image of a kitten playing with a ball of yarn. Perfect for Bree.

"Hey there, sis." Bree's curly blond hair was pulled into a damp bun on top of her head, and her forehead was wrinkled into a frown. Her blue eyes looked big and a little wild. "What brings you to my neck of the woods?"

Renee shifted her weight, slightly jarred by Bree's unusual appearance. Her face was usually soft and smooth, her eyes bright and excited. "Sorry to pop in on you unexpectedly."

"No, that's okay. I just finished a shower. Is everything all right?"

She studied her younger sister. She definitely looked a little frazzled, a little distracted. "Mostly, yeah. Did I come at a bad time?"

Bree hesitated before shrugging. "Sort of. I'm getting to the middle of this wicked sweater, and it's got me pretty, um, occupied."

Strange. Depending on their difficulty level, Bree's knitting projects always relaxed her or excited her. She didn't even open the door. Clearly, she wanted to be left alone.

Stranger still.

"Ah, well...I'll leave you to it then. I was just in the neighborhood and decided to stop by." Which was mostly true. "Why don't you come over tomorrow night for dinner?"

"Um, maybe?" Bree faltered.

"Since when don't you jump at the invitation of a free dinner?" Renee smiled, though Bree didn't return the smirk. "I can make one of your favorites—maybe that brown sugar–crusted salmon?"

"I just, I have a lot of stuff going on. But, um, thanks."

Okay. So, Bree was definitely hiding something, but what? The sisters shared everything. To the best of Renee's knowledge, a secret had never existed between the pair. From the time Renee had accidentally left the medical practice unlocked for an entire weekend (nothing had been stolen, thank goodness) to Bree asking her sister to take her to the doctor for birth control in high school, they felt comfortable telling one another *everything*.

"You're acting weird," Renee said, going the blunt route. Suddenly, an idea struck. "Do you have a guy over right now?" Like her, Bree wasn't exactly active on the dating scene.

"Ha, good one. But no. Just knitting a sweater. Like I told you before."

She pulled Renee in for a weirdly tender hug. Renee squeezed back, wondering just what was going on.

"Enjoy the rest of your bike ride," Bree said, gently, but firmly closing the door.

With a heavy sigh, Renee peddled back home where she drew a hot bath. She poured lavender oil beneath the faucet and lit a candle. Then she settled into the warm water, positioned her gel eye mask, and skimmed an idle finger along her collarbone.

Imagine if Dr. Dan visited the pie shop.

"Oh, we're about to close," she'd say. Behind him, the windows would show off a gilded sunset. "Can I package you something up to go?"

"Better make it sweet." Dan would then flip the sign over, from open to closed, and lock the door behind him. "And I'd prefer to eat in."

He'd prowl behind the counter with a determined urgency, press her against the back wall and kiss her fully, nipping at her lower lip. His tanned hands would caress her arms, tease the sides of her breasts, the crease of her butt. He'd drag her hips to him, and she'd feel every bit of how excited he was…

With a start, Renee sat up in the tub, slid off her eye mask, and sucked in a few deep breaths.

Good lord. Her body hadn't felt so hot since she fell asleep last summer sunbathing on her patio and could barely stand to wear pants for a week.

Do not have sex fantasies about your boss, Renee.

The Coastal Kids Medical Group had been a godsend after Russell left her. Dr. Brewer had hired Renee despite the fact that she had an English literature background rather than a scientific one. She was paid generously and been privileged to work a flexible schedule, meaning she could see Tansy off in the morning and be waiting for her at home in the afternoons.

Even though Tansy's childhood days were long gone, Renee would never jeopardize her position at the practice.

It kept her feeling balanced, stable, needed.

Dan Hanlon was hot—but so what? The last handsome man who made her heart flutter had left her alone and rejected.

She released the drain and fumbled with the faucet.

Time for a cold shower.

Chapter Nine

I really don't think they're up there."

"Well, I really think they are," Sadie retorted to Ethan, giving the creaky ladder a shake to make sure she didn't break her neck. Gingerly, she stepped on the first wrung.

"Please get down from there," he sighed, placing his hands on her hips protectively. "I don't want my pregnant wife climbing a rickety old ladder."

She was on a quest to find the family's Easter decorations, and even though Ethan swore the only items he'd ever stored in the attic were Christmas lights, she had turned the house inside out looking for the cardboard box of plastic eggs and miniature wicker bunnies. If they weren't in the basement storage area, garage, or the catchall of a hall closet, where else could they be?

Ethan stood below and spotted her as she made the rest of her way upstairs. "Shout for me when you want to come down, okay?"

"Okay," she agreed.

Ethan and his laptop disappeared back down the staircase. Not only had he spent most of the workweek in Boston, Ethan had spent nearly every minute he was home on his computer. He would join Sadie and Lincoln for a quick dinner, and then retreat to his office until bedtime. Every day was filled with apologies, but that didn't change the fact that today he'd set an alarm for six and had been staring at the screen ever since.

She'd tried asking him more about his current project, but all he did was rattle on about Java until she felt like she needed a triple-shot latte.

She knew he wanted her patience. And she was trying to find some the best way she knew how, by decorating.

Etched-glass eggs, floral bunny serving platter, and seagrass Easter baskets—here she comes!

Dust motes floated in the dim light of the attic. When they first moved to Seashell Lane, this area was supposed to be part of their home renovation. Sadie had fantasies of a home office with angled ceilings and skylights. That's when she thought she'd be doing freelance work after the baby was born. She and Ethan would have split the space evenly, setting up their respective workspaces on either end and convening in the middle for coffee breaks and cuddles with their new babe. They would set up a Pack 'n Play for the baby to nap while they worked, and everyone would be one, happy family.

Sadie sighed. If only that dream had come true.

She peered around now. There was the box of Christmas lights Ethan had mentioned, as well as the reindeer and snowman that perched in the front yard last December. But most of the boxes were ones Sadie didn't recognize. She wondered if the previous owners, the Brewers, had left them behind. Dr. Reggie Brewer had been Renee's former boss at the Coastal Kids Medical Group. He and his wife had retired to North Carolina to be closer to their son, which was when Ethan had swooped in and purchased the cottage.

When Sadie was up here in the attic, the musty air reminded her of Grandma and Grandpa. Despite Grandma Hester's expertise in the kitchen, she'd never been much of a housekeeper. And once Grandpa Hank's sight began to go, he wasn't great about catching all the dust bunnies either. Sadie liked this smell just as much as the scent of Grandma's pies baking. It made her feel cozy and warm. Safe.

"Hello gorgeous," she murmured catching sight of an antique steamer trunk in the very back corner. Maybe she could refinish the piece and use it as a coffee table.

She crept over, fumbled with the brass latches, and pushed it open.

The chest was filled with old photographs and countless sheets of yellowed paper. Some of the photos were in black-and-white but most were in faded color, and the paper was covered in elegant cursive. She picked up one of the photos, presumably of a mother and her young daughter. The woman was wearing some amazing plaid bell-bottoms and holding a pigtailed little girl in her arms. They both had the same button nose as Sadie, and her same sprinkling of freckles. She turned the photo over and read: "Hester and Melissa, May 1975."

It was Grandma Hester and her mom!

Her heart beat faster.

This wasn't from the Brewers. This was *her* family.

Sadie carefully pulled out photo after photo of family members past and present. There was her mother holding up a Barbie in front of the Christmas tree, and a snapshot of Grandpa Hank deep sea fishing. She set aside the pictures she wanted to share with her parents and Ethan, plus a picture of Grandma Hester taking a pie out of the oven to show Renee. She read the letters quickly, knowing she would read them again, much slower, much more carefully, later. They were love letters shared between Grandpa Hank and Grandma Hester.

What a treasure trove!

But when Sadie stumbled across a weathered notebook of sorts, its leather cover peeling off, she sensed she was uncovering something extraordinary. It was dusty and fragile but seemed to radiate a sort of power and happy energy. Gingerly, she opened the book and read the first page.

"Hester's Recipe Collection," the author had written proudly.

Sadie flew through the pages, reading recipes for potato casserole and oyster stuffing, before she found the section she'd been looking for: Desserts.

And the very first recipe that was listed: Grandma Hester's Whoopie Pies.

Not burned. Not lost. Simply forgotten.

"Mommy! Mommy, I awake!" Lincoln cried out, startling Sadie.

"I'm coming, babe!" she called back, then raised her voice a little louder. "Ethan? I'm ready to come down the ladder now!"

Brushing her hands off on her jeans, Sadie gathered the recipe book and assortment of family photos before Ethan appeared at the bottom of the ladder. He held his arms out as she carefully made her way down, ready to spring into action and catch her should she slip.

"Thanks, honey," she said with a smile, a warmth in her chest.

"Of course." He kissed her forehead. "Gotta get back to work."

Right then.

Her smile fading, she set her findings on the dresser in her bedroom before going to retrieve Lincoln from his.

"Hi sweetie. Did you have a nice nap?" She'd kept Lincoln up too late the night before playing and snuggling and the cranky toddler had definitely needed a little morning snooze.

"Yes. I dream about robots."

Sadie loved this about Lincoln. He seemed to dream every single time he went to sleep, just like Sadie did (just last night she'd dreamed about being on HGTV's *Design Star* and having to fashion a coffee table out of licorice). As Lincoln found his words and started to talk more and more, Sadie was getting to enjoy how he flexed his imagination.

"I love robots." Sadie widened her eyes. "But guess what I love more? Swimming! After spring comes summer, and that's when we get to play in the water."

"Beach?"

"Yep, baby. All beach, all the time."

Summer was her favorite time in Cranberry Cove. She loved getting to the beach early, setting out a giant umbrella and striped towels, using their large canvas tote as an anchor. Then, they'd build elaborate sandcastles and hold hands as they jumped over waves, laughing hysterically each time they stumbled. They would eat strawberries and peanut butter sandwiches for lunch, washing it all down with lemonade. While Lincoln took an afternoon snooze, Sadie would read a romance novel, the only background noise the roll of the waves and the call of seagulls.

Heaven.

"We go now?" Lincoln asked her excitedly. "Now!"

Sadie shrugged. "Well, okay! But no swimming, buddy. Too cold."

"Good idea," Lincoln agreed so seriously, so rationally, it made Sadie giggle.

She plopped a little baseball cap on Lincoln, and a far less adorable one on her own head, before packing the tote with sand toys. They stopped in the doorway of Ethan's office.

"Lincoln and I are going to walk on the beach. Come with?" she asked brightly.

"Can't," Ethan replied absently. He had started to hunch forward as he worked, and she worried about his shoulders and back. "Lincoln, will you bring me back a seashell? A really special one?"

"You come! Come!" Lincoln ordered. "Daddy come!"

"Daddy has to work," Ethan replied, turning back to his computer screens, his dual monitors looking like a command center. "Sorry, bud."

When had Ethan's job become so demanding? Why was her husband suddenly more absent when he was home than when he was in Boston?

Renee was outside gardening and waved to the pair. She looked put together in a beige pullover with her hair tied into a neat ponytail. Her pair of red Keds looked pristine, and her jeans were weathered in a chic way.

Sadie looked down at her own outfit, which had become a uniform of sorts: sneakers, black yoga pants, and one of Ethan's old Ohio State sweatshirts, which had a hole in the right elbow.

"Lincoln and I are going to walk on the beach. Want to join in the fun?" She hadn't gotten to see much of Renee this week and was surprised to realize how much she missed her neighbor's company.

Renee paused for only half a second before nodding. "I'd love to!"

She tossed her gardening gloves on a small bench and strolled over to Sadie and Lincoln. The trio made the short walk down to the shore. Lincoln ran off in front of them, giddy with excitement.

The two women were quiet at first, merely appreciating the warm spring sun and the rhythmic pulse of the waves.

"How are you feeling?"

"Not as nauseous as the first go around, touch wood," said Sadie, pausing to rap on a log. "It's still there, but at least I can be out in the world without dive bombing every trash can in sight."

"That's great. And how goes it with the mother-in-law?"

"It had its moments." She stayed at the stupid B&B the rest of the visit to make a point. "But Lincoln thinks she's the best thing since hot fudge on ice cream."

Renee cocked her head, gaze probing. "And you not so much?"

"No, she's fine." Sadie tucked a loose hair behind her ear and shrugged. "We're just, well, different. Oil and water."

"What does she do back home?"

"Babysit her local grandkids a lot and volunteer with the Junior League."

Renee nodded. "Well at least she was game to fly in for Lincoln's party."

"She is a great grandma." Sadie wished she could also add that Annette was a great mother-in-law, but the lie stuck in her throat. "Hey, how's Tansy doing at USC?"

"Busy, far too busy for me," Renee said before clearing her throat. "Not to change the subject but Essie Park has hit me up with the most outrageous idea."

"Outrageous ideas are Essie Park's bread and butter." Sadie remembered the time Essie found a two-for-one deal at some float therapy spa and had tried to get Sadie to come along. "What's she dreaming up this time?"

"So I guess the Old Red Mill sold and is open for leases?" Renee's voice tinged with nervous excitement. "Well, Essie wants me to open a pie shop, one that can serve as the anchor store and lure other small shops to follow."

"Shut up! That's the most amazing idea! Clearly you need to share your blueberry pies with the world."

"I don't know." Renee deflected even as her eyes shone. "It feels so risky."

Sadie's heartbeat quickened as she thought of her morning's discovery.

"Look at me." She held her neighbor at arm's length. "I really, truly think it's an awesome idea. And you won't believe what I found this morning in the attic—Grandma Hester's recipes. All of them. Including the whoopie pies."

Renee let out a sharp exhale and laughed. "Stop. You're kidding me."

"It's kismet. I'll bring them over. Maybe we could even try one out tonight. Your pie shop could include your own masterpieces as well as Grandma Hester's. It would be a perfect mix of new and nostalgia."

"I love it. Yes, let's bake some whoopie pies tonight and see if we can even come close to Grandma Hester's greatness," Renee said with a nod before growing quiet. "It's just…about the pie shop. I don't know the first thing about running a business. And apparently the space needs a ton of work. Have you seen my house? I haven't changed a damn thing since I moved in. All I do is add more finds from my antique adventures."

"I love your house. It's perfect," Sadie said with a smile, meaning it.

And yet, there was an excitement bubbling away in the pit of her stomach because she knew quite a lot about renovating spaces. She studied Renee's face, trying to read what she was feeling. Would Renee even want Sadie's help with this venture? Or would Sadie be stepping on her toes? What would Ethan say? They were already underwater as they tried to prepare for a second baby…Would he totally flip over the idea of Sadie working again?

Sadie pushed all of these thoughts aside and threw her hat into the ring.

"What if, well, what if I helped?" she volunteered shyly. "I'd be thrilled to design the space for you, Renee. I would think of every last detail, I can promise you that. I'll make the place perfect."

"Really? You would do that?"

"Absolutely." Sadie was on a roll now. "And, well, I'm also really great with numbers. I could even help you with the books and manage the business end of things."

Renee stopped walking on the beach. Sadie beamed back at her.

"You and I would be kick-butt partners," Renee declared without hesitation.

Sadie let out a squeal and hugged her friend tight, more optimistic than she'd been in months. Time to dig out the old sketchbooks and start working up concepts. Hopefully Essie would be available to show them the space tomorrow. It should feel snug and warm, yet fresh and bright. There had to be gingham fabric involved, that was for sure, and maybe they could frame some of the old photographs she'd found today of Grandma Hester.

She started, suddenly back in the present, looking at the quiet beach ahead, and then immediately out to the rolling sea.

Lincoln.

Where was he?

"Oh my God," Sadie breathed, turning left than right. "Where's Lincoln? He was just here, wasn't he?"

Renee looked wildly around the empty beach, as Sadie broke into a panicked run. "Lincoln? Lincoln! Where are you, baby?"

Chapter Ten

*H*ow *in the hell did Lincoln just up and vanish?*

Stupid question. Two-year-old boys were like lightning bugs...popping up here, there, and everywhere—then *poof* gone in a flash.

Renee could have sworn the little boy had been skipping just ahead, throwing driftwood and chasing gulls. But then, she'd gotten so stupidly carried away about the pie shop that a 747 could have landed on the dunes and she wouldn't have noticed.

A wave gnawed at the empty beach, hungry and heavy. An invisible band squeezed her chest. Most of the time she found the ocean's vast emptiness calming, a welcome counterpoint to all the hustle and bustle back on land. Yet the North Atlantic wasn't just fodder for oil paintings and tourist brochures. It was also cold, dark, full of hidden secrets, sharks, and drowned sailors. Unspeakable fear mounted in her throat, holding her tongue hostage.

Lincoln hadn't wandered near the shore break, right?

Sadie sprinted ahead, head swiveling from side to side. "Lincoln, honey!" Her frightened voice cracked. "Are you hiding? Are you playing a silly game? Come out, come out, wherever you are!"

Renee had lost Tansy once during a trip to Washington, D.C., in the National Air and Space Museum. Those five minutes had felt like fifty. It only took a second for something terrible to happen to a child. A single second to rearrange the world. A second between there and…not there.

Her vision dimmed at the edge as she spun around. Maybe he'd somehow got behind them. Something caught her eye out in the water, floating just behind the breakers. Her pulse pounded in her ears as she lurched forward, her limbs struggling to function. The dizzy relief was almost crippling when she realized it was just a log.

She cupped her cold hands around her dry lips and was finally able to shout. "Lincoln! Come back!" Deep breaths. He'd be scared if he heard the hysteria in their voices. "Lincoln!"

And then, quick as their terror had started, it ended. Dr. Dan rounded the headland, Lincoln perched on his broad flannel-clad shoulders, waving in delight.

"Oh my God!" Sadie stumbled, crashing to one knee before bouncing back on her feet. Twin tears slipped down her flushed cheeks. "Thank you, Dr. Hanlon. Thank you so much. I'm sorry. I don't know how he got out of my sight. I was about five seconds from completely losing my mind."

Dan lifted the boy over his head and handed him to Sadie.

"It's okay, Sadie. Everyone is safe. Lincoln is all right." He smiled kindly, somehow knowing exactly what a mother would want to hear. His blue eyes were gentle with empathy. "This big boy is quite the birder. He was chasing a pack of sandpipers right around the corner."

"I wanna catch dat little birdie!" Lincoln announced, all

business. "Member book, Mommy? Birds! I like those funny guys."

Sadie nodded, before turning to Renee and wiping her eyes. "We read a book about birds at the beach last night."

Renee rubbed her back, not quite sure what to say except, "I'm so sorry, Sadie. That was all my fault."

"What? No," she said, shaking her head. "Of course it wasn't. I'm his mother. I'm the one who is supposed to watch him, to…to…keep him safe no matter what."

Sadie burst into fresh sobs and Renee felt her own eyes itch with tears.

Dr. Dan made a soothing sort of "shhh" sound before tousling Lincoln's hair. "Sadie, this could have happened to anybody. I'm not a parent myself but as a pediatrician I can pretty much guarantee every parent has experienced this sort of scare. Right, Renee?"

Renee nodded earnestly, also taking note that this confirmed her suspicions that Dan did not have children. A small part of her had always worried he had kids and was simply an absent father who never spoke of them.

"Absolutely. Do you remember that scar Tansy has on her forearm?" she asked, to which Sadie nodded mutely. "Tansy got that when I stupidly had a pot of soup cooking on the front burner. She reached for it, and it spilled all over her little arm. I had to rush her to urgent care to be treated for a second-degree burn. I felt horrible."

Sadie's eyes widened slightly before she sniffed. "I'd better get on home. Thanks again, Dr. Hanlon. Talk to you later, Renee."

As they walked away, Sadie could be heard muttering, "God. As if I could design a shop right now. What was I thinking?"

Renee turned toward the steely sea and offered a silent prayer of thanks that Lincoln was okay.

"Are you all right?" Dr. Dan asked, turning to face her fully. He didn't look away. She wasn't used to holding such intense eye contact and it hit her like a slug of whiskey, spreading low through her belly like a slow, deep burn.

She held up a still trembling hand and fought for a rueful smile. "Still rattled, to be honest. Guess I feel responsible for that scare."

"Hey now," his voice was calm and reasonable, "don't beat yourself up. Nothing bad happened."

"I was filling in Sadie about Essie's pie shop idea." Renee brushed the hair from her face as the wind picked up. "I guess we both got pretty excited."

"That's because it is exciting." Dr. Dan crooked his mouth in the half smile she couldn't get enough of, the one that revealed the secret dimple that hid in his left cheek.

She cleared her throat and forced herself to focus on something, anything, else. She settled for a jet high up in the sky, flitting between the clouds. "Sadie offered to design the space and then possibly manage the shop. We got carried away." Renee peered up at Dr. Dan, towering over her. What would it feel like to reach up and wrap her arms around his neck? He had a delicious neck. One that begged to be licked.

Oh my God, what am I doing?

"You must think I'm ridiculous, the way I keep going on and on and on about this idea."

He shook his head. "Actually, I've been plotting how to get another taste for days." A splotch of red appeared on his neck. "Of your pie I mean."

Another frisson of heat. This one wasn't in her belly. It was lower down and more like the sharp crack of kindling. His words were nothing, just polite small talk, right? But why did they sound so dirty?

And why did she love it?

"Ahem." She squared her shoulders and summoned all her courage. "Well actually, I…um…happen to have a fresh strawberry pie cooling in my kitchen if you'd like to stop in for a bite." Her eyes widened as she realized her own moxie. Quickly, she tried to backtrack. "I mean, you probably have plans for today. I just meant—"

"I'd love to." His reply had a quiet intensity that made her heart rate accelerate for the second time that morning, this time for a much better reason.

As they strolled back to her little cottage, she tried to recall the state of her house. It was clean, of course—her home was always clean, with only one tidy person currently living there—but had she left out anything embarrassing? She often draped bras to dry over the backs of the kitchen chairs, and she was reading that one very steamy cowboy romance. Shoot, she'd left that on the nightstand, yes? Or was it tossed on the sofa after she indulged in a few chapters along with a glass of merlot last night?

But as the sun broke free of the clouds and the warm rays kissed the back of her neck, she made a conscious choice. Time to cut loose worry, let go of insecurity and simply allow herself to bask in her proximity to Dr. Dan. The way their hands almost brushed against one another's. The faint smell of citrus that clung to him—either shampoo or soap. The tiny shaving nick on his otherwise perfect jaw.

Were neighbors watching them from behind their curtains?

Hopefully.

Even though she hadn't had the heart to get another cat after Smudge died last year, she often wondered if Cranberry Cove considered her a fuddy-duddy cat lady, one who was forty-three going on eighty. Sure, Myles was relentless in his blind-date setups, which Renee humored a few times each year, but nothing ever panned out. The last one had been with a man named Thad Maxwell. An insurance salesman from Freeport, Thad chewed with his mouth open in an unsexy way and tried to sell her a whole term life insurance policy over dessert.

There had been a few charming guys over the years, but no one special enough for Renee to risk getting her heart shattered all over again. She wondered if *anyone* was worth the sheer devastation of being abandoned the way Russell had left her. That sort of pain was huge and crushing, and she would do anything to avoid experiencing it all over again.

Besides, she had her daughter, her garden, her baking, and wine and romance novels for when the nights grew cold and lonely. She didn't need a man or his affections to make her life complete.

But there was a big difference between need and want.

And what did she want?

Good question.

"This is me." Renee held her hand out toward her cute little house as she and Dr. Dan came up Seashell Lane. She was proud of her home and gestured toward an empty space beside her bottom step. "I'm going to create a little succulent garden here this year. Maybe a jade, a few *sempervivum*. It will have to be something I move inside during the winter, but that shouldn't be a problem because with central heating my living room gets as dry as a desert."

"Ah," he said with his usual brand of grave politeness.

Wait, no. What was she talking about? She resisted the urge to face-palm—less succulents, more sizzle.

Renee fumbled with the lock she only used every, single day, before pushing open her front door.

"Great place." Dr. Dan entered the foyer, which was packed

with antique shop finds. The chandelier was a special one she and Bree had found in Vermont.

Renee couldn't help but beam. "Thanks. One of the benefits of being on my own all these years—I never had to consult a husband regarding my, um, eclectic choices."

"I'm still adjusting to the single life myself," he murmured. Again with the eye contact. His jaw flexed like he wanted to say more but was biting it back.

She nodded, not wanting to pry into the backstory of his widowhood. If and when he wanted to share, she'd be there.

He followed her into her warm kitchen with its terra-cotta floors and chipped white cabinets. The Formica countertops were scarred from various baking projects over the years and the refrigerator was decorated with photos of Tansy and magnets from various vacations, like a Liberty Bell from Philadelphia and a cactus from their trip to Tucson.

"Make yourself comfortable." Renee nodded toward the built-in booth where Tansy used to hunker down with her homework. "What would you like to drink with your pie? Coffee or tea?"

"Green tea if you have it." He slid his big frame onto the seat.

"I do. Citrus and matcha." Renee busied herself preparing a kettle and tried not to sneak too many glances at Dr. Dan surrounded by her grandmother's china and the wobbly mug stand Bree had made in woodshop her sophomore year. Dr. Dan simply fit in her home. He added to its coziness. He felt as right as her fraying but beloved kitchen towels and crocheted pot holders.

Renee set a plate of warm pie and a mug of tea in front of him. She brought her own tea over as well as the sugar canister.

"I already ate a piece for breakfast," she admitted. "Two actually."

Dr. Dan took his first bite, closing his eyes and offering a not-so-subtle moan of appreciation that sent her thoughts straight to the gutter and all her neck-licking fantasies.

"I don't know how you have the willpower. I want to bend over and lick the plate."

The idea of *him* bending down to lick anything was not at all unpleasant.

She tried not to choke. Nothing sexy about spraying tea from your nostrils. "So, which flavor do you like more? Raspberry or strawberry?"

He polished off his piece and gently pushed the plate away. "That's easy. Strawberry."

"Why's that?" Her curiosity piqued.

He cleared his throat. "Because that was the slice I got to enjoy here with you. In your home."

"Oh," Renee inhaled. "Oh." It was all she could manage.

Blushing furiously, she darted her eyes around the kitchen, trying to find anywhere to focus other than her boss's striking blue eyes and his crooked smile.

Don't look at me that way. There's nothing to see here. Just someone who enjoys baking, gardening, and romance novels. You would be bored with me and my quiet life in weeks—no, days—and then what? We go back to being boss and employee? How would that work?

"So! Seen any good movies lately?" Renee asked lamely.

A small smile on his face, Dr. Dan shook his head. "I tend to only rewatch the classics. Probably a sign that I'm getting old."

"I have the same bad habit," she admitted. "Tansy and I used to watch so many Nora Ephron movies together. I bet I could tell you every line of *When Harry Met Sally*."

A sudden sparkle in his eyes, Dr. Dan leaned closer to Renee and murmured, "That first bite of pie? Well, I nearly reenacted Meg Ryan's 'I'll have what she's having' scene."

Renee burst into wonderful laughter. She shook her head. "I don't even know what to say right now."

She stared down at the kitchen table, images of Dr. Dan orgasming in her head. Her ears burned hot.

"Say I'm not the only one feeling something here." His voice was gravelly, slightly hoarse.

Renee's eyed widened, her heart pounding in her chest. Was this a dream? Had she somehow slid into an alternate universe? This couldn't be real life. No, she was about to wake up in her sleigh bed with a book against her chest and a mug of cold chamomile on her nightstand.

"Renee?"

Oh god. This was not a dream.

"Um, no, you're not the only one feeling something, but…" She trailed off. "Well…"

"We work together."

"Right." She nodded. "Right."

"But that doesn't mean we can't get to know each other better. Spend some time together doing…things."

"Like Scrabble?" Her frantic gaze landing on the forgotten game. Why was that on top of the kitchen cupboard anyway? She hadn't played since last summer, before Tansy left for USC, and here she was the reigning queen of awkward banter.

Dr. Dan chuckled. "Scrabble?"

Renee stood, walking toward the board game and holding it out like a shield or a peace offering. "We should play."

He narrowed his eyes. "Didn't you major in English literature? You trying to hustle me?"

"You remember that?" She stared in disbelief.

"Of course I do. When I first started you were making your way through *Pride and Prejudice* for your, I think twelfth time?

And you told me you had studied English lit at Binghamton, and there's that 'Jane Austen is my homegirl' bookmark pinned above your desk."

When was the last time someone had taken the time to notice her? Notice things that mattered to her? She simply nodded, too touched to speak.

Finally she got her vocal cords working. "Well lucky for you, I'm a little rusty with board games since my daughter moved out. Plus, you have the upper hand when it comes to medical jargon. Talk about words with high point values!"

"Oh yeah." He flashed a good-natured grin. "Look out! I'm coming for you with 'colic,' 'asthma,' and 'varicella.'"

They settled in her living room, Dr. Dan sitting on the edge of her linen sofa and Renee cross-legged on the rug, with the board game spread across the coffee table.

"Sternutate?" Renee laughed half an hour into their game. "That is not a word!"

"It is, too!" Dr. Dan waggled his eyebrows. "It's the official term for sneezing."

"I don't believe you." She giggled, lunging for the dog-eared Scrabble dictionary.

He laughed, reaching for it and accidentally grabbing Renee's hand. He held it gently before tightening his grip, interlacing his fingers with hers. His skin was rough, but warm...just as she dreamed it would be. She never wanted to let go.

They both went silent and the air between them crackled as if filled with invisible embers.

"Renee?" His voice was a rasp, a request for permission.

Her throat dried even as her palm grew damp. This was a moment where what she did mattered. If she played her cards right, he would come closer and touch her with those big hands in other, softer places. Their lips would meet and oh good God, she'd kiss him, she'd kiss Dr. Dan and— *Brrrrrrrriiiiiiinnnnnng!*

Cursed by the phone.

"Oh!" She fell back, her hand covering her mouth.

Dr. Dan cleared his throat and awkwardly rubbed his fingers up and down his thighs.

"Um, excuse me. Let me grab that." She hurried to the phone in the other room, answering with a breathless, "Hello."

"Are you okay?" Tansy immediately asked. "Were you on the elliptical?"

"What? No, why?" She'd been about to kiss a hot doctor. As much as she wanted to talk to her daughter, she wanted to know if he tasted as good as he looked.

"You sound out of breath. Hmm. Maybe you should start using it if you're that out of shape."

She frowned at her daughter's unfamiliar sass. Who was this kid? "I actually gave that to your aunt Bree this fall."

Dr. Dan had risen from the couch and was milling around her family room, examining each painting and photograph.

"Well, I was just calling because…" Tansy paused.

Renee could tell something was up. Had she bombed an exam? Or was there roommate trouble?

"So, look. I won't be coming home this summer."

"What!" Renee curled in like the wind had been knocked out of her. "We must have a bad connection because it sounded like you said you weren't coming back to Cranberry Cove."

"*Mother*, dial down the dramatics," Tansy groaned. "I got invited to go stay with Beckett. I met his mom last night and she totally loves me and they supposedly have this killer place in Vail and—"

"Back up. Who is Beckett?" Renee sputtered. "And Colorado?

For the whole summer? Have you been out in that California sun too long today and lost your mind?"

Dr. Dan turned and studied Renee curiously.

"Beckett is my new boyfriend. We met in geology," Tansy said matter-of-factly. "And he wants to take me hiking and rock-climbing and they have an indoor pool and a home movie theater."

Her daughter didn't even like to walk barefoot in grass, nor had she ever looked twice at a rock. "You're taking a geology class? You have a boyfriend? You want to rock climb?" This was all baffling news. Didn't she miss Cranberry Cove? Didn't she miss her mom?

"Yes. As a science elective. Things are serious with Beckett, and I think I'll like camping. Okay? Does that answer all of your questions? Weren't you the one who told me college was a time to try new things?"

"Yes, but…" Renee's head spun. Too much to process at once. "How long have you been dating—what's his name? Bennett? Why am I just hearing about him?"

"Beckett, Mom. Beckett St. John if you want to be a psycho and Internet stalk him. We've been together for about six weeks." Tansy sighed, clearly exasperated with her mother. "And I don't know why I didn't say anything. Maybe because there was never a reason to bring him up until now."

No reason? Since when did Tansy need a reason to tell Renee something so important, so essential?

"I just figured I should let you know about my change of summer plans, you know, as a courtesy, just in case you were preparing for me to be home." Tansy had made her plans and they didn't include seeing her mother. For the whole summer. And that would turn back into the school year and…

Renee could almost hear her heart shatter.

Just in case? Just in case? Renee had planned the entire summer under the assumption Tansy would be home! She'd already requested her vacation time and was counting down the days until Tansy would back down the hall. She couldn't wait for rom-com movie nights and leisurely mornings spent making French toast casserole and reading magazines. She wanted to hear her daughter's footsteps on their creaky hardwood floors and come home from work to find Tansy sitting on the front porch steps, absently nibbling her fingernails while flipping through a novel.

"I knew this would be high drama with you. Look, I've gotta go. We can discuss this more later."

Click.

Renee stared at her phone screen, shell-shocked. Discuss what? There was to be no further discussion. Yes, Tansy was eighteen, but being a legal adult and being an actual adult were two drastically different things.

"Everything okay?" Dr. Dan asked, coming into the doorway.

Tansy used to tell Renee everything, from the moment she got her first period (during a seventh-grade science test, poor thing) to her various crushes throughout the years. Tansy had always been an open book, so the thought of her having a boyfriend, especially one she liked enough to venture off with his family for the entire summer, and never saying a word was mind-boggling.

Renee's mind whirled: she'd lost track of a toddler for a few terrifying minutes this morning, nearly gotten busy with her boss this afternoon, and now her daughter had announced she was basically never coming home.

What a day.

Things were definitely not okay.

And Renee's quiet, orderly life?

Well, it wasn't so neat anymore.

Chapter Eleven

Still clutching Lincoln against her very tender boobs, Sadie nudged open the front door of the house, gasping to find Ethan in the foyer. "Oh! You scared me!"

"You okay?" He narrowed his eyes and gave her a slight frown. "You look pale. Is the morning sickness back?"

Sadie had experienced horrible bouts of vomiting while pregnant with Lincoln, and they tended to hit her at the worst times, though puking in an elevator crowded with her firm's executives definitely topped the list. She'd never forget the sight of her morning Cheerios splashed across Stuart Dillon's shiny loafers.

"It's actually been a lot better this time around." She briefly considered telling Ethan about her scare with Lincoln on the beach but ultimately decided against it. Her legs hadn't stopped shaking, and her heart was continuing to race over all of the what-ifs. With a second child on the way and now this pie shop possibility—as improbable as it was—Sadie was more determined than ever to appear calm and capable.

She was already fumbling as a stay-at-home mom. What made her think she could handle a job in addition to parenting? She was certainly not her own mother, who seemed to manage both motherhood and a career with such effortless ease.

And Ethan was so damn practical.

How was she going to convince him that this was a good idea? How was she going to convince herself?

"Yeah? Well, that's good to hear. I wish your pregnancy headaches weren't so awful, though," he said, genuine concern in his eyes. "A package just arrived for you. It looks like it's from my mom."

The only other time Annette had sent Sadie a package, it had contained a variety of cleaning products, an issue of *Midwest Living*, and a throw pillow embroidered with famous Ohio landmarks. She'd even included a note about the importance of keeping a clean home and encouraged Sadie to "reach out with any questions you may have."

"I bet it's some sort of Easter surprise for Lincoln," Sadie guessed. "Why don't you take him into your office to play for a bit? I don't want him sneaking a peek at any treats."

Ethan nodded. "Good idea."

There was a phrase she hadn't heard from her husband in a while.

She carried the small box into the kitchen and set it on the countertop. Using a pair of poultry shears, she sliced open the packaging tape.

There was a lilac envelope on top with Sadie's name written in Annette's beautiful penmanship. Her mother-in-law's stationery was heavy and expensive, the note cards embossed with AL in metallic gold. She'd actually bought Sadie a matching SL set last Christmas, though Sadie had yet to use it.

Dear Sadie,

I'm sorry for losing my temper during my visit. It was out of line and completely inappropriate. I told my sisters about the ordeal, and they suggested you read this book. It's all about being a calm and peaceful parent—serene moms promote serene children! It makes perfect sense. You'll have to call and let me know how it is. I figured you could use all the advice you could get with another little one on the way. Oh, how I cannot wait for my next grandbaby!

Love,
Annette

P.S. Have you given any thought to getting a dog for Lincoln? You know, Ethan grew up with Apollo, and I'm sure he'd be the first to tell you that every child deserves such a companion! Think about it!

Gripping the letter in one of her shaking hands, the book in the other, Sadie stormed down the hall.

"Is she serious with this?" she shouted at Ethan, who was sprawled across the floor playing with Lincoln.

"Mommy mad!" Lincoln observed, both awed and slightly amused as she thrust the note at his father. "Mommy, why mad?"

"Could her apology be any more backhanded? I don't even know why I'm surprised. Who else could manage to say sorry and then sneak in a kick in the ass?"

Ethan skimmed the letter with a growing frown.

"There's no way we're getting a dog," she fumed as he quietly read. "I know you loved Apollo but I'm a hard no on a Saint Bernard. The last thing we need in this house is lots of dog hair and drool."

"Of course not." He shook his head. "I'm not a masochist. Maybe someday when the kids are much, much older."

She paused, realizing he was on *her* side and felt strangely ashamed of throwing the Saint Bernard under the bus. Their imaginary dog hadn't done anything wrong here.

She handed over the heavy hardback, which featured a picture of a mother who looked like Gwyneth Paltrow snuggling a cherubic little girl. They were both blond and bright-eyed. "She also sent me a parenting self-help book along with her congratulations on our second child."

"Come on, Mom." Ethan's neck grew red and he fumbled with his words. "I'm sorry she did this. It's partially my fault. After our fight last Saturday, when Lincoln and I went to see her at the B&B, I felt like I should explain where you were coming from. I wanted her to understand how much stress you're under and that your hormones are out of sorts."

"What?" So much for calming down. Annoyance blazed into something more searing and bright.

"You felt the need to explain me to your mother? Like my reaction to our fight was so crazy that I not only required explanation, but a biological excuse?"

Seeing the look on her face, he studied the floor, unable to meet her gaze. "Please don't say things like that. You know that isn't true."

Her fingers twitched. God, she longed to throw the stupid book at him. But Lincoln was still watching and his little face reminded her she was the adult here. Instead, she spun on her heel and stalked back into the kitchen, opening the trash and dropping the contents of the package inside. The simmering resentment boiled down to one clear idea.

The pie shop.

She wanted to do it. She needed to do it. It was too easy

for a woman to forget who she was after becoming a mama, to remember what filled her bucket and made her come alive. She loved being her son's mother, but she needed a professional life to bring balance. It might not make her serene, but it would make her happier.

"Honey, I need to nap and cool down. Will you take Lincoln for a bit?"

She could tell him about the pie shop right now and be done with it, but the idea was so new, so fragile, that she didn't want him to burst the bubble with some ill-timed practical questions or concerns on how she'd manage to balance the workload.

Right now she just wanted to…well…*want*.

"Of course," he agreed quickly.

Sadie climbed up the stairs, burrowed beneath her comforter, and took a deep breath, feeling calmer than she had in a long time. Before long she fell asleep with visions of sugarplum pies dancing in her head.

* * *

The next morning, at nine o'clock sharp, she knocked on Renee's cheerful red door.

Eight o'clock was too desperate she had decided the night before. But if she waited until ten, Renee may already be out and about for the day.

"Good morning, Sadie. Hiya, Lincoln." Renee had her hair tied into a French braid and a smudge of flour on her cheek. "What's up?"

She shoved Grandma Hester's recipe book into Renee's hands. "Let's do this." She blew right past all the usual pleasantries. "I know the pie shop is a big leap, but I need it. Heck, we both need it."

"You're serious." Renee's head whipped back with shock. "Come on in and we'll chat. I just pulled a batch of scones out of the oven and they need to be eaten."

Relieved to be invited in and not laughed at for showing up and acting like a crazy woman on a mission, Sadie walked right in.

Renee's cottage was the definition of adorable. While her own mom had an affinity for trendy, modern art and leather furniture, Renee's decor had always been warm and sentimental. Every item in her house, from the mismatched plates to the upright piano, had a story.

"Smell good!" Lincoln cheered.

"It always smells yummy in here." Sadie nuzzled Lincoln's little nose with her own. "Miss Renee is a magical baker. Do you remember what a baker does?"

"Cuppy cake! Bread!"

"Coffee?" Renee held up a French press.

"Please, oh, please, oh, please. I'm allowed one cup a day and could use every ounce."

Renee filled two ceramic mugs. She transferred the scones to a wicker basket lined with a tea towel that said "Sweet Dreams Are Made of Cheese" and placed it in the center of the kitchen table. She then spread a classic star-pattern quilt on the floor and handed Lincoln a few plastic bowls and measuring spoons to play with.

"You're always so prepared." Sadie sighed, both awed and defeated. Renee was the sort of wife and mother Ethan and Lincoln deserved. If he was smart, Ethan would take Lincoln and move into Renee's cottage and never look back. "I'm always two steps behind."

"You're too hard on yourself." Renee smothered her scone with butter. "It's just the stage you're at. Trust me on this, I'm old and wise."

"S-sometimes…" Sadie stammered, staring down into her cup of coffee. "Sometimes, I feel like I'm a bad mom. I think about my grandma…and my mother…and how much better they were at this whole mom thing than me."

There. She'd done it. Spoken the ugly fear out loud.

"Grandma was so great at involving me in fun activities, from having me help her bake to collecting different shells and driftwood during our nature walks on the beach," Sadie continued. "And Mom always had me signed up for something educational or enlightening. She banned frozen food from the dinner table and never lost her temper. *Ever.*"

"Okay, that? That just isn't human." Renee reached for Sadie's hand and gave it a squeeze. "I'm sure your mom had her moments. I used to be a shower crier myself."

"A what?"

"A shower crier," she said, smiling sadly. "I would bottle everything up during the day and then let it all go once I got into the shower at night. Because God forbid I show my daughter that I was a real person with real human feelings."

"Maybe I should give that a try."

"Listen, Sadie, you're not a bad mom. I swear. All of us mothers try our very best, but let's face it. Kids don't come with instruction manuals. As much as we love them, they push our buttons and put us through the wringer. We may have the best of intentions, but we're only human."

Sadie nodded, trying not to cry yet again. She was becoming quite a waterworks lately.

"I'm feeling like a pretty lousy parent myself these days," Renee admitted in a confidential tone.

"You?" Sadie's eyebrows flew into her bangs. "Yeah right. What's happened? You only sent three care packages this month?"

Renee sighed and took a slow sip of coffee. "Ever since Tansy went away to school, it's like she's becoming a different person.

114

I knew college would be a change, but I didn't anticipate a total transformation. It's impossible to get ahold of her these days. Just yesterday, when she finally did call, it was to inform me that she didn't want to come home this summer. She wants to go and live with her new boyfriend and his family in Vail, Colorado."

Renee looked near tears herself. She swallowed thickly. "I had never even heard of this boyfriend until that phone call."

Sadie thought of the photos and videos Tansy frequently posted on both her Instagram and Facebook accounts. Her former—and favorite—babysitting charge was now taking photos of herself drinking White Claw and filming videos of her friends doing keg stands. She seemed to favor crop tops and could often be seen hanging on the arm of a fraternity brother.

"You aren't on social media much, are you?" she asked, just for confirmation.

"Like Twitter and stuff? No, I hate all that." Renee shuddered. "Tansy created a Facebook profile for me at some point, but I forgot my password and never bothered to update it. I just don't have a need for it. If I want to talk to someone I call or text. It makes me sound ninety, but it's how I roll."

"Right." Sadie debated if she should tell Renee about the posts. Even though she wasn't completely sure it was her place, she figured she would want to know if Lincoln was getting involved with the wrong crowd. "I have something to show you."

She pulled out her iPhone, and Renee huddled close.

She scrolled to Tansy's Instagram profile, and sure enough, the girl had posted a photo just last night. She was wearing a bikini top paired with a pair of jean shorts that revealed half a toned buttcheek. She had a red Solo cup in one hand and was in the arms of a well-muscled guy with a giant tattoo on his shoulder and a backward baseball hat on his head.

"What the," Renee inhaled.

"Ayuh. That's a pretty standard post for her." Sadie handed Renee the phone so she could scroll at her own pace. "Her pictures started changing last fall. I don't know. Maybe it's just innocent and fun. I mean it is her freshman year."

She peeked over Renee's shoulder at Tansy holding up a bottle of vodka while wearing a white dress with an absurdly deep neckline. She had a cigarette dangling from the corner of her mouth and made a vulgar gesture with her vodka-less hand.

Sadie shook her head. *Nope. Not so innocent.*

The color drained from Renee's face. "Smoking? She hates smoking. We both do. There's no way a student could party like this and have time for studying. What if she loses her scholarship?"

"Tansy was always exceptionally smart," Sadie said helplessly, hating that she was the messenger here. "I'm sure she's got it figured out."

Renee pushed the phone away and closed her eyes. "I feel so freaking out of the loop."

"Tansy is thousands of miles away. How could you have known any of this was going on?" Sadie countered. "Kids go a little wild their first time away from home. I know I did. Tansy is smart and was always a good girl. She'll find her way."

"But I let her become so distant. I should have been more persistent."

"She's living on her own now. You can't be there every minute. She has to make her own mistakes. It's like you said, all of us are just trying to do our best."

"You best!" shouted Lincoln. "Pies best!" The two friends hugged and laughed.

And for the next hour they talked about pies and business plans. It felt fantastic.

Chapter Twelve

Renee sat and stared at the phone in her hand. After a great business-brainstorming session with Sadie, she now had to switch gears and deal with Tansy. Tipping her head back, she blew out a long raspberry. How was she going to handle this?

Should she play it cool for the first few minutes, and then let it rip?

Or start off full Mama Grizzly with angry shouting and threats to kick her butt off the Santa Monica Pier? Tempting, but probably not productive.

Good lord, the fact she even needed to have this conversation felt insane. Smoking, drinking—who knew what else?

Renee didn't want to shame her or put even more distance into their relationship. But she couldn't condone binge drinking. And if Tansy was having sex with this Beckett, it better be protected. She'd suffered through not one, not two, but *three* painfully awkward talks with Tansy about birth control pills, condoms, IUDs, oh my!

She closed her eyes as the reel of Instagram pictures played past like a disturbing movie starring a stranger. How could Tansy have changed so much in such a short time? Not too long ago, she had been too self-conscious to wear a bikini or ask her crush to the annual Sadie Hawkins dance. Renee had to cheerlead every single tentative step Tansy took toward being less shy and more confident with boys or her body.

And now she was running half-naked around Los Angeles. Renee wasn't stupid—she assumed Tansy would have her fun. But sipping on the occasional cocktail was a lot different than beer bongs and shots.

"What do I even say?" She shoveled in a third scone before choking on the dry bite. So much for eating her feelings. "It's like she's throwing everything away, and for what?" she said, once she finished coughing. "I have no idea."

"I'm not sure either," Sadie admitted. "But the first step is just to be honest with her. I think I would approach it from both an emotional and logical perspective. Tell her how seeing those posts made you feel, and make sure she knows the implications. Like she doesn't want that to be what people look at if she applies for an internship."

Renee squeezed her eyes, feeling the beginning throb of a migraine. "I hadn't even thought of that."

Sadie gave her a squeeze. "Good luck. Come over later if you want to debrief."

After Sadie left, Renee made her way upstairs. She'd call from Tansy's bedroom, with its creamy yellow walls, crowded bookshelves, and loft bed. Her prom dresses still hung in the closet, and her stuffed lamb perched on the nightstand. It still smelled like her, a sweet mix of vanilla and brown sugar–body lotion. Renee needed to be here for this phone call, surrounded by Tansy's old, familiar things. She needed those physical reminders of who her daughter was before she'd moved to California.

She sat on the multicolored rug and leaned her back against the mostly empty dresser.

"Oh Mother, hi."

Renee heard giggling in the background, and the slam of a car door.

"I'm a little busy. Mia—you remember Mia, right? The girl who lives across the hall? We're heading—"

"No," Renee replied immediately, her tone serious and commanding.

"No what?"

"You and I are going to talk now. I don't care where it is you and your friend were going, I want five minutes."

"Um, okay?" she replied, taken aback. "What?"

"I just, I just called to say," Renee took a deep breath. "You'll be spending your summer in Cranberry Cove, not in Colorado. I'd be open to you going for a week or two, but that's it."

"Um, yeah. That's not happening. Beckett already told his parents I'm coming," she sniffed haughtily. "I won't risk upsetting them."

Renee felt some of the wind escape her. Apparently, Beckett's parents' disappointment was more concerning to Tansy than her own mother's.

"This isn't some joke, Tansy," Renee said, her nerves frayed. "I finally got wind of your social media this morning. From the kegs to that shirtless boy you're constantly draped over like a curtain, your behavior isn't exactly scholarship material. And smoking cigarettes? Really? What the heck are you thinking? Remember Grandpa's lung cancer? Hello? I thought you were smarter than that."

"B-but," Tansy started to stutter, "you hate social media! How do you even know what I'm posting?"

"A friend brought it to my attention." Renee decided not to out Sadie. She didn't want Tansy to know her former babysitter had ratted her out. "You've worked your talented little butt off to get where you are. Why risk blowing it? You're going to be the next Nora Ephron, remember?"

Tansy snorted. "Beckett thinks rom-coms are stupid."

"Too bad for Beckett then." Renee stared at the *Sleepless in Seattle* poster over Tansy's desk for so long that Tom Hanks and Meg Ryan were reduced to blurry peach-colored blobs. Tansy was nine the first time they watched it together. As the credits rolled, she'd declared it the most romantic thing she'd ever seen, and asked to watch it again the next day. It had felt so pure, and so fun, to bond over movies, squee during the grand gestures, and bury faces in pillows during the dark moments. "Since when are you the kind of girl to change yourself based on what a boy thinks?"

She'd raised her better than that, hadn't she?

"Whatever." Renee could tell Tansy was rolling her eyes. "Anyways, that was just a kiddie dream."

"It's kiddie to want to write great comedies?"

Tansy exhaled. "Look, I get that it's hard for you, but I've grown up a lot since moving out here. I'm changing. I'm not some helpless child who needs Mommy holding her hand all the time."

Renee closed her eyes, her migraine going up a notch. "If you're such an adult, how are you keeping up with your schoolwork? It looks like partying is your new major."

"That's a stretch."

"Is it, though?" Renee snapped. "You know, when you came home for winter break, I never considered asking to see your first semester's grades. And now I'm starting to think that they weren't as stellar as you claimed."

When Tansy had reported she'd received straight As her first term, Renee hadn't thought to ask for actual proof. Tansy was a hardworking, dedicated student. She always had been. One afternoon during her sophomore year, Tansy had actually arrived home in tears, practically inconsolable over receiving a B+ on a history paper.

"I'm not even close to failing out, but thanks for the vote of confidence." Hurt filled Tansy's words. "I'm totally maintaining the GPA required to keep my scholarship. I'm not an idiot. So, calm down. Please. I know this must come as a shock but I can chill at frat houses *and* write an essay on Emily Dickinson. The two aren't mutually exclusive."

"Since when do you even care about Greek life? Let me guess. Mr. Shirtless is a frat boy. What a shocker."

"His name is Beckett! And I am going to Colorado this summer, for as long as I feel like. I'm legally an adult, and I can make my own decisions. And I choose Beckett. I want to spend my summer with him." Tansy's anger erupted. "You know what? You're probably just jealous because when's the last time you've had a boyfriend since Dad left? Oh wait, I know…never!"

The phone went dead.

Renee sat in stunned silence, looking at her phone as if it had smacked her across the face.

Whoa.

She blinked, trying to focus, but the room felt blurred and unreal.

What the hell just happened?

Her daughter had never spoken to her that way; they used to

joke they were like the *Gilmore Girls*. Now it felt like they were starring in a nineties *Jerry Springer* episode or something. Except, what Tansy had shouted had some truth to it, even if she did spit it out like a brat.

She hadn't slept with anyone since Russell left. And she hadn't slept with anyone before him either. The tall and lanky Russell Rhodes, with his green eyes and shaggy blond hair, had taken her virginity, and she'd married him thinking they'd be together forever.

Her almost-kiss yesterday was the most romantic action she'd received since she'd bought a battery-operated boyfriend off Amazon five years ago.

Good lord. She was practically a nun.

And what had she been thinking anyway, moving in for that kiss? Sure, she had a giant crush on the tall, dark, and handsome Dr. Dan, but he was first and foremost her boss. And she had forgotten how awkward it was to share your feelings. Did he really like her? After all, she was a woman who loved going to Target or watching HGTV.

Renee pushed herself from the bedroom floor and trudged downstairs in dazed, plodding steps.

Restless, she needed company—some light conversation and distraction.

Sadie, she thought, grabbing a jean jacket and heading next door.

No one answered though. She must be putting Lincoln down for his nap.

From there Renee grabbed her bike and headed down Seashell Lane and eventually turned onto Bree's street, Starboard Court, head down, lost in thought.

Maybe she should join a dating website.

There were dating sites for just about every type of person, right? It would be like online shopping for the perfect man. She would request someone tall and tanned.

Eyes? Blue. Definitely dark blue like the ocean she loved so much.

He'd have to be sweet-tempered, giving, and passionate about doing good in the world.

Widowed, divorced, or never married. No preference there. But he'd need a healthy appetite and an adventurous palate. He wouldn't be one for trendy fad diets. He'd have to love bread and pasta.

Dan.

She was describing freaking Dan Hanlon.

Frustrated, she propped her bike by Bree's front steps and rapped on her sister's antique door knocker with extra force.

"Whoa, tiger. Don't break it." Bree wrung a dish towel in her hands. Behind her, the house looked darker than usual, most of the blinds pulled shut.

"Can I come in?"

Bree hesitated but nodded after a too long pause, motioning her forward.

"Sorry to barge in." Renee studied Bree carefully. She had pale purple circles beneath her eyes, and her burst of curly blond hair hung lank. She was wearing a pair of worn jeans and an old oatmeal-colored sweater. She looked tired and slightly sad. Nothing like her usual serene self. "What's wrong?"

"What? Why? Nothing. Everything's fine." Bree walked into her kitchen, filling the kettle with tap water and setting it on the stove. She pulled a carton of half-and-half out of the fridge, sniffed, and then poured it down the sink. "Hope you weren't set on cream though I think I can manage sugar."

Renee narrowed her eyes. Her sister radar detected trouble, but what?

"Rooibos or black tea?"

Renee nodded toward the Lipton.

"Quit staring." Bree spun on her heel and began stacking papers on the kitchen table.

Renee leaned against the island and examined a pile of cowls in cherry-blossom pink, persimmon, and sky-blue yarn that Bree must have recently finished up. "You took terrible."

"Did you come over to visit or pass judgment?" Bree wouldn't meet her eyes. "What's up?" Bree had a point.

"I almost made out with my boss," Renee announced dramatically, having to keep herself from shrieking like a lovesick teenager.

She stared at her sister, waiting for an awed or shocked reaction.

"Dr. Dan?" Bree raised a brow. "What the heck does 'almost made out' mean?"

Maybe Renee hadn't set the story up well—Tansy had always been the storyteller, not her. She was better at playing the part of the captive audience.

"Well, I ran into him walking on the beach. Technically Sadie and I did. We were with her toddler, Lincoln. You remember Sadie, right?"

Bree nodded, looking impatient.

"You would have been so proud of me. I asked him to come over, and he agreed. I served him a plate of my strawberry pie, and then we played Scrabble. I reached for a dictionary at the same time he did, and he grabbed my hand. I started to move toward him. He started to move toward me. But Tansy called at that exact second!"

Renee widened her eyes and waited for her sister to burst into laughter or perhaps squee. But Bree did neither.

"O-kay?" She sounded slightly exasperated. "So you almost

kissed him. In that case, I almost kissed Brad Pitt that one time I ran into him at an airport ten years ago."

Renee blushed, looking down at her lap and suddenly feeling more like a thirteen-year-old girl than a forty-three-year-old woman. What was she going to swoon about next? Dan giving her his letterman jacket or asking her to the big school dance?

"I'm not trying to be mean, but if you really like him, quit doing things halfway. Stop almost kissing him and actually making your feelings known." Bree poured their mugs of tea. "Believe me, life's too short. You're forty-something not four hundred. This is your sexual prime. Get after it."

"The man is my boss." Renee stirred a spoonful of sugar into her tea, the silver clattering against the ceramic. "I have to tread lightly here."

Bree looked at her with such pity, Renee felt her skin crawl. "You've been treading lightly for twelve years now."

There it was, the unspoken words she'd sensed flowing right under the surface were cresting. Her lungs filled. Taking a full breath was an impossible idea. It was one thing to know, vaguely, in the back of your mind that you were stuck. It was another thing to be unexpectedly doused in the face by the cold truth.

"Seriously?" She scooted away from the table and headed for the front door, needing an escape hatch, to hit the fresh air, to be able to breathe. "Isn't that the pot calling the kettle black? I don't recall you exactly setting the town on fire since Ian broke off your engagement."

The only sound was the scratching of her mother's favorite lilac bush against the window pane.

Renee rubbed the bridge of her nose. *Shit*. She didn't mean to fight dirty. "Bree—"

"Did you really just throw Ian in my face? Nice. That's great. Real mature."

Ian had been Bree's boyfriend starting in high school. Comfortable, predictable Ian Doring was an accountant who was about as exciting as a glass of water. Still, her sister had seemed...content with the relationship. Accepting.

Or was it resigned?

Privately, Renee had been relieved when Ian got cold feet and called off the wedding five years ago. Bree might love knitting and be something of a homebody, but Renee felt like Bree's heart was too big to be given to an auditor who seemed more passionate about duck hunting and the New England Patriots than her little sister.

She'd been meaning to talk to Bree. More and more she'd seemed to be going through the motions. Never fully engaged or happy.

But Renee was suddenly too exhausted for a deep and meaningful conversation. Plus her stomach had begun to hurt, like she'd been punched in the gut too many times for one day.

"I can't fight with you too," she announced with an air of finality.

"What do you mean 'too'?"

"Tansy. I had it out with her today. It was awful. She doesn't want to come home this summer. And I saw these pictures of her, and she was smoking...smoking! Like hello! Was watching Dad die of lung cancer not enough?" Renee pressed a hand to her mouth as Bree's eyes widened. "Never mind. Coming here was a bad idea. I don't want to get into it with you, or Tansy, or anyone. I'll go home and garden. Yell at the weeds."

"Wait a second." Bree hurried behind as she made her way toward the door. "Don't leave in a huff. I was only being real! That's what sisters do!"

Renee didn't answer. She nearly tripped down the front steps and could hear Bree gasp from behind, "Be careful!"

She thrust her hands into the air. "I'm fine!"

For once she wished she could say those words and actually mean them.

It was time to add a few sprinkles to this smushed cupcake of a day.

When she got home, she stalked passed her garden without giving the dandelions a second glance. Instead, she marched up to her favorite Adirondack chair on the porch, took a seat, and whipped out her iPhone.

Tansy, Bree—heck, probably the whole frigging town—thought she was some cautionary tale of broken hearts and broken dreams. She'd show them. She'd show everyone.

Heart in her throat, she selected her message thread with Dan, which included painfully professional topics such as restocking their *Sesame Street* sticker supply and the missing address of an insurance provider.

"Here goes nothing," she muttered.

Hi. Sorry yesterday ended so abruptly. Poor Dan had excused himself after Tansy's unexpected phone call, saying they would catch up later. Now was as good a time as any. I had a lot of fun with you.

There. If that wasn't a sprinkle, she didn't know what was.

Renee shoved her phone back into her pocket, suddenly exhilarated by her own small act of boldness, and headed for the beach. She felt her jacket buzz but waited until she was sitting on the cool sand to look at the message.

I had fun, too! ☺

She smiled, loving the little smiley face emoji.

And then, another message came.

127

Are you free tomorrow night? Want to grill on my boat?

Renee screamed—a wonderful, guttural exhale.

Yes. That sounds great! She beamed as she pressed each letter. What time?

She wanted to twirl barefoot at the waterline. She wanted to dig a hole and hide down with the crabs.

This all felt thrilling and terrifying.

Her moves may be rusty, and her playbook completely blank, but she was ready to get on the field and put her heart back in the game.

If only she could send it off with a helmet and protective padding.

Chapter Thirteen

I t couldn't hurt to take a peek, right?

Sadie and Lincoln had gone to celebrate the warmer weather and her intense pregnancy craving with a trip to Sprinkles Ice Cream. Maybe it was the pralines-and-cream-fueled sugar rush, but before she'd even finished her double scoop waffle cone, she'd strapped Lincoln back into his car seat and lead-footed it to the Old Red Mill. It was a blue-sky April afternoon, and daffodils and tulips lined the street. It was a short distance to the mill's location on a quiet bend of the Indigo River, maybe half a mile at most. Sadie drove with all four of her windows (plus the moon roof) open. The rearview mirror revealed Lincoln in all his chocolate ice cream smeared glory.

She wasn't going to fret about the sticky mess she'd have to deal with later. She was too busy licking her own cone, deliriously happy with possibility. She had discovered Grandma Hester's missing recipes. There was a new life quietly taking shape inside her. She might be returning to the design world with an exciting new business venture.

Hope bloomed through her chest like a sunflower.

She parked the minivan by the river and got Lincoln out to take a look around. That's all she was doing, she told herself as she tried to focus on the mill's faults. After all, the red paint was chipped in places, and some of its boards looked rotted. The waterwheel was impressive, though it had been decades since it had been in use. But the stone foundation appeared solid, and the roof had no missing shingles or obvious leaks. Not only was the mill adjacent to the river, it was also surrounded by mature maple and ash trees and all sorts of wildflowers.

"Gorgeous." Sadie breathed in the fresh air and potential of this place.

The Old Red Mill was always stunning during the fall, with the red, orange, and yellow foliage on display. If she squinted hard enough, she could imagine customers at farm-style tables, smiling over warm slices of Renee's pies, cozy and content as they enjoyed the view.

"Well well well! Hey there, Sadie. Hiya, Lincoln! Fancy seeing you here."

Sadie jumped two feet as her cone hit the ground.

Essie Park posed on the front steps of the Old Red Mill in knee-high boots.

"Essie, hi," Sadie sputtered, embarrassed by both her nosiness and clumsiness. Hastily, she bent to pick up the fallen ice cream cone. She may be a snoop, but she was no litterbug.

"Oh leave it." Essie smoothed a lock of perfectly straightened hair over her camel-colored blazer. "You're about to make some raccoon very happy."

"Ha, right." Sadie shuffled awkwardly. "Lincoln and I were exploring."

"Beautiful day for it." Essie's smile held a glint of glittering resolve. "But not all who wander are lost. What's the deal? You interested in a lease?"

Busted.

Essie had a spectacular BS detector, and right now it was almost audibly pinging.

"Renee told me about her pie shop idea," Sadie confessed. "And I want to help."

"Smart girl." Essie gestured toward the heavy front door. "Smart Renee, too. Why don't you both come on in for a tour? I'd love to show someone with your design background around the place. There's oodles of potential."

Sadie nodded, cheeks pinking from Essie's straightforward compliments. Scooping Lincoln into her arms, she followed Essie inside, her heels echoing briskly against the hardwood floors. Sadie could hardly keep up, and she was wearing a pair of Pumas with her signature yoga pants and oversized sweatshirt ensemble.

The first thing that stood out was the abundance of natural light.

She'd expected the mill to be dark and maybe a little damp and cold. But it was quite the opposite.

"Wow." She did a little spin and made Lincoln giggle. "Just...wow."

An entire wall was lined with floor-to-ceiling windows, allowing sunlight to pour into the space. Even better, the windowed wall was on the side of the mill that faced the river. It boasted a fantastic view of burbling rapids, rustling beeches, and stony banks. The wooden ceiling beams were exposed, making the height of the space all the more impressive while also imparting a more modern, industrial feel.

"How long was the space used as a mill?" Sadie was amazed at the positive energy radiating throughout the building. "I don't really know much about the history. It hasn't been operational since I've been alive."

"It's something special, isn't it? The new owner is an investor who lives in Manhattan, but he grew up rurally and appreciates the place's character and potential. I'm determined to find him the perfect tenants." Essie stood silent briefly, lost in her own thoughts. "But it was an operating mill until the 1960s. There are a few books that reference it in the library. You should check them out. They're worth a look for the old photos alone."

Sadie nodded, knowing she would.

"These are the original floors and beams. The windows were added by the mill's next tenant, a restaurant that had a very brief stint here. Probably only a few years at most. I bet your parents came here for a date or two. It was called the Miller's Wife. Ring a bell?"

Sadie frowned, shaking her head. "Vaguely."

"I forget how young you are." Essie winked.

Ouch. While Essie had likely meant it as a compliment regarding Sadie's maturity, she couldn't help but wonder if she'd said it because she thought Sadie looked old. It didn't help that Essie, who must be twenty years Sadie's senior, had clearer skin, brighter eyes, and a better figure.

When was the last time Sadie wore her favorite heels? And where even were they? Probably collecting dust bunnies in the hall closet. Dressing like an adult and doing a job that fulfilled her on a cellular level, now there was an idea that was almost sexier than Chris Hemsworth shirtless.

She cleared her throat and refocused. "When did the restaurant close?"

"Late nineties. You'd have been tiny." Essie walked toward one of the large windows, admiring the river below. They'd had a few days of heavy rain, and the current looked powerful while a heron stalked the shallows. "Between you and me, their food wasn't much to write home about. But they did add quite a kitchen. Wanna see?"

"Shut up." Sadie's eyes widened. "There's a commercial kitchen?"

"You betcha. Come on, I'll show you."

Sadie followed Essie toward the back of the mill where a slightly dated—but absolutely usable—kitchen was located. She poked her head inside the giant stainless steel refrigerators and opened the oven doors.

And the built-ins! The built-ins were incredible. They must be over one hundred years old. Sadie traced her hand across one, its white paint peeling.

All this space needed was a good scrub and a little bit of love.

For starters, they could paint the cabinets. Maybe a cheerful periwinkle paired with light yellow accents or a grayish, sea-side blue…Sadie would pull color swatches tonight. Schoolhouse lighting would look fantastic in here or even retro globe fixtures. A window over the deep porcelain sinks overlooked the river and she could imagine it outfitted in the same gingham curtains they'd use for the shop.

Gosh, and this was only the kitchen.

Beside the space for the pie shop there were all sorts of other interesting rooms. Main Street was special, but this space was something else entirely, and would be a welcome respite from the constantly changing weather. Besides the pie shop there could be a bookshop, an old-fashioned candy store, a craft cider tasting room, a yoga studio, a boutique toy shop, or a small hair salon. So many options.

"Okay, this place is insane." She laughed, breathless in her excitement. "And I mean that in the best possible way."

"I know it, right? We just need to convince Renee." Essie's phone started to blast a Beyoncé song for a ringtone. She glanced at the screen and raised her perfectly micro bladed brows. "I need to take this call, but you stay as long as you'd like. Afterwards, let's regroup, and you can ask me any questions you may have. I'll be just outside."

Sadie nodded. She set Lincoln on the ground and walked back into the main area.

Her mind whirled.

The mill was huge—it had enough space for at least five shops and oh, maybe one of those trendy shared working spaces for free-lancers. Chickadee Studios and Castaway Yarn were both bursting at the seams. She wouldn't be surprised if the two shops would want the space.

Best of all would be the pie shop, the heart of the new Old Red Mill.

Her fingers itched for a sketchbook and pencil as the design ideas came fast and furious. She would keep all of the Old Red Mill's original details intact—that was important—and add modern touches where appropriate. The space should feel creative, innovative, and slightly industrial, yet warm, inviting, and cozy—and through it all the scent of Renee's addictive pies wafting in the air.

That rich brown-sugar scent.

It was the same sweet way her grandma had always smelled, of love, comfort, and safety.

Oh God—what if they named the pie shop "Hester's"?

"Do you like this place?" Sadie asked Lincoln, as two-year-olds are known for their honesty. "Is it cool?"

"Yes!" Lincoln exclaimed. "We go to park now? Swings?"

"I like the way you think," Sadie said with a grin. "And yes, buddy. I promise we'll head to the park next."

Gosh, maybe the Old Red Mill could even have some sort of play area and indoor jungle gym. It would be a perfect spot for parents to take their children on rainy days, or when the weather turned cold. Plus, how many times did Lincoln grow impatient and cranky during errands? Busy parents could take a short play break between their stops at the shops.

Sadie held Lincoln's hand as they walked out to meet with Essie once more.

She was finishing up her phone call and jotting something down in the sleek, black planner she always carried.

"I have another bit of exciting info," Essie said. "That was Mayor Peterson calling to let me know the city council approved funding for a riverwalk during last night's meeting."

"Yeah?" Sadie was only half listening. She was mostly watching Lincoln, who had started playing with a pile of rocks. Knowing her luck, he would break one of Essie's car windows. "Well, that sounds nice."

"Girl." Essie arched a brow. "Have you been following the riverwalk news?"

"Honestly, no." She shrugged. "I'm a little out of the loop on local news."

"The boardwalk trail is going to go right past the Old Red Mill." She beamed. "Can you imagine the extra business it will bring? People will be able to stroll from the harbor to Main Street to here, no problemo."

Sadie gave a low whistle. "This certainly feels like kismet, all right."

"Mommy?" Lincoln tugged on the hem of her sweatshirt. "Mommy, we go swing now! Peas?"

Lincoln changed favorite activities by the week. While this week's obsession was swinging, last week's had been his bathtub toys. Who knew what next week would bring? He was growing so fast, doing so many new things.

A chill dampened her spark of excitement. Would she be able to keep up with everything once the new baby arrived? Would she be able to give Lincoln the love and attention he deserved? What if instead of racing Matchbox cars and building block towers together, Lincoln ended up plopped in front of the television as Sadie devoted all of her focus to the baby and design?

She wanted happiness and personal fulfillment, but not at the expense of her child.

Having it all was easier in theory than in practice.

"Let's hit the swings." Sadie squeezed Lincoln's hand tight. "Can you tell Miss Essie thank you for showing us the mill? Wasn't that cool?"

"Tank you," he said solemnly, just like a little man.

"You are quite welcome, doll baby." Essie winked. "How old is he now?"

"Two." Sadie dug around her oversized, seemingly bottomless tote. She retrieved a packet of wet wipes and began to rub the sticky ice cream off Lincoln's cheeks and hands.

"Have you started to look into preschools?"

"Preschool?" She shook her head. "No, I guess we'll start researching them next year when Lincoln turns three. Isn't that the standard age?"

"My cousin runs Little Acorns—the spot near Dr. Hanlon's office? They have an award-winning two-year-old program." Essie said. "I figure if you and Renee are serious about the shop, you'll be in need of child care, yes? Might as well go with the best."

Oh god, this could really work. It didn't have to be a pipe dream. It could be real...real and wonderful.

Her heart sped up at the idea of working again, of returning to her beloved career. Imagine waking up, showering, putting on makeup and styling her hair. She imagined eating overnight oats with Ethan, Lincoln, and the baby before they all started off on their separate days. Maybe they could hire a part-time nanny, Sadie carrying the new babe around in Lincoln's old BabyBjörn on the babysitter's off days.

Did it make her a horrible mom, how much she craved that picture?

But a happy mom and wife would make for happier children and a happier husband.

"Yes, I guess that's true," she replied, trying to keep her voice even despite her excitement. "Thanks for the recommendation."

"Of course. I bet Lincoln would love it, too. He seems like such a smart, social little fella." Essie swung her purse over her shoulder and hit a button on her key fob. Her white BMW convertible beeped twice. "I must run. Be sure to tell Renee every amazing detail, and have her call me, gosh darn it! I want her to see the space for herself."

Sadie waved. "I will. Promise."

She buckled Lincoln into his car seat and drove to their favorite park, the one that overlooked the ocean.

"Yay! We go swing now!"

She gave him a tickle, setting him in the baby swing and pushing him gently.

"Higher, Mommy! Higher!"

Sadie daydreamed about the pie shop as she pushed Lincoln on the swing set, lost in her own little world. And how perfect that Essie had mentioned Little Acorns! She would have never thought Lincoln was old enough, and she was certain he would love the interaction with other children his age, not to mention all the activities.

Maybe they even taught the children a second language. Now wouldn't that be something? Even Annette would be impressed if Lincoln suddenly began speaking French at the dinner table.

"*Plus de jus, s'il vous plaît,*" Lincoln would say, his pronunciation perfect.

"*Mon Dieu!*" Annette would gasp.

Sadie would take a delicate sip of her white wine, the new baby sleeping docilely in her arms, and smile, "Why yes! Didn't we mention Lincoln is now bilingual?"

Perfect.

She'd talk to Ethan tonight.

She was going to finally tell him about the pie shop idea, especially now that there was a childcare option for Lincoln. She sent her husband a quick text.

Hi! What time are you getting home tonight?

Bad news... I'm not. Stuck in Boston for the night, forgot to mention it. SORRY!

She stopped and simply stared at his words.

Was he really stuck? Was he really "SORRY"?

And was Ethan even going to be receptive of the pie shop? He seemed to take pride in telling people that Sadie stayed at home with Lincoln, that he was able to support their little family on his sole income. Plus, he talked about his Cincinnati childhood like he'd been raised in Mayberry, always raving about the brownies his mom would have waiting for the children after school and how she was always around for homework help.

"Mommy! No stop push!"

"Whoops. Sorry, sweetie." Sadie gave Lincoln a few extra generous pushes. "Wow! Look how high you're going!"

Sadie watched her giggling toddler soar, all the while completely lost in her own thoughts.

But Ethan had always been very supportive of Sadie's design skills. She knew he believed in her. But would he think she could manage balancing everything?

She honestly didn't know. But she never used to be the kind of woman who asked permission for anything. She took what she wanted and wrangled her dreams into submission.

Maybe it was time to be that woman again.

Chapter Fourteen

Renee rummaged through her top dresser drawer.

She must look unhinged, her hair flying every which way, her pale pink pedicure was still drying, and most of her wardrobe was spread across the bed.

She held up a pair of white cotton briefs for inspection.

Functional, yes. Sexy? Nope.

Why didn't she own thongs? Or anything silky or lacy? Even prudes should at least own more than Hanes.

This was ridiculous. It wasn't as though anything was going to happen tonight. For all Renee knew, Dan had simply invited her to his sailboat as a friend.

Men and women can't be friends.

The famous *When Harry Met Sally* line ran through her head. She wished Tansy was here. Her daughter would help her choose the right outfit. Although, judging by her new Internet personality, maybe she'd put her in a crop top and low-rise jeans before suggesting they move their date to Ye Olde Watering Hole to do body shots.

After settling on a pair of black briefs (black cotton had a whiff of sensual, right?), Renee chose a floral wrap dress and nude wedges. She tamed and twisted her red hair into a sleek and simple updo, and smacked her lips with sheer gloss. She stood in front of her full-length mirror inspecting herself with the sort of scrutiny a woman so unfairly reserves for her own appearance and did a final twirl. Hmmm. Her boobs didn't look half bad. The mascara brought out her eyes and—

"Crap!" she gasped, pulling the back of her dress out of her underwear.

That would have been quite the statement.

She spritzed perfume on her wrists and neck. She loved the floral, slightly spicy scent. Why didn't she wear it more often?

She carefully walked down the stairs and stood in front of the window, waiting for Dr. Dan in the very spot Tansy used to stand while watching for rides to soccer practice or National Honor Society meetings.

At exactly six thirty on the dot, he pulled into the driveway in his black Toyota Highlander.

She liked that he wasn't the sort of guy to drive a flashy sports car. And she liked that he always seemed to have a few stubborn hairs out of place on the top of his head. She liked, well she liked *him*.

Here went nothing.

She gathered her purse and locked the door behind her.

"Oh! Do you need to use the bathroom?" she asked, surprised to see him coming up the front walk. He was wearing khakis and a crisp, button-up shirt. He had the slightest five-o'clock shadow and smelled like woodsy cologne.

"I wanted to escort you out." Dr. Dan smiled, checking her out from head to toe. "But you beat me to it."

So, this is a date.

He opened the passenger-side door for her, and she slid inside as neatly as possible, trying to keep her skirt from hiking up. "I'm not used to SUVs."

"Yeah?" He fastened his seatbelt. She did the same. "I keep wondering if I should downsize, but I get a lot of use out of all the space. I like to go camping, and I can fit my tent, fishing poles, and, most importantly, Moe in here."

He was very attached to the nearly one-hundred-pound hound.

"Will Moe be joining us tonight?"

He nodded. "Is that okay? He's already on the boat, but I can drive him home if that's a problem."

"No way. I'm the guest here! It's Moe's sailboat." She smiled, even though she was a little nervous about remaining upright on her unsteady wedges with Moe running around. Maybe she should have gone more casual.

He parked his SUV in the small lot outside of the Cranberry Cove Harbor and held her arm as they made their way down the dock.

"This is it," he said a trifle shyly, standing beside a gorgeous schooner. He stepped aboard, lending his hand to Renee.

She grasped it, and he pulled her toward him. She lost her footing and ended up crashing into his chest. It was big and hard, the perfect size to rest her head on.

"Sorry!" Her cheeks heated. "Bad call on the elevated footwear."

He smiled. "Well, they're sexy as hell." His gaze blazed a trail down her body to linger on her pink-painted toes. "I gotta say, you look amazing tonight."

"Thanks." She stared down at her feet, suddenly grateful for the wedges and their unpredictability.

He opened the door that led to the boat's cabin, and a speckled dog leapt out to greet them.

Thankfully, Moe wasn't the jumping type. He simply leaned his body against Renee, pleading for a pet.

"He's going to act like no one gives him any love." Dan rolled his eyes. "Don't believe him for a second. He's an attention hound who is particularly fond of pretty women."

Her heart sank with the sudden implication, and she blurted, "Do you entertain a lot of pretty women on your boat?"

He cleared his throat, "No, no...I... Well, you're the first one to come on this boat. I bought it when I moved to Maine. Meggie...um, that's my late wife's name...Meggie and I always talked about buying a boat in Seattle, but we never got around to it."

Renee nodded. "I see."

"Can I get you a glass of wine?" He eagerly changed the subject. "I'd love to show you around. It's a small but mighty vessel."

He poured her a glass of sauvignon blanc before showing her the tiny kitchen and living area, full bathroom, and modest bedroom. The floors were mahogany and he'd made the entire space feel inviting. The sofa had navy cushions and a flannel blanket draped over it. A leather framed photo of Moe on a fishing dock somewhere hung on the wall.

"This is cozy." Renee approved.

"That's a compliment coming from the Queen of Cozy."

"Huh?"

"Your cottage might just be the warmest, most welcoming place I've ever visited."

He held a chair out for Renee, and she took a seat as he lit the tea lights on the bistro table.

"Fancy!" She settled in, loving that he went to so much trouble.

He smiled at her as he searched for something on his phone. A few moments later, John Legend crooned over the boat's speakers.

He set a basket of fresh dinner rolls between them and a Caesar salad at each place before taking a seat. Moe settled in himself, lying against Renee's feet, keeping them warm.

"Wow…this looks delicious." She smiled bashfully, thinking she'd never been treated to a dinner with so many thoughtful details. "Thank you."

They kept the conversation light through their salads and the dinner rolls. She told him more about Tansy and her prestigious scholarship, making sure not to mention any of her daughter's recent behavior.

"Is it hard having her across the country?"

"Extremely." Renee's heart ached with missing her. "She was, she *is*, my life. When she first left, it felt like a part of me was missing. That phantom limb feeling hasn't quite subsided."

"Bet you can't wait for summer vacation." Dr. Dan removed her salad plate as well as the breadbasket. "Ready for the main event?"

Renee tried to smile through the flash of sadness as he set a platter of lobster in front of her. A cup of melted butter was beside it as well as a baked potato with all the fixings.

"This is gorgeous." She swooned, her mouth already watering.

Time to forget Tansy for a moment and be in the present.

He lifted his head and toasted the starry sky. "I had to serve something special to accompany tonight's meteor shower."

"Wow, really?" Was she dreaming? There was no way she was on this incredible boat with this incredible man, being served the best dinner she'd had in years.

He grinned and nodded. "Meggie used to have this giant telescope. We kept it in the attic of our house, and she'd sit up there with a glass of wine at night, gazing at the sky." He looked down at his lap. "I'm sorry. I shouldn't be talking about her like this. It's my first date since, well, since she died. I'm an amateur."

144

Renee wasn't offended. "I'm glad you shared your memories with me. And not to worry, I guarantee I'm rustier at dating than you." She paused, wondering if he would find the next detail off-putting or just plain pathetic. "I haven't dated anyone, seriously that is, since Tansy's dad, my ex-husband, left me. And that was…oh, twelve or so years ago?"

He looked flabbergasted. "You're joking."

"Let's put it this way, the last time a man took me out to a fancy dinner, I'm not even sure the iPhone was released yet," she joked, trying to lighten the mood.

He looked at her with such big, sincere eyes, her stomach suddenly hurt. "What the hell did your ex-husband do to you?"

Well, let's see. Russ completely blindsided me, giving me an eternal feeling of being on edge, of never being able to truly relax. He robbed me of my self-confidence. He left me to raise our child alone. He took away my ability to trust.

"Russell had an affair with Tansy's kindergarten teacher," she said, her voice small. "He didn't even tell me to my face. I woke up on a Saturday morning late in May, and there was this stupidly clichéd 'Dear Renee' note sitting on his pillowcase."

It wasn't even two-sided—Russ was much too concise for that. He wrote that he and Ms. Samantha had fallen in love after he helped chaperone the Halloween party. (Renee had only missed it since she came down with the flu. Go figure.) He didn't take much. Just a few suitcases. And her hopes and dreams.

"They moved to Vermont, thank God, so I don't have to see them around town." She sighed, trying not to let the hurt show. "They got married and have three kids now. Tansy visits them occasionally, but not much. It's a shame. He may have broken my heart, but he's still her father."

And there it was, the truth: Russell had broken Renee's heart.

145

Torn it into pieces, stomped on it.

She remembered tearing his devastating letter into shreds before balling a corner of the down comforter in her hands. She sobbed into the duvet. She screamed into it. She leapt from their bed and grabbed their framed wedding portrait. The sound of the glass shattering against the hardwood floor had been shocking, painful, and strangely satisfying.

She would never forget glaring at the photograph lying there amid all the glass and thinking, *You stupid girl. Why didn't you see this coming?*

Russell had a wandering eye and a restless spirit from the moment Renee met him. She'd thought it was exciting and dashing.

She's been an idiot.

"Mommy?" Tansy had appeared in the doorway only a few minutes later. "Are you okay? I heard a big bang."

Quickly, Renee had wiped her tears and plastered the hugest, fakest smile across her splotchy face. "Yep! I was just trying to kill a spider. What would you like for breakfast, sweetheart?"

And that was that.

Renee was forced to dust off her knees, get up, and move on. She had a daughter to raise and a house to take care of. She would need to start job-searching on Monday. She was the breadwinner now.

There simply wasn't time to fall apart.

Over the years, her heart continued to feel that pain quite keenly. The horrible memories from that morning in May were etched into her soul.

But when she was with Dan? Her body relaxed, her fears quieted.

He reached for her hand and squeezed it.

"I'm sorry that happened. No one deserves that." His low, soothing voice turned gravelly. "You must already realize this, but your ex-husband is an idiot. He'd have to be to give you up."

Renee blushed. "Thank you. I appreciate that."

Before the meteor shower began, Dan carried their dishes to the cabin. He brought back a flannel blanket and the bottle of wine. They moved to the cushioned, leather seats that ran the perimeter of the boat's deck.

"Let me," he whispered, wrapping her shoulders in the warm fabric. He refilled her glass and sat beside her, their thighs barely grazing, yet touching enough it was hard to focus on anything else.

They gazed up at the sky, to the soaring rays of light.

"I don't even want to blink," she sighed.

"Growing up, my dad used to take my brother and me to this a nearby conservatory. He loved astronomy. He could point out every constellation. I think if he was born in a different time, with different circumstances…"

"He would have been an astronomer?"

"Yeah," Dan said, with a nod. "Maybe even an astronaut. His family was pretty poor growing up. He got a job as a mailman when he was eighteen years old and never looked back. He appreciated the dependable nature of his government job."

"He must be so proud that you became a doctor."

"He is—though if I ever told him the amount of student debt I graduated with, he would have been appalled. Probably would have asked me why I didn't just become a mail carrier like him." Renee smiled at him, relishing every bit of this family information. "He and Mom still live in Indianapolis, where I grew up. They're in their late seventies now."

Dan pointed at an especially bright streak of light, and Renee inhaled in appreciation. "Tom, my brother, still lives in Indy. He's a sports writer for the *Indianapolis Star*."

"Are you two close?"

"I love him, but we're guys. We could do a better job at keeping in touch."

"I guess I'm lucky my sister lives nearby, and well, that we're women," she laughed, with a pang thinking of how distant she had felt from Bree lately. "Makes me sad I never gave Tansy a sibling."

With their faces still tilted toward the spectacular cosmic show and not at one another, she pushed on. "So, no kids for you then?"

God. Could she have chosen a more awkward way to ask such a personal question? She wanted to slip under the flannel blanket and hide.

But Dan didn't seem insulted or bothered.

"Meggie and I tried until she was around thirty-six or so." He squinted his eyes. "And we only stopped when she was diagnosed with ovarian cancer. It's what would eventually take her, nearly six years after the initial diagnosis."

He took a ragged breath. "We had access to the best care, the best doctors in the world. I credit them for keeping her alive so long. But in the end, it just wasn't enough."

Renee reached out and took his hand, holding it between her own. "I am so sorry."

"I stuck around Seattle for a few years after she passed, but eventually needed a change of scenery. Everything reminded me of her, and it became too much. So, Moe and I packed up for the very opposite end of the country." He rubbed the dog's chin. "It's been good. Maybe it sounds corny but Cranberry Cove has been healing. I love it here—I love the small-town vibe, the scenery, the people, especially one person…"

"W-we're lucky to have you," she stammered, her insides going off like a sparkler.

Though they were quiet for the remainder of the meteor shower, Dan moved his arm around Renee and held her close. She rested her head against his broad chest and listened to his steady heartbeat, trying to determine if his heart was racing as fast as her own.

Afterward, Renee tried to help him clean the dishes, but he refused.

"I'll get to those tomorrow. I don't want to waste a single second tonight."

They returned to the ship's deck where they talked about their favorite places and most memorable trips, both good and bad. Renee mentioned the antiquing trips she and Myles took occasionally around New England.

"I once went to a conference in Amsterdam and tried ordering a latte at a 'coffee' shop," Dan said with a grimace. Renee laughed, immediately understanding the joke. "My brother tagged along on that trip, and set me up."

"One time Bree and I visited the Grand Canyon," Renee said. "She surprised me with a helicopter ride, and I vomited the entire time. She was so embarrassed!"

"Hey, it was her idea in the first place!"

"Right? That was my defense!"

After a final glass of wine, Renee began to smooth her dress and gather her clutch. "Suppose I should get going. I'd hate to overstay my welcome."

"Impossible," he replied.

She rolled her eyes playfully. "So you say. But really, I'd better get going."

It may have been a long time since Renee had been on such a

fabulous date, but she remembered the importance of leaving on a high note.

"So, any updates on the pie shop?" he asked during the drive back to Renee's cottage. Moe panted happily in the backseat. "Do I need to start looking for a new front-desk associate?"

"Still considering my options," she replied.

"Well, as much as I'd miss you at the office, I hope you go for this." They stopped at the town's sole traffic light. He reached over and held her hand. "You deserve this next adventure."

When they pulled into her driveway, she realized with a sudden panic that she wasn't ready for the night to end. Not by a long shot.

Hell with leaving the man wanting more. She wanted more of this, more of him, this very instant.

"Why don't you and Moe come inside for a nightcap?"

He looked warily at his furry friend. "Are you sure? He sheds."

Renee laughed. "The last time I checked, I owned a vacuum cleaner. Bring him on in. I'll get him a bowl of water while we enjoy our wine."

As Moe lapped up water from the plastic mixing bowl on Renee's kitchen floor, she fumbled with the bottle of merlot. Her hands were shaking as she retrieved a pair of wineglasses, and her breathing had turned shallow.

Renee racked her mental repertoire of every *Sex and the City* episode she'd ever seen. She was no Samantha, but what would Charlotte do in this situation? Turn on some jazz and discuss art as they sipped on their wine, waiting for her sophisticated date to make a move?

When she turned around to hand Dan his drink, he was staring at her with such desire, such urgency, it took her breath away.

Locked in his gaze, she asked, "Still want a glass?"

"Nope." He shook his head once. "Just you."

She set the glasses back on the countertop just in time.

He reached for her wrist and raised it to his mouth. Warm lips pressed to her skin as he gave her a gentle kiss right where her pulse fluttered. He lifted his gaze to hers and while the expression was still gentle, it was overwhelmingly certain. He wanted her. He was sure of it. Something surged in her chest and before she could second-guess, she leaned in, angling her head to brush his lower lip with hers.

It was so light, just a graze, the faintest suggestion of a kiss.

And that was all it took.

"God, Renee," he growled her name in a rasp that fell somewhere between a plea and a prayer. His hands flew to her hair, where he pulled her updo loose, sending her curls cascading over her shoulders. He pulled her closer, her body practically vibrating the moment their tongues touched, stroking once, twice, then tangling together in delicious strokes. Her whole body arched, like a plant starved for the sun, reveling in his heat. He shuddered when a hitched sigh escaped her lips, hiked her onto the table, and kissed her like she'd never been kissed before.

Chapter Fifteen

When was the last time she'd felt so good on so little sleep?

Sadie made the bed, fluffing both her and Ethan's pillows as though he'd been here last night, sleeping beside her. It sucked that he'd had to stay in Boston, but at least he'd called when he'd finished up work for the evening. He sounded exhausted, but had ended the conversation with, "Thanks for taking such great care of our little guy, Sade, and our new babe on the way. I don't know what I'd do without you."

They were only two sentences of appreciation, but they were exactly what Sadie needed to hear. Especially as she was heading to her first doctor's appointment for the new baby the next day, something Ethan would have to miss because of work.

After tucking Lincoln into bed, Sadie had fixed herself a giant bowl of popcorn and hunkered down on the living room floor, surrounded by fabric samples, design books, and every magazine she owned. For hours she'd worked. She cut inspiration photos out of magazines and bookmarked fabrics. Most of all she sketched.

Sadie mapped out the Old Red Mill, detailing where each shop would go and what the vibe would be of the common spaces: welcoming, bright, happy. She actually stirred herself a mocktail before focusing on the most important shop of all: Hester's.

By the time Sadie finished her work, it was one thirty in the morning. And with Lincoln typically waking up at dawn, she should feel exhausted. Instead, she felt more rested than she had in years.

And when Lincoln woke up at six fifteen, she got him dressed and fed in record time. Normally, she'd plunk him in front of a television show for thirty minutes as he ate his Cheerios and sipped on his smoothie pouch, but today she was dying to see Renee. She couldn't wait to tell her all about her tour of the Old Red Mill and to share her design plans for Hester's.

"Lincoln, we're going next door." She slid tiny sneakers onto his feet. "How about you choose one book and toy to bring with you?"

He shook his head. "I like Miss Renee toys. Bowls!"

Sadie laughed. "Of course."

She grabbed a cardboard book and Lincoln's LeapFrog cash register anyway before gathering her own giant binder. The pair marched next door.

"Hi!" Lincoln shouted happily. "Hi doctor!"

Whoa.

Sure enough, there was Dr. Hanlon coming out of Renee's front door, slightly disheveled and dressed too nicely for the morning hour in his slacks and button-up shirt.

He actually blushed when he saw them standing there in the side yard.

Busted.

"Oh, um…Hello, Lincoln," he replied, still as good-natured as ever. "Hi, Sadie. Gorgeous weather, huh?"

Sadie nodded, pretending like she was more interested in the ocean than his walk of shame. "Uh-huh."

"Well, I'll see you around." He paused, before saying, "Make sure you're eating plenty of fruits and veggies, Lincoln!"

"Me am!" her toddler replied.

Sadie tried to cover her smile as Dr. Dan (and his dog!) got into his black SUV and drove away. She practically jogged to Renee's front door and rang the bell three times in her excitement.

"Did you forget—" Renee stopped short on those words when she realized it was Sadie and Lincoln standing on her doorstep and not her new, hot boyfriend. "Oh! Hi you two."

She was wearing a thigh-grazing robe, and her hair was in a tousled updo of sorts. She and Dr. Hanlon had definitely not been meeting for business purposes.

"Oh. Em. Gee. Did you and Dr. Dan just…" She looked at Lincoln, wondering what was the most appropriate term to use here. "Do it?"

Renee blushed a deep crimson before launching into defensive mode.

"Dan was just, um, dropping off some forms," she stammered. "You know, for the practice."

"At eight o'clock in the morning? With his dog?" Sadie frowned. "Seriously though, why was his dog here?"

"Doggie! I want doggie!" Lincoln cheered.

Yeah, yeah. You and your grandma both.

"He brought Moe along on his errands." Renee clasped her hands together, trying to convey an air of formality. "Would you two like some breakfast? I whipped up some Greek yogurt pancakes this morning."

"Gotta love the fancy morning-after food." Sadie smirked.

"Oh, fine." She exhaled, as the two followed her into her

kitchen. Renee handed Lincoln his beloved mixing bowls and a wooden spoon to rap against them. "We had the most incredible night. He invited me to his sailboat for a lobster dinner. We sat under the stars and watched meteors."

Sadie whistled. "Now that's what I call a first date. It was the first one, right?"

Renee smiled and nodded. "Yes. And then he drove me home, and one thing led to another."

"Got it." She grinned. "That's awesome, Renee. That man's a total catch, and I've always wondered when a guy was going to come along to sweep you off your feet."

"You have?" Renee paused, a forked pancake suspended midair.

Sadie nodded. "Everyone has. You're beautiful. And you're one of the kindest people I've ever met. You've basically been Cranberry Cove's most eligible bachelorette for as long as I can remember."

Renee snorted. "Oh, please. You don't mean that."

"I do. Anyway, I promise I've come here with something useful to say, not to barge in on your booty call bliss."

"Sadie!" Renee laughed, setting a small plate in front of Sadie and a second for Lincoln to snack on.

"Please, sit down." She motioned to the other side of the table, and Renee took a seat. She pushed the binder toward her. "Lincoln and I were being nosy yesterday and poking around the Old Red Mill. Essie ended up being there and gave us a tour. It's amazing, really."

"Yeah? How's it look on the inside?"

"The exterior needs a little love, that's for sure. The good news is, Essie has already had the building inspected by engineers and it's structurally sound. It has a solid foundation. And the inside is amazing. All it needs is a little reconfiguring and some design magic, which is what this binder is all about."

Sadie flipped through the pages of her night's work, showing Renee everything from paint color choices to the hardware she had fallen in love with for the cabinets and doorknobs. She also showed Renee how the entire mill could be set up, with Renee's pie shop in the back center and a handful of stores on either side of a central pathway that led to the anchor shop.

"And, well, if you don't already have a name chosen," Sadie began awkwardly. "I was thinking we could call the shop Hester's. You know, after Grandma Hester."

Renee nodded. "I love that. It's a perfect name for what our shop will stand for—embracing the new while appreciating the old. Yes. The shop should be called Hester's."

The two women simply grinned at one another for a few moments, overwhelmed by the happiness of the moment, of the possibility of what was in front of them, before breaking into excited squeals.

"Can we do a happy dance?" Renee asked.

"Rule number one of happy dances, you don't ask to start them." Sadie reached for her phone. "Are you ready for this treat, Renee?" She turned on the "Baby Shark" song, which made the women burst into laughter. Even Renee knew the tune beloved by children everywhere and loathed by their caregivers.

"Yay!" Lincoln cheered, as Sadie gathered him in her arms, and they all danced around the kitchen. "Baby shark, doo doo doo doo doo doo!"

After their impromptu dance, Renee and Sadie discussed more specifics, how Sadie would be responsible for not only the remodel and design, but running the front of the shop once the renovations were complete, while Renee would be in charge of the kitchen and all the baking.

"I need to talk to Ethan about all this," she admitted, "but I'm sure he'll be on board." She glanced down at her Fitbit (it had been a Christmas gift from Annette, accompanied by a comment about Sadie's habit of running late) and sighed, "I've actually got to get to the doctor's office. It's my first OB visit for the new baby. I'll get to hear the heartbeat today."

"Fantastic! You and Ethan must be so excited."

"He's actually in Boston," she admitted. "What's new?" Maybe if she acted casual and breezy, she would actually start feeling that way.

"Are you serious? He won't be there?"

"No, but I'll have Lincoln." Sadie tried to sound bright and positive. "Besides, the baby is basically a gummy bear at this point. And it's not like Daddy can be there for every appointment, you know?"

"I can come along with you," Renee said automatically. "As you well know, it's pretty emotional hearing your baby's heartbeat for the first time. I can call in a bit late for work." At the word "work," she blushed.

Sadie thought about how nice that sounded, having eternally calm and soothing Renee by her side. But Renee had work. And besides, she could do this.

"I'll be fine. Promise. Lincoln, tell Miss Renee goodbye and thank you. We've got to go to the doctor's office now."

"We see Dr. Han...Dr. Han-don?"

Renee blushed one final time, and Sadie laughed as she picked Lincoln up and they waved goodbye.

As they drove to the OB-GYN's office, Sadie wondered if she should tell Lincoln about the new baby. While it felt a little wrong doing it in the minivan, with Ethan not even there, they were also about to hear the heartbeat for the first time. The cat was out of the bag.

"Honey, I have some exciting news." She turned down the Disney song that had been playing over Bluetooth. "Mommy and Daddy made another baby. You're going to be a big brother!"

Lincoln's eyebrows shot up. "Baby?"

"Yes! Isn't that exciting? A surprise. Just like you were." Maybe they'd find out the sex this time. Make it easier to plan. Naturally, she and Ethan hadn't discussed it yet.

"Okay!" Lincoln called back, clearly not understanding the magnitude of this discussion.

Sadie parked the van in an expectant mothers spot for the first time of this pregnancy and was humiliated when she saw a woman waddle by just a few moments later, clearly in the last trimester of her own. And, on second glance, that woman was Maria Gonzales—who'd lived on Sadie's block when she was growing up.

Even worse, she had to sit beside Maria in the waiting room.

"I'm so sorry I parked in that spot."

Maria looked up from her phone. "Don't worry about it, Sadie! I try to park far away. I'm aiming to get all the exercise I can. My friend told me I'll have a much easier labor and delivery that way." The woman nodded toward Lincoln. "Did you work out much with him on the way? Do you think it helped?"

"Um, yep! Absolutely," Sadie lied.

The truth was, Sadie had hardly worked out at all when she'd been pregnant with Lincoln, save for a handful of prenatal yoga classes sprinkled over the nine months. Instead, she'd spent entirely too much time working at the design firm, determined to prove she was as indispensable as ever and would continue to be so once she was a mother. She'd get to the office at seven and be anchored at her desk for nearly twelve hours a day. In addition to sitting around a lot, there may have been some stress eating too.

Always fit and athletic, Sadie had struggled to embrace her pregnant body the first time. She was so insecure about her appearance, she hadn't even let Ethan take many pictures. This time was going to be different. Not only was she determined to take better care of herself physically and emotionally, she was going to love every bit of this pregnancy. She would take those monthly photos where she stood in the same exact place so they could marvel at her growing belly. She would wear a two-piece at the beach this summer. She was going to appreciate every rumbling, every kick.

"Sadie Landry?" a nurse called from the door, holding a clipboard. "You can come on back now."

"See you around, Maria."

Holding Lincoln and his medley of toys in her arms, Sadie followed the nurse down the long hall and into an exam room. After a lengthy conversation regarding Sadie's medical history and last menstrual cycle, the nurse took a few vital measurements and a blood sample.

"Dr. Jennings will be in soon. Your gown is on the table." The nurse motioned toward the aforementioned paper gown, one of the many humiliating parts of any gynecological visit. "Will anyone be joining you today?"

"I'm afraid my husband couldn't get away from work." She kept her voice overly bright, but the room felt too big, too empty without Ethan here. She rubbed her hand on her jeans, suddenly aching for him to hold it.

The nurse gave her a "men, they get us into this mess then leave us to deal with it" smile, before exiting the room.

Sadie changed into the embarrassing paper gown and tried to sit as politely as she could on the examination table, attempting to be cool and composed like meeting her future child via ultrasound was something she did every day. Thankfully, Lincoln was happily occupied with his beloved cash register. She wondered if the new baby would be a budding checkout person too.

Dr. Jennings, a middle-aged woman with tawny skin and thin black braids, knocked on the door a very long ten minutes later. "Hi Sadie," she said with a smile, revealing perfect teeth. "Nice to meet you."

Sadie typically saw Dr. Monroe, who happened to be on maternity leave herself.

"Nice to meet you, too," she said, overly polite. Why did she always try to kiss up to doctors?

"And what's your name?" Dr. Jennings bent to Lincoln's level.

"Link," he said cheerfully, not taking his eyes off his toy. "Want buy something?"

Dr. Jennings pulled a book about a teddy bear visiting the doctor off a nearby shelf and handed it to him. "This book, please."

"That will be two dollar."

"Perfect." She rummaged in her pocket and pretended to hand Lincoln money. "Looks like I have two dollars exactly. Thank you, sir!"

"Welcome!"

Sadie smiled. She liked Dr. Jennings.

Dr. Jennings stood beside her. "So, baby number two. How are you feeling this time around?"

"Nervous," Sadie immediately replied, before trying to backtrack. "I mean, absolutely excited, too, of course. I'm not entirely sure how it happened. I mean I *know* the mechanics or whatever, but I was never great about tracking my periods. I was actually on the pill when it happened. I think I missed one...or two."

Sadie braced herself for some sort of judgmental comment from Dr. Jennings, but it never came. "Maybe an IUD would be better after this pregnancy," she said instead, her voice kind and understanding. "It's hard to remember to do something at the same time every day, and when you put a toddler into the mix? Yikes."

Sadie smiled. "Seriously."

"Now, let's take a look." Dr. Jennings pulled on a pair of gloves and did a quick pelvic exam. "Everything looks good. Are you ready to see your new addition?"

Sadie took a deep breath as the ultrasound went between her legs.

And then?

A grainy little gummy bear came into view on the screen. Dr. Jennings squinted.

"Is everything okay?" Sadie asked, her voice suddenly thick and anxious.

Dr. Jennings adjusted the wand two, three, four times. "Hmmmmm." Dr. Jennings frowned slightly, making Sadie nervous. "I'm not seeing a heartbeat. Given the gestational age, I would have expected to see one by now."

Sadie shivered, a coldness flushing through her veins. "What does that mean?"

"It's too soon to make a call. I'd like you to come back in a week and we'll try again." Dr. Jennings furrowed her brows. "The pregnancy might not be a viable one. I'm so sorry."

"Oh. Oh, okay," she murmured, numb as an Arctic winter.

Dr. Jennings offered both reassurances and possible medical explanations as to why this had happened, but she wasn't listening. She couldn't focus on anything except the sound of Lincoln cashing out again and again.

"I'll see you back here in a week?" Dr. Jennings repeated, maybe understanding that Sadie was hardly comprehending. "And please call the office if you start cramping or bleeding."

"Right. Yes. Good."

God, no. Not good. Bad. Very bad.

Sadie crumpled the paper gown and left it on the exam table. She pulled on her panties and jeans and held her hands against her lower abdomen. Was this her fault? Did she manifest a potential miscarriage? It was no secret she'd been upset to discover she was pregnant once again.

Sadie and Lincoln walked back outside, the warm spring sun burning her skin. She stared at her SUV, the short walk to the expectant mothers space suddenly insurmountable. Why had she even parked there to begin with? She was nothing but a phony, a fraud.

She had never been religious, and yet, Sadie wondered if this was the universe's way of saying she didn't deserve a second blessing, that she wouldn't be able to handle another child.

Now that the new baby's fate was in jeopardy, she wanted him or her more than anything else she had ever wanted.

Everything felt different. And she wanted her husband very badly.

Chapter Sixteen

"Whoa. You look different." Betsy Franklin, the town's mail carrier commented as she set a stack of envelopes on top of the reception desk.

"Do I?" Renee feigned innocence, taking a sip of her morning coffee.

"Haircut?"

"No."

"Facial?"

"Ha. Not in this decade. Maybe it's the scrubs. I watched that Marie Kondo show over the weekend. *Tidying Up*? Well, I discovered all sorts of things I'd completely forgotten about in the closet."

Betsy nodded. "My sister was just telling me I should watch that show. She thinks my snow globe collection has gotten out of hand."

"How many are you up to now?"

"Seventy-five. I officially had to move a few to the guest bathroom."

That sounds like way too many snow globes.

Betsy shrugged. "Anyway, maybe I'll check it out. See you tomorrow."

Renee fingered the hoops in her ears. She was wearing a pair of earrings from Chickadee. Just a little fancification.

Dan came in through the front door and her body tensed, pulling tight as a bow.

Good lord, his eyes looked extra blue today. Had he always looked so gorgeous in his crisp white shirt and tan slacks? And now she knew exactly how good he looked under those clothes.

She smiled a huge smile, her heart swelling at the sign of him.

But for some reason, he looked nervous? He cleared his throat. "Er, good morning. How was…um, how are you doing?"

"Pretty great!" Did she need to say it with the enthusiasm of a cheerleader? "You?"

"Super." He set the word of the day on her desk.

Gawky: awkward or clumsy.

"Isn't it ironic," Renee murmured.

"What's that?"

"I said the mail's here." She reached for the stack and handed it to him with increasing uneasiness. It had been less than two hours. Why was he acting weird? Her happy zing started fizzling.

"Thanks." He slid the envelopes beneath his left arm. "So, uh, we should—"

"Dr. Hanlon! Dr. Hanlon!" Seven-year-old Mia Waters exclaimed, trampling through the door and up to the reception desk. Even on her tiptoes, they could only see the very top of the little girl's head. "You've gotta see me quick. My mom told me if I'm brave today I get a pet hamster!"

Rachael Waters pulled up the rear with Mia's two younger siblings, a set of boy-and-girl twins.

"I've resorted to bribery." She sighed, stopping to wipe a piece of banana off her son's chin. "At this rate, I'm going to end up with a zoo."

"Happens to the best of us." Renee checked them in on the computer. "It looks like all of your paperwork is up-to-date, Rachael. Why don't you all head on back with Dr. Hanlon?"

Mia Waters was getting a wart removed today. Even though it was a routine produce, wart freezing even gave Renee, a rational adult, the heebie-jeebies. A pet hamster seemed like fair compensation.

What had Dan been about to say? It didn't sound like he was leading in to sharing what an amazing night he'd experienced.

Warmness pooled between her legs as memories of their night together ran through her mind, making her heart beat faster.

She wasn't the most experienced of partners, but even she could tell he was a good one. He'd made her feel like the most beautiful, most desirable woman in the world. The way he'd looked at her, the way he'd touched her…ravenous yet gentle. Afterward, coming not once, not twice, but *three* times, she'd slept more soundly than she had in years, his warm body nestled beside hers, his protective arm holding her close against his broad chest.

That next morning, Moe had found his way into her bedroom and curled at their feet. He looked as happy and content as she felt, his eyes peacefully closed and softly snoring. She'd slipped into a nightshirt the evening before, but a quick peek beneath the covers confirmed that Dan had slept naked.

Renee let out a small squeal at the thought.

Her boss had spent the night naked in her bed.

How was she ever supposed to wash her sheets again?

Twenty minutes later, Renee reviewed the office charge with Rachael Waters while trying not to imagine the clever tricks Dan had done with his fingers. "What color will your new hamster be?"

"Black and white with a pink nosey!" Mia's little brother volunteered.

"His name's gonna be Fluffy," Mia announced with an air of pride.

Rachael thanked her one last time, and the family trooped back outside.

Renee briefly wondered where one bought a hamster in Cranberry Cove before looking at the clock—their next patient wasn't expected for another ten minutes. Now would be an excellent time to make a move. She could go back to his office, check if he needed anything. Would he press her against the wall, tickling her neck with his bristly face as it made its way toward her cleavage? Or would he be softer, gentler than that, perhaps pulling her to his chest as she luxuriated in the feel of his hands spanning her waist.

She tiptoed up the hall, heart pounding in anticipation, and just as she was about to step into his office with a flirty, "Hey, handsome," she stopped short.

He stood with his back toward her, holding a framed photo of his dead wife.

Suddenly it felt wrong to stand there, too voyeuristic and intrusive. This moment felt private and not for her. It felt wrong to *want*. What if his wife was watching from above thinking "Hands off my man."

Goose bumps broke out along the back of her arms. She retreated to her desk and took a sip of coffee with shaking hands.

Everything had felt so magical that she'd never fully considered

Dan's position. He'd lost his wife. His wife! Who knew how he was feeling right now. Losing her own parents in quick succession a few years ago had been a devastating blow. Some days she'd feel fine, and then out of the blue, it would feel like the earth had opened up and threatened to swallow her whole.

The remainder of the morning, Renee quietly freaked out. What should she say? What should she do? Share that she caught him in that moment? Let it go? For Dan's part, he was more introspective than usual, and certainly more gawky. They were constantly bumping into one another in the carpeted hall, each mumbling apologies and evading eye contact at all cost.

Then Essie Park burst through the door at noon.

"There's my favorite future pie shop owner in all of Cranberry Cove!" She removed her straw sunhat with a flourish and shook out her impossibly perfect hair. "How goes it?"

"That's an awfully specific title, especially for a woman who hasn't signed the papers yet." Renee couldn't help but smile, though. That would be a pretty amazing title to have.

"Tell me you're thinking about it."

"Yes," she promised. "Sadie told me about her and Lincoln's tour of the mill. It sounds pretty special."

"'Pretty special' doesn't begin to cover it. The space is outstanding." Essie reached into her tan leather handbag and procured a crisp white envelope. "Hey, do me a favor and pass this along to Dr. Dan?"

Renee took the envelope, examining the beautiful calligraphy.

"What is it? A wedding invitation?"

Essie leaned in close, her Joy perfume heavy in the air, and lowered her voice. "It's an invitation to the Spring Fling Gala. Seems criminal not to invite the hottest bachelor in town. And you know how I love me some silver fox."

Renee studied Essie's pretty face, her perfectly arched eyebrows, her clear skin, and her full, red-painted lips. She had a vintage Hermès scarf tied around her neck and wore her signature diamond studs.

Next to her, Renee felt like the definition of frumpy.

"Oh. Okay." What was the alternative? She couldn't say Dan was hers. For all she knew she was a rebound, an appetizer as he got back in the game. Maybe he regretted their night. She didn't have a claim here. "Do you want to wait out here while I give it to him?"

Essie gave a sly smile. "I actually wrote on the invitation that he should give me a call."

"I see." How long could she plaster this stupid fake smile across her face before her cheeks shattered?

"Thanks, girlfriend. You're the best." Essie secured her hat back on her head as well as a pair of Chanel sunglasses. "Call me later this week. We can grab coffees and stroll around the mill grounds."

"Yes. Great." Renee gave a robotic nod. "Goodbye."

"Talk soon!"

With a deep breath, she trudged back toward Dan's office. This time he was seated at his desk at least. The picture of Meggie back up on the bookshelf.

"You've got mail."

He slid off his thick-rimmed reading glasses and rubbed the bridge of his nose. God, she loved when he did that. And adored how his office smelled like eucalyptus thanks to a diffuser he kept in the corner.

He leaned forward. "What's that?"

She set the posh invitation on his desk and took two steps back. "A personal invitation to the Spring Fling Gala from Essie Park."

"Oh." He frowned, staring at the envelope but not picking it up.

Tell me you don't want to go with her. Tell me you were going to ask me.

"Oh. Right," was all he said.

Awkward. This silence was so freaking awkward.

"Guess I'll be seeing you guys there," she found herself saying.

"You're going?" Did he look crestfallen or was that wishful thinking?

"Uh-huh. Yep, it's been lined up for weeks."

Totally not true. But the last thing Renee wanted to be was a charity case. *If a boy likes you, you'll know it,* her mother used to tell them. *Don't waste a second playing silly games.*

Renee still held the sentiments close. She wasn't going to throw herself at Dan. If he wanted to go to the dance with Essie Park, then he should go right ahead. This was a free country and all that jazz.

Plus, he was a middle-aged man who'd been to hell and back. He deserved to do whatever—and whoever—he wanted.

"Right." Dan looked down at his lap. "Well, thanks for being the courier."

"Happy to." If she smiled any harder her teeth would break.

That night, Renee poured herself an extra stiff gin and tonic. She squeezed fresh lime juice over the top and gave the drink a good stir.

She was not a heavy drinker, particularly with cocktails, but tonight she needed something to numb the confusion swirling inside. She wanted Dan, yes. But her life had been so simple for so long. And simple was nice. Simple didn't break hearts. Simple didn't leave you.

The image of Dan holding the framed photo of Meggie was

seared into her mind. The slump of his shoulders, the wrinkles in his forehead.

A woman like Essie would be better for Dan. She was vivacious and outgoing. She would break him out of his dating cocoon, show him the dazzling sunlight. Renee was too timid, too shy for any of that. If anything, she'd be responsible for a regression.

"I thought I was lonely, but *then* I met Renee," she could imagine him saying to his sports writer brother. "Talk about a strikeout. She was so boring, I'd rather be celibate the rest of my life."

Cringe.

She plunked Grandma Hester's recipe book on top of the kitchen counter and began to sift through the yellowed pages, each one filled with the woman's neat cursive. In addition to the recipe itself, Grandma Hester had written little notes in the margins.

Melissa's favorite. That child asked me to make this every day for the rest of her life.

Renee found herself laughing and made a mental note to show the page to Sadie.

She turned to a recipe for a chocolate–peanut butter torte.

The combo of chocolate and peanut butter could cure all the world's problems. I dare say, we'd have world peace if everyone enjoyed this evening dessert.

If this torte could inspire world peace, it could certainly help mend her crumbling heart. She searched for a jar of crunchy peanut butter and the highest quality chocolate she could find. And then, set to work.

For hours she sifted, stirred, measured, and baked. She lost herself in the world of Grandma Hester, reading her bits of wisdom with delight.

This is my family's preferred Christmas treat. I think holiday indulgences are so important.

That "too much of a good thing" saying does not apply to this peach galette, and I dare anyone to prove me wrong.

Almost any nut can be substituted for the crust—and you'd have to be a nut not to love it!

She wished Hester was sitting here in her kitchen, chatting and cooking. She'd never seemed intimidated by anything. Renee vividly remembered the afternoon she and Myles ran into Hester at the clothing shop that predated Stripe. It was called "Femme" or something insufferably pretentious, particularly for Cranberry Cove.

"Lordy, have you seen the prices here?" Hester had held up a pretty sunhat, glaring at its tag. She dramatically whipped out her readers. "Thirty-five bucks for this. Why, I could make you one of these with the straw from my brother's barn for an eighth of the cost."

Myles had whistled in approval, and Renee, a timid twenty-something suddenly felt not so different from this beloved town fixture.

"That hat is imported from Bali," the boutique's owner had said with a sneer.

"Could have fooled me." Renee recalled the smile that tugged at Hester's lips. "Looks like old Maine hay to this New England gal."

I realized something today—all I need in life is my family and my baking. I am a happy woman.

By the time Renee pulled the final creation—pecan tassies—from the oven, she had half a dozen desserts crowding her kitchen counters, a slight stomachache, and a more positive mind-set.

She'd gotten by just fine without a man all these years, she reminded herself. She certainly didn't need one now.

But what if she was sick of simple?

What if it was time to put herself out there—finally—and brave a few complications?

Chapter Seventeen

Sadie woke up to a nearly forgotten sensation: her husband's big hand sliding up her inner thigh and his hot mouth nibbling her earlobe.

She shivered as tiny goose bumps broke out down the backs of her arms. "Well, good morning to you, hot stuff." She cracked her eyes open and smiled lazily. She'd passed out before Ethan had finally returned from Boston last night. She'd tried her hardest to stay up and share the distressing news about the pregnancy, but all that fear had knocked her out. "What time did you get home?"

"Mmm...ten?" He began to gently trace her nipples with the tip of his tongue, always so deliciously sensitive during pregnancy.

Her eyes rolled back in her head. Okay, now *that* felt good.

Ethan hadn't initiated early-morning sex in ages. Even though she woke up early by anyone's standards, for the past few months, her first sight every morning was Ethan's empty side of the bed. He logged on to his computer as early as five forty-five some mornings, and on other days, drove to Boston even earlier than that.

"Happy anniversary." Ethan working his way back up to pay a

visit to the hollow of her neck. "Three years ago today, I finally worked up the courage to ask the hot designer out on a date."

Her grin widened at the memory of that spring afternoon when Ethan had awkwardly approached her desk, his usual swagger replaced with a nervous energy.

"Something I can help you with?" she'd asked absentmindedly, the majority of her focus being given to a tricky seating arrangement.

He cleared his throat. "Actually, yeah. I was wondering if you're busy tonight?"

Sadie had stared at him blankly, her mind struggling to make the leap between desk dimensions and dinner plans.

"Would you like to go out with me?" he'd sputtered.

"Like on a date?"

"No, to hang at the laundromat and compare detergent. Yes, of course as a date."

She'd been attracted to the cute software engineer at her current assignment. She'd had a little crush since they'd bonded over Frank Lloyd Wright while waiting for the coffeemaker to brew. But she didn't want to be appear *too* eager.

"That depends." Sadie chewed on the end of her pen. "What did you have in mind?"

Ethan had wanted to take her to a trendy new bistro a few neighborhoods over, known for its wine selection and tapas. But when they'd arrived, they discovered the restaurant was closed for a private event.

It had been Sadie who suggested they duck into the hole-in-the-wall bar next door, an establishment with sticky floors and an abundance of Red Sox paraphernalia. They'd split a pitcher of cheap beer and a platter of chicken wings as they chatted about their hometowns, their families, and their friends. Ethan had called an Uber at the end of the night, and when the sedan pulled up outside Sadie's apartment, he'd insisted on walking her up the three flights to her front door. He'd given her a swoon-worthy kiss goodnight and left like a proper gentleman.

It had been Sadie's last first date, and her most favorite.

Now, three years later, she kissed her husband fully, passionately.

"God, I missed you," Ethan murmured, pulling her toward him. He ran his hands over her stomach and cupped her breasts. He inhaled in appreciation. "I forgot what pregnancy does to these babies."

A sudden coldness ran through Sadie's veins. She felt herself constrict, tighten up. Her arms instinctively hugged her belly.

The pregnancy. Their baby. Their child, whose fate was now completely up in the air.

"Sade? You okay?" Ethan stopped the sensual caressing. He propped himself up on his elbow, looking at her with furrowed brows. "What's the matter? You just completely shut down."

She stared at him, swallowing hard.

"Whatever's wrong, you can tell me," he said softly. "I'm your husband. Your partner."

She nodded. Again more swallowing.

"Remember how I had my first doctor's appointment yesterday?" she said.

"Oh my God. Sadie, I am so, so sorry. I completely forgot." The color drained from Ethan's face. "I feel so shitty right now. How did it go? How's our baby?"

She bit her lip, clenching the linen duvet in her hands. "Well—"

"Mommy? I pee-pee! I pee-pee in my bed!"

"Shit," Sadie and Ethan said together, in a rare demonstration of synchronization.

* * *

Ethan had insisted on cleaning up the soggy mess, which included throwing all of Lincoln's bedding into the wash before the toddler himself received a proper scrub. "You take a shower while I tackle all that," he told her.

Sadie simply nodded, unable to blurt out the news while Lincoln was standing there cold and wet.

In the shower, she cranked the water as hot as her skin could stand and stood beneath the rain showerhead. She glared at the razor sitting inside one of the herringbone-tiled niches, knowing she should shave her legs on this rare occasion when she actually had the time. "Screw you," she murmured in its direction.

After her shower, she made an effort to use the blow-dryer for the first time in months. Amazing the difference it made. Had her hair always been capable of such volume and shine?

Ethan gave a low whistle as she walked into the kitchen, wearing a white sundress, jean jacket, and red espadrilles. "New outfit?"

"Just something I haven't worn in a while," she said.

He seemed to have forgotten about the doctor's visit news and she decided to tell him after their outing. No need to ruin a perfect family day.

They loaded up and drove to Cranberry Cove's annual May Day Festival, holding hands like the very picture of domestic bliss. Except for the fact she felt her insides scorching under the pressure of keeping the news to herself. After they parked and walked to Main Street, she kept sneaking glances at her husband in his worn Cincinnati Reds baseball cap. He gave her a wry smile and whispered, "When we get home? Let's pick up where we left off this morning."

She nodded and murmured some sort of agreement, her

stomach even more unsettled. *Where you think we left off, and where I think we left off are two very different things.*

Lincoln perched on his broad shoulders and gestured excitedly at every spring-themed float that passed by. "Daisy flower!" he cheered. "Ooooh! Look! Butterfly!"

The town's annual May Day celebration started with a twelve o'clock parade. The high school and junior high marching bands performed, and every local business put together a creative float to welcome the new season. This year, Chickadee Studios had even created flower crowns to pass out to the crowd.

"Pretty crown for a pretty gal?" Jill Kelly smiled at Sadie. "I had so much fun making these. Makes me want to add a floral component to Chickadee. Think people would like that?"

"Uh-huh. Sure." She graciously accepted the ranunculus, spray rose, and blue thistle crown and set it atop her head. She smiled and offered a weak thank-you, thinking how wrong it felt to wear such a cheerful crown when she felt so anxious, so scared.

"You look like some sort of pagan fertility goddess." Ethan winked.

"Ha, right." Sadie instinctively set her hands over her stomach.

"You okay?" Ethan looked down at her, wrapping a protective arm around her shoulders.

She smiled up into his handsome face, the same one that always made her go a little weak in the knees—that is when she wasn't wanting to bang him over the head with a whiffle ball bat. "I'm just glad to be with you," she said truthfully.

He planted a soft, perfect kiss on her forehead.

Castaway Yarn's float made its way down the street. Every year, the shop's float featured a giant ball of yarn surrounded by volunteers holding various rescue cats and kittens. By the end of the celebration, most of the precious pets were already adopted.

"Kitties!" Lincoln pointed at a small tabby. He was orange with green eyes. "Dat one. Dat one mine?"

"Sorry, bud. Daddy's allergic," Ethan replied smoothly.

"Lergic?"

"It means cats make Daddy sick," he explained. "I sneeze and cough! We don't want that to happen, do we?"

Lincoln stared before shaking his head solemnly. "Daddy no sick."

She watched the bank's float go by. They'd crafted a "money tree" surrounded by springtime blooms—a joke, of course, but slightly cringe-inducing. Next year, when she and Renee had opened Hester's, they would create a wonderful float, something imaginative, thoughtful, and clever. Maybe they could bake up tiny hand pies to give out to the crowd as they sashayed down the main drag.

"Sade, you getting hungry yet?" Ethan asked.

Her stomach growled, a reminder she was eating for two. God. At least she prayed she still was. "Maybe a little bit."

Lincoln clapped. "Me too! Me hungry."

"Lobster rolls?" she suggested.

"You read my mind," he said with the confidence of a man whose wife knew him so completely that *of course* she could guess his appetite's desires. "Let's head over to the Lobster Shack before it gets too crowded."

As they stood in line, Lincoln gleefully climbed up Ethan's strong, well-muscled legs, his father's hands gripped around his tiny wrists and holding him steady. Sadie stood beside them, overwhelmingly sad and exhausted. Lincoln might not be a big brother after all. Ethan might not get to be a dad again. She might not get to be a mom for a second time.

"Sadie?"

She whirled around. It was her gynecologist, Dr. Jennings, also known as the absolute last person she'd hoped to run into today.

"Hi, Dr. Jennings," she said, pushing a strand of hair behind her ears. She noticed a little girl standing behind Dr. Jennings's legs and waved. "Hello. I'm Sadie."

"This is my daughter, Ava." She scooted the shy girl forward. "She's waiting very impatiently for the Maypole dance."

"I used to love that part of the day. What color ribbon are you hoping to get?" Sadie asked.

"Orange!" Ava beamed. "I want my mama to braid the ribbon into my hair!"

"Excellent choice. I always went for purple myself." Sadie squeezed Ethan's hand. Her handsome husband turned, Lincoln now hooked around his middle. "Honey? This is Dr. Jennings. She's my OB while Dr. Monroe is on maternity leave."

Ethan flashed her one of his charmer grins and shook her hand. "Great to meet you, Dr. Jennings. Thank you for taking care of my beautiful wife. We're so excited to be parents again. Can't wait for Lincoln to be a big brother."

Sadie only had a moment to blanch before Lincoln began to shout, "Potty! Potty now! Now, *now*! Can't hold it!"

"Why don't you take him and I'll grab our lunches. We'll all meet up by the picnic tables," Ethan suggested

"Right! On it," she said, regretfully leaving Ethan in the company of her doctor.

"Hurry, Mommy," Lincoln urged. Sadie knew he wasn't kidding. Just a few weeks ago, they'd been at Shopper's Corner when Lincoln suddenly proclaimed he had to pee. Unfortunately, another patron was occupying the grocery's single restroom, and by the time Sadie got Lincoln next door to Castaway Yarns, he'd let loose…all over the front of her sweatshirt.

At this point, Sadie could write a book called *The Poorly Timed and Horribly Misaimed Pee-Pee Chronicles*.

"Yay! We did it!" Lincoln exclaimed the moment his mother sat his little butt on the toilet seat. "Yippee! M&M now?"

Wiping the sweat from her brow, she smiled weakly. "We did! Just in time. Great job, buddy. And how about a very special ice cream cone instead?" She held him over the porcelain sink afterward and washed their hands together beneath a stream of warm, soapy water.

They walked back toward the picnic table area slowly, Sadie feeling as though she could collapse beneath all the worry she was carrying.

As soon as she saw him at the picnic table, she knew he knew.

Lincoln scooted onto the bench and began to grab for the hot dog pieces Ethan had neatly cut up for him. "Slow down there, buddy," Sadie warned. "Have some of your juice between bites."

She sat down in front of her own lobster roll and La Croix.

"Thanks for grabbing our lunches, honey. Did you happen to talk to Dr. Jennings?"

Ethan nodded. "Sweetheart. The baby. Why didn't you tell me?"

Her eyes immediately filling with tears. "I tried, this morning."

"I know. I know you tried."

Sadie suddenly felt sick. She pushed the lobster roll away.

"I tried staying up last night," she whispered. "I wanted to tell you when you got home from work. In person."

Ethan nodded patiently.

"And then this morning, I tried again. But Lincoln..."

"Wet the bed," he finished for her, "and I didn't really listen." He suddenly pulled her close. "Oh, Sadie...God. I don't even know what to say. I'm sorry."

She hiccupped. "For what?"

"For not being there yesterday. I should have been there with you during your appointment." He ran his hand up and down her arm. Sadie felt a tear leak down her cheek. She didn't care if they were in the middle of the park during the May Day festival. "You shouldn't have had to go through that alone."

An announcement boomed over a nearby megaphone: "Calling all children! It's Maypole time! Please report to the gazebo where Ms. Park will assign you a ribbon color!"

Sadie watched as dozens of kids made a dash for Essie Park, who was standing inside the gazebo with a clipboard in her well-manicured hands. Lincoln began to push and pull on them, as toddlers are wont to do. "Come on, guys! I get ribbon now! Come, come!"

"Hey buddy, Mommy isn't feeling so great right now." Ethan knelt down in the grass, holding Lincoln out at arm's length. "Let's get her home, so she can be comfy and rest in her bed."

"Oh, Mama! You sick?" Lincoln held a tiny hand against her forehead.

Sadie burst into tears.

"I love you so much, Sadie," Ethan whispered in her ear. "Love you forever."

With her two favorite guys on either side, Sadie gratefully left the fair behind, feeling a bit lighter. No matter what happened, they'd get through it together.

Chapter Eighteen

"O uch!" Renee yelped, dropping the eyelash curler into the bathroom sink. "Oh, damn it."

"Everything okay in there?" Myles knocked on the door. "Do I need to call the paramedics?"

"Yep!" She tossed the beauty tool that felt more like a medieval torture device into a drawer and slammed it shut. She repeated the line she'd given poor Myles ten minutes ago. "I'll be ready in five."

When Renee texted Myles in a panic over her lack of a Spring Fling date, he'd immediately come to her rescue. "As it turns out, Nathan is going to be in Chicago for a conference," he'd texted. "I'd be honored to be your escort. Just don't wear anything green. It's unflattering for my skin tone."

"Lol!" Renee returned.

And now poor Myles was stuck waiting as she fussed and fumbled with her appearance.

Was her eye makeup too simple? Was her red lipstick too much? Renee propped open an *Allure* magazine and attempted to contour her cheekbones. My God, this was harder than it looked. She regretted every dismissive comment she'd ever made about the Kardashians. This felt like an Olympic sport. After a few aggressive swipes of bronzer and its immediate removal, she decided to dust on her normal blush and call it a day. She scrunched a little floral-scented gel in her hair and threw the magazine in the trash can.

For as long as she could remember, Renee and Bree had gotten ready for the Spring Fling Gala together. Bree would pop a bottle of champagne, and they'd sip from Renee's antique flutes and primp. They wore the same size and loved to swap outfits.

"So! What time are ya coming over on Saturday?" Renee had asked her sister earlier this week. "I've already got a bottle of bubbles chilling in the fridge, and I'm going to bake a snack mix for us to nibble on."

"About Saturday," Renee knew the first sound of a flaky excuse all too well. "I'm sorry, but I actually have to work late."

"What? Come on! Castaway has to be closing early for the Fling!"

"We are…" Bree paused. "But I, um, volunteered to do some inventory work after the shop closes."

It was an unexpected response and a strange excuse at that, particularly since the gala was a huge deal in the Cove. There was no way that Nina, Bree's sweet boss, would expect or request the extra hours on that day.

"Bree, what gives?"

"I'm actually in the middle of an episode of *Big Little Lies*—chat later!"

"Press pause!" Renee had shouted back, but the line was dead. Bree had already hung up.

Regardless, what did it matter that Bree wasn't around to help her look her best? Dan was escorting Essie to the gathering. And she wasn't at all sure he had enjoyed their night together. Maybe he wasn't as ready to move on after his wife's death as he'd thought. Not even gorgeous Essie Park could compete with that.

"Yes, queen! Do your thing!" Myles crowed when Renee finally made her grand entrance downstairs. He'd mixed himself a drink and had settled into her sofa while he waited. That was Myles all right. He never failed to make himself comfortable. "What are we calling that color?"

"Dove blue. But I have to be careful around the wine, it's only on loan."

She'd gone online to Rent the Runway and splurged on the Badgley Mischka off-the-shoulder gown with its sweetheart neckline. It wasn't because she was trying to make Dan's eyes pop out of his head. No, of course not. Not in the least. She most definitely was not trying to show Dan what he was missing out on. Nope. No way. But yet, despite the fact they had had only one night together, she missed him terribly.

Myles helped her with the zipper and winked. "You should treat yourself. It matches your eyes."

She kicked off her stilettos as she drove them downtown, having never mastered driving comfortably in heels. The parking lot was already crowded when they arrived, and she immediately recognized Dr. Dan's Toyota Highlander. Her stomach dropped, and she felt slightly sick. Taking a deep breath, she drove to the opposite side of the lot where she squeezed her little sedan in a spot between two SUVs. Myles gallantly extended his arm, and the pair waltzed inside.

The Spring Fling Gala was held in the Cranberry Cove Town Hall the first Saturday of May. The women all wore cocktail dresses in pastel hues while many of the men opted for seersucker suits.

Fern Nielsen, the town florist, provided whimsical decorations and place settings, and a band had driven in from Portland.

"Hey, do you see Bree?" Myles squinted his eyes. "She said she was going stag. Again. When is the last time that sister of yours was with a man?"

Renee smiled. "More recently than me?"

"Oh honey." Myles arched a brow. "That's not saying much. You two need to get out there. Live it up. Stop hiding all that gorgeous sparkle in the shadows."

"You're just saying that because you're one of my best friends," she said. "I just hope Bree made it by now. She said she had to work late. That's why she couldn't get ready with me like we usually do."

"Work late? The night of the Spring Fling?"

Renee shrugged. "I tried fighting her on it, but she's so stubborn."

"Something is up with that girl," Myles said. "Do you know she's canceled on our Wednesday wine night two weeks in a row now?"

Renee had always been slightly envious of the fact that one of her best friends had a standing weekly hangout with her sister. The two split a bottle of wine and a fancy charcuterie board while watching celebrity cooking shows. She'd joined them a handful of times but had a hard time keeping up with their passionate love of Hollywood gossip.

"I'm worried about her," Renee admitted. "And a little bit hurt too."

"Talk to her," Myles advised. "There has to be something going on. It's not you...it's her."

Huh, something to think about. Worry started winding its ugly tendrils through her already overstimulated brain.

Just then, Sadie and Ethan approached.

"Oh my God! Look at you." Sadie engulfed Renee in a hug that went on an extra beat. It felt wonderful. "That dress is stunning."

"You look pretty amazing yourself. Hello, Ethan!"

Ethan kissed her cheek. "Hi there. Hey, Myles."

Sadie wore a coral eyelet dress that set off her dark hair. And while Ethan's khaki suit expertly complemented Sadie's ensemble, the couple seemed a little sad, a little tired.

"Have you two seen Bree?" she asked them. "She had to work late, but she should be here by now."

"I feel like I saw her earlier." Ethan craned his neck.

"But you know who we did just bump into? Dr. Hanlon." Sadie gave an innocent, wide-eyed shrug. "Oh, there he is right over there, near the bar."

Renee blushed furiously as her eyes moved toward the center of the room where Dan was handing Essie Park a pink cocktail. Essie wore a striking white dress that looked unnervingly similar to a bridal gown. It was strapless and clung in all the right places. Dan looked dapper in his navy suit, his salt-and-pepper hair close cropped and his face freshly shaven.

"I need my smelling salts. Take me over!" Myles practically purred, and Renee regretted not filling him in on the situation. If he knew what had happened between them, there was no way he'd drag her into such agony. Myles may be a flirt, but he was a fiercely loyal friend. "No offense, Ethan. I'm just more of a Tony Stark than a Captain America sort of guy."

"None taken," Ethan laughed.

"What would Nathan say?" Renee elbowed him, trying to save herself from this impending doom.

"That there's nothing wrong with window-shopping." Myles

was already walking toward Dan and Essie. "It's not as though I'm going to try anything on!"

Rolling her eyes, she helplessly trailed behind him.

Dan's eyes widened when he first saw them, and Renee immediately gazed down at her dress, regretting the plunging neckline. Why hadn't she worn that yellow swing dress with the scoop neck? Or the darling vintage number with the polka dots? She looked ridiculous with all this cleavage, like a try hard cougar.

"Renee, Myles," Dan said, nodding toward them. He shook Myles's hand and gave Renee a chaste kiss on the cheek. "Great to see you two. Renee, you look beautiful."

"Thank you." She plastered a smile across her face, even as her skin burned where his lips had grazed. "You both look super."

Super? She did a mental face-palm.

"Essie Park, you're slaying it! White—how virginal!" Myles dramatically fanned his face. "About to be touched for the very first time."

"Oh, stop it, Myles Morrison." Essie swatted at him. "But if you must know, I had a business meeting in the city a few weeks ago, and I made a trip to Bloomingdale's while I was there."

"Speaking of business, you should really take a leap." Essie gave her a pointed look. "What could go wrong?"

The thought of the pie shop served as a pick-me-up, but she wasn't in the mood to talk business. She had no right to be jealous and yet here she was slowly turning the same color as split pea soup.

"Still thinking it over," she murmured.

Dan cleared his throat. "I, for one, think it's an outstanding idea."

"Yes, well." She shuffled awkwardly. Her feet were already hurting from the stilettos, and she could practically feel the blisters forming on the sides of her pinkie toes. "If you'll all excuse me, I need to use the bathroom."

Smooth, Renee. Real elegant exit.

She hurried toward the ladies' room, pretending not to hear Dot Turner call her name and avoiding all eye contact. Once safely inside, she leaned against the deep basin sink and glared at her reflection. She regretted coming tonight. Seeing Dr. Dan coupled up with Essie was breaking her heart in all sorts of new ways.

"Bree?" Renee startled when she saw her sister slinking out of a bathroom stall, her face splotchy and tear-stained. "Oh my God. What's the matter?" Was there some new man in Bree's life causing a ruckus? "What did he do to you?" she spat.

"Who? Who did what do to me?" She quickly wiped the area beneath her eyes. Bree clearly thought she'd been alone. She took in Renee's appearance and tried to smile. "New dress? It makes your boobs look eighteen. Every guy in this place must be wanting to motor boat them."

Renee shook her head. "Thanks, but no changing the subject. Why is my favorite sister crying alone in a bathroom stall?" If there was a man behind those tears, he was going to have hell to pay for whatever he'd said or done to hurt her sister. Especially considering all she'd been through.

A look of alarm shot across Bree's face. Every part of her sister looked exhausted, from her smudged eyeliner to her slightly wrinkled dress. "I'm fine, really." Bree hastily washed her hands, her eyes set downward. "Just springtime allergies. Freaking hay fever."

"You don't get allergies." Renee narrowed her eyes. "In fact you brag about it every year while the rest of town is sneezing up a storm. Seriously, cut the crap. What gives? I'm worried about you."

She moved forward, ready to engulf her in a warm hug, but Bree stumbled backward.

"Here's an idea. How about you stop acting like everyone's mother?" she snapped.

"Excuse me?"

"I'm not Tansy. I'm not your responsibility." Bree's voice was defensive. "If I need you, I'll let you know but right now I just really need to be alone."

"Wow, okay then." Surprised and overwhelmingly hurt, Renee hugged herself close. "I get it. I'm sorry. I just love you, sis."

"I love you too, more than words can say, but please get out of here. I'm begging you. Go enjoy the party."

As if. As soon as she exited the bathroom, she knew she had to get out of here. She was worried about Bree—really worried. She had to get to the bottom of this. And yes, she was feeling a bit sorry for herself too. She barged back into the party. With the strands of lights and flowers it looked like a fairy tale. Too bad it felt like a nightmare.

Myles was still chatting with Dan and Essie, though Jill Kelly had joined the group. Essie was resting her hand on Dr. Dan's forearm and laughing at something he'd just said.

Essie was so outgoing and effervescent, the very sort of woman to entertain him without expecting more from him than he was able to give.

She needed to let the fantasy go. Let the ship sail.

She discreetly tapped Myles on the shoulder.

"Hey," she murmured. "I'm sorry, but I'm getting a crushing migraine. Do you think you can get another lift home?"

"You poor thing!" Myles exclaimed entirely too loudly. "But don't worry about me, sweet pea. Dr. Hanlon here passes my place on the way out to his cabin. I'm sure I can beg a ride from him."

"Who said I'm letting this babe go home alone tonight?" Essie winked, making the small group burst into laughter.

Renee and Dan locked eyes. He quickly glanced to some mystery spot on the ceiling. Her stomach muscles clenched. She felt like she was going to throw up. "Thanks again for joining me tonight," she told Myles quickly. "Have a nice night, everyone."

Turning sharply on her foot, she made a beeline for the door.

Once outside, she sucked in deep breaths of the salty air, trying to fill her lungs to bursting. Maybe that would put her out of her misery. She leaned against the brick building and closed her eyes, willing the tears to stay put. She had been through hell and back with Russell. She was not going to let this man who she'd slept with one measly time drive her to tears.

"Renee?" She looked up sharply. Dan. His eyes were narrowed with concern. His movements cautious, hesitant. "I didn't realize you get migraines. Will you be okay driving home?"

She couldn't deal with a pity gesture, not right now.

"Oh it's just one of those things. Boring really." She made an offhand gesture. "I'll manage."

And before he could say another word, she fled to her car.

Chapter Nineteen

S adie could hardly breathe.

Here they were, the first appointment of the day on Monday morning, after an agonizing remainder of the weekend, which even included a ridiculous attempt to have fun at the Spring Fling. As if that was remotely possible when the only thing on her mind was the health, the very viability, of her unborn child.

"Our baby is going to be okay." Ethan nestled his nose into Sadie's hair, resting it just above her ear. "Just think, this time next year? We're going to be sitting on the beach eating peanut butter and banana sandwiches and building sandcastles together. All four of us."

Sadie loved that image. She thought of Lincoln digging a moat while Ethan molded turrets from wet sand. She would have the baby snuggled against her chest, maybe breastfeeding or reading a story to the happy infant.

"But what if he or she isn't?" A wave came crashing into the frame, knocking them all to their backs, helpless.

"We have to think positively." His words were more convincing than the thick emotion in his voice. "We're his or her parents. If we aren't in the baby's corner, who is?"

Sadie nodded, resolute. She rubbed her stomach. "You can do this, little one. We believe in you."

"We love you," Ethan said so quietly, it was nearly a whisper.

Thank God Renee had volunteered to watch Lincoln this morning. If this pregnancy wasn't viable, she wasn't sure how she was going to react. Would she burst into ugly sobs? Quietly cry? Scream? Any of these possibilities would scare Lincoln, and the last thing she wanted to do was upset her boy.

"Good morning." Dr. Jennings's tone was serious and somber. Sadie appreciated that the doctor wasn't trying to pretend like this appointment was anything other than tense. "I know this all must be incredibly scary."

They both nodded, their voices caught in their throats.

"Are you ready?"

Again, more silent nodding.

Sadie gripped Ethan's hand as they watched Dr. Jennings move the ultrasound wand inside her. They didn't make a sound, their hope spread as thin as tissue paper, as if any noise could rip their hopes in half.

Please be okay, Sadie prayed. *Please be okay in there.*

Ethan squeezed her fingers, and she looked up at him, locking gazes. They didn't need to talk—their eyes said it all. While this pregnancy had startled them, they wanted this baby.

Their baby.

Then the corners of Dr. Jennings mouth lifted up and suddenly everything was all right.

"There's the heartbeat."

Sadie's eyes welled up with tears, and she let out a giant exhale. Nervously, she asked, "So the baby is going to be okay?"

"Yes. Your baby is fine." Dr. Jennings nodded. "Would you like to listen to the heartbeat?"

"Yes, please," Ethan said quickly. Sadie noticed his own eyes were glassy. He let out a small exhale and collapsed into a nearby chair, running his hands through his hair. "Christ. I don't know if I've ever been so worried in my life."

"Exhausting, isn't it?" Sadie said, though she couldn't agree more. The couple listened to the soft whoosh of their child's heartbeat, relief making her shaky. "That's our baby, honey. Listen how strong they sound."

Ethan reached over and stroked her thigh before holding her hand once again, this time looser, more relaxed.

Dr. Jennings let them listen a while longer before asking if they had any other questions. "No? Well, I'll see you at your next scheduled appointment then," she smiled, tossing her gloves into the trash. "And congratulations to you both."

They talked about baby names the entire drive home.

"I want something old-fashioned and elegant for a girl, like Tabitha or Theodosia," she mused. "And if it's a boy, maybe Harrison or Alexander."

"Not bad." Ethan drummed his fingertips against the steering wheel. "Theodosia is a mouthful though. Maybe Thea?"

"Wouldn't it be fun to have a girl? Of course, two boys would be great, too. I'd get to be the queen bee of my own wolf pack."

"I love imagining Lincoln as a big brother. He is such a sweet kid…He reminds me so much of Stephen."

"Yeah? I like that comparison." Stephen Landry was Ethan's older brother, a public defense lawyer who spent his downtime coaching his kids' sports teams and volunteering at the Ronald McDonald House.

When they turned onto Seashell Lane, Ethan suggested Sadie

pick up Lincoln from Renee's house while he made them breakfast. "How do croque monsieurs sound?"

"Oh my God, yes, please!" Sadie loved Ethan's gooey grilled cheese sandwiches with their slices of crisp, buttery bread, and savory folds of ham. "Thank you, honey."

When Renee opened her door, she eyed Sadie cautiously, her brows furrowed but her eyes hopeful. "How did it go? Would you like to sit down?"

"The baby's okay," she sighed. "We got to hear the heartbeat, and it was the most glorious sound you can imagine."

Renee took Sadie into her arms and gave her a wonderful, warm hug. When she finally released her neighbor, she was wiping tears from her eyes. "Sorry about the waterworks. I was just so worried."

Sadie gave her a second hug and wondered if Renee knew how good it felt to have someone worrying about her. She hadn't even bothered to tell her own parents, figuring it didn't make any sense to worry them when everything could turn out okay.

The thought made her smile all over again: everything was okay.

"Let me go get Lincoln. I know you have to get to work. Thanks so much again." She followed Renee inside and giggled at what Lincoln had been up to all morning. He had built a fortress using Renee's dozens and dozens of books. From chick lit favorites like *Jemima J* to literary classics like *To Kill a Mockingbird*, the castle was built on a foundation of wonderful literature.

"Look, Mommy! Castle!" Lincoln smiled proudly. "Big one."

"A book castle! I love it." She bent down and kissed Lincoln's cheeks, making him giggle. "I think it's the most magical castle I've ever seen."

"Yay!" he cheered.

"Are you hungry? Daddy's making us breakfast right now. Well, breakfast number two for you, I'm sure," she added. Sadie pushed his baby soft hair away from his forehead.

"Okay," he agreed.

"Can you help me get these books back on Miss Renee's shelves? And then thank her for playing with you this morning?"

Sadie went to move a book, and Lincoln shrieked, "*No! Mommy, stop it! My castle! You hurtin' my castle!*"

Uh-oh.

"Honey, you can build another one at our house." Sadie thought about her paltry collection. Best-case scenario, Lincoln would have a book hovel. "Now help me clean this up so Miss Renee doesn't have to. It was so nice of her to let you play with her books, wasn't it?"

Lincoln's bottom lip trembled before he began to howl.

"That's okay! We can leave the book castle up." Renee swooped in. She lowered her voice. "Seriously, Sadie, don't worry about it. It'll take me ten minutes tops to get all of these books put away."

"Really?" Renee had already done her such a huge favor this morning. She hated the idea of leaving her with an additional mess. "Are you sure?"

Lincoln wailed louder.

"Yep! Now get home to that yummy breakfast. Thanks for coming over, Lincoln. I had a lot of fun!" Renee rubbed his back. "Come visit again soon, buddy."

Sadie and a hiccupping Lincoln returned home, where Ethan was plating hot, melty sandwiches. He cut each diagonally, just like Sadie preferred, and filled a bowl with freshly cut fruit.

"OJ or water?" he asked her.

"What is this, a restaurant?" she marveled. "OJ, please!"

As Sadie used airplane noises to fly strawberry slices into Lincoln's mouth, she was struck with how much she loved being a mother and how excited she was about the new baby. This pregnancy felt like a fresh start, a new beginning.

Sadie cleared her throat, her heart beating with excitement. "Honey, there's something I've been meaning to bring up."

"Yeah?" Ethan took a bite of his sandwich. He looked relaxed, as if he was expecting Sadie to tell him the furnace filter needed changing or that she wanted to paint the guest bathroom for a third time. "What's up?"

She used the end of her fork to push a green grape around her plate, taking a deep breath. She had to set this up right, explain everything best as she could. It would be a big change for their family, and Sadie wanted Ethan to know every detail.

"As much as I've loved and appreciated this time at home with Lincoln—" Almost on cue, Lincoln began to cough. Sadie handed him his juice and waited until he had three successful swallows to continue. "Ethan, I would like to go back to work."

Ethan stopped eating. "At the design firm?"

Sadie colored. "No, not the design firm. I would be up here in the Cove. I'd like to work with Renee."

"At the doctor's office?"

Good God she was doing a lousy job of explaining this.

"No, honey." She took a moment to pause, to catch her breath. "Renee and I are considering opening a pie shop together."

"A pie shop," Ethan repeated.

"A pie shop," she confirmed. "Remember those pies she made for Lincoln's birthday party? Well, we'd be serving a mix of Renee's recipes as well as Grandma Hester's. The Old Red Mill has a space up for lease, and Renee has the money to take it. We would be the anchor shop. I thought it was all a little crazy...but then I visited the space, and it just, it just feels right."

Not waiting for Ethan to reply, she continued. "Renee would be in charge of the kitchen, and I would run the front of the house. I would also get to oversee the renovation. But before we move forward, I wanted to discuss it with you. Of course. Obviously." She stopped. She was clearly rambling.

Ethan stared at his half-finished plate, shaking his head in a sort of stunned silence.

Finally, he spoke.

"Sweetheart, while I think the pie shop is a fantastic idea for Renee, why do *you* need to be involved?" His words stung. "Running a restaurant is extremely hard work. It's long shifts without much profit—particularly in the early days when you'll have a newborn and a toddler to look after."

His words made Sadie see red.

"Don't you mean when *we'll* have a newborn and a toddler to look after? They're your kids, too." Sadie used all of her strength to keep her voice calm because Lincoln was in the room. "But I don't see you thinking twice about *your* long hours and extended time away from your family."

"Of course I know that they're my kids, too. I work hard so that you don't have to. I want to provide for you guys the same way my dad did for us," Ethan responded as though that was obvious.

"Seriously?" She forced a laugh. "I mean, Ethan, come on. It's not 1950."

He made a noise of frustration. "That's not what I mean. I'm not trying to force you into high heels to serve me pot roast on Sundays or something. I just want you to feel like I can take care of you."

"And I appreciate that! I truly do," she said, her voice shaky. "But, well, your mom chose a path that made her happy, and *that's* the same luxury I want. I want to choose my own path, a path that makes *me* happy. I want you to take care of me, but not be so focused on the material part. Take care of my heart, my well-being, and I'll do the same for you."

Ethan shoved his glasses up onto his forehead and ground fists in his eyes. "Can't you see how hard I'm working to take care of your well-being? And our son's! And, now, the baby! Don't you see how much I love this family?"

"I get that, but I need you to get something too." She swallowed. "Don't you remember who I was when you met me? When you fell in love with me? I was the woman who stayed at her desk working until six thirty, seven o'clock every night, the one who looked forward to tough problems and creative solutions. I'm still that same person, that same ambitious woman you fell in love with. It's not like the second I pushed Lincoln out, I suddenly changed."

He nodded but remained quiet.

"I know it seems counterintuitive, but I believe I would be a better mom if I got that part of myself back. I wouldn't feel like I was always drowning. Plus, Lincoln is the perfect age to start at Little Acorns. He can go to preschool while I'm at work. I figure we can find part-time sitter help for the new baby, and I can carry him or her around in the Björn on other days." She reached for Ethan's hand. He let her take it. "Please say something."

"I mean…wow. It's just, things are a little unpredictable right now…" He scooted his chair away from the table, stood, and gently placed his plate in the kitchen sink.

"Unpredictable?" she repeated. "Because of the baby?"

Something else—anxiety, uncertainty?—flashed through Ethan's eyes, but he eventually nodded. "Yeah, exactly. We don't know what it's going to be like juggling two little ones. It's just…I'm excited for you, sweetheart. I really am. I can see why this would be a really wonderful thing for you, for *us*, but I need a little time to process."

She nodded. She got that.

"I worry about you getting overwhelmed or feeling spread too thin. Restaurants are such risky endeavors. And I would hate to see you put so much into it and have it fall apart; since it's not like you can get the time with the kids back." He reached for a towel, wringing it in his hands. "I just worry. You know how good I am at that."

Sadie smiled sadly. "You'd earn gold at the Olympics if it was a sport."

"Ha, tell me about it." Annette's favorite story to tell involved Ethan finding a sickly kitten in their backyard. The vet was closed for the evening, so what did Ethan do? Swaddled the poor thing with an old sweatshirt and bottle fed it every two hours until morning despite uncontrollable sneezing. That's how they discovered he was allergic.

"Why don't you go take a nap? Or get some mama time in? I'll clean this all up and keep an eye on Lincoln."

"Um, okay. Thank you." It was a kind offer, but Sadie wasn't ready for the conversation to end. Not like this, with no solid resolution or understanding between them. "Can we talk about this later then? After you've had time to, um, process?"

Ethan gave a distracted nod, suddenly hyper focused on transferring the leftover fruit to Tupperware.

She could do this: juggle being a mom and helping run a business. But it seemed like Ethan doubted her?

What if he simply thought she wasn't up to the challenge?

* * *

Sadie tried to lie down and rest, but her mind was racing. She stared at the fan spinning above her, at the tiny crack in the otherwise perfect ceiling.

She'd finally gathered the courage to tell Ethan about the pie shop idea, about working again, and his response had been disappointing. He didn't seem to have confidence in her, and he also didn't seem to really get what made her tick. His wife.

Was the pie shop a silly idea?

Maybe it was like he had said—fantastic for Renee, not for Sadie.

It was Renee who had this marvelous talent, not Sadie.

Was this the hill she wanted to die on?

Frustrated, she tumbled out of bed. Sadie stood at the top of the stairs and called down, "Honey? I can't sleep. I'm going to pick up Lincoln's room instead. You guys doing okay down there?"

"I'm showing Lincoln that documentary my mom sent us!" he shouted in return. "The one about the Cincinnati parks?"

Great. Sadie couldn't wait to hear Lincoln ask if they could visit some random playground in Southwest Ohio. But now wasn't the time to argue.

"Wow! Sounds fun!"

Sadie opened the hall closet and pulled out their Shark vacuum cleaner, a wedding present from one of Annette's sisters. Naturally, Ethan's Aunt Celia had gone for the pet hair model, as it was "only a matter of time" before the family adopted a furry friend.

What was it with the Landrys and their dogs?

She dragged the vacuum into Lincoln's bedroom and removed the childproof cover plate from an electrical outlet so she could power up. She and Lincoln both had a bad habit of tracking sand throughout the house, and his bedroom could certainly use a good sweep.

She also liked to disinfect his toys every few weeks and straighten up his crowded bookshelf. And more often than she'd care to admit, she found herself wiping the walls down with a

Mr. Clean Magic Eraser. But as she gathered up Lincoln's dump trucks, stuffed animals, and blocks, a new idea came to mind.

The cushioned bench she'd had specially made for the family room would work great up here. Lincoln could store his toys inside, and the top would serve as a cozy reading spot. And if she moved that bench to Lincoln's bedroom, that meant she could put the gorgeous steamer trunk she'd found in the attic downstairs.

It had been her grandparents', a family heirloom that deserved to be in a more prominent area.

So once again, Sadie found herself making the trip to the attic.

"What is it you're looking for?" Ethan asked, holding the ladder securely behind her. Lincoln tugged on his shirt, demanding they return to their film.

"I've already found it," Sadie said. "I just need to clean it out first."

"Let me know when you're coming down then," he replied with a shrug, disappearing back downstairs with Lincoln in tow.

She unfastened the straps of the trunk and pushed open the top. *There's more stuff in here than I thought.*

Sadie bundled up a large stack of papers and photographs and brought them downstairs to her bedroom where she could properly sift through the lot. She spread the assortment across her and Ethan's king-sized bed, organizing the material into various piles. She couldn't wait to show her parents some of these pictures. There was one of her mother as a toddler with brownie batter all over her chubby face and a wooden spoon in her hand.

Had Sadie ever seen her mother eat a decadent dessert? Melissa was extremely careful about what she ate, usually deferring to sliced berries and yogurt as an "indulgence." Seeing her dig into a bowlful of brownie batter—even as a three-year-old—was positively mind-boggling. Sadie imagined her mother came out of the womb requesting a tossed salad with the dressing on the side.

A small notebook with a worn, leather cover caught Sadie's eye. DIARY was neatly embossed against its cover, is gold ink legible despite its age and wear. She wiped her hands against her thighs, sensing this was something special, a family heirloom that should be treated with care. Gently, she opened it.

Sadie instantly recognized Grandma Hester's distinctive cursive.

"Oh my God. Grandma's diary," she breathed, her eyes going glassy.

January 1, 1974

Hank and I missed Charlie and Louise's New Year's Eve party last night—the first time ever, too! Little Melissa had a wicked fever, and I'm sure the boys will soon enough. As they say, when it rains, it pours. Knowing my luck, we'll all come down with the stomach bug to boot. Now won't that be a treat—and not the kind of chocolate and peanut butter. Anyways, instead of a New Year's Eve spent enjoying oysters Rockefeller and champagne, the five of us feasted on minestrone soup and Sunny Delight instead. It was a pissah.

Sadie giggled, recognizing Grandma Hester's signature Maine spunk. She was also reminded of what Grandma said whenever she dared complain: "No one likes a spleeny, Sadie doll. Get yourself a diary for your grievances."

January 3, 1974

Jack went back to school today, so once again, it's just Brent, Melissa, and me at home during the day. Melissa's fever broke yesterday, and no one else in the house caught it before then. I think that's a good sign for the year ahead, don't you?

January 5, 1974

Oh, LORDY!!! Yesterday was right out straight. Tried baking Nantucket cranberry pie for Hank's birthday, and had only just started when Brent scampered into the kitchen and dropped an entire carton of eggs on the floor. A dozen eggs— SPLAT! GONE! And then poor Melissa slipped and landed on her behind. For a split second I felt like crying, but thankfully, my urge to laugh was much stronger.

Sadie sighed. Why couldn't she be more like Grandma Hester? Making a special pie from scratch for her husband's birthday, finding the ability to laugh at the day's imperfections. If that had happened to her? She probably would have sat right in the broken egg mess and sobbed, shells clinging to her butt.

January 7, 1974

Nantucket cranberry pie was a success! All the guests loved it and Hank teased, "Hester, I think you owe it to this entire town to open a bakery!" He was only joking. I know he was. But it got me to thinking…what if I did? Not to sound boastful, but I am a mighty fine baker. My pies are especially wicked. All our family and friends say so.

Oh my God. Grandma had thought about opening a pie shop?

January 8, 1974

Still daydreaming about that bakery of mine. I think I would call it Hester's—does that sound conceited? I think it would be just the nicest thing, having a little shop that's all my own. I've even been doodling designs—see them below?

Sadie gasped. Hester's. It was the name she and Renee had selected. Amazing.

Sadie traced her fingertips over three logos. The first was "Hester's" written inside the shape of a rolling pin. The second was an illustration of a pie, complete with squiggles of "steam" overtop, and the third featured the most darling sketch of a woman, presumably a self-portrait of a young Hester, wearing an apron and proudly presenting a pie. "These are wonderful," she murmured.

January 21, 1974

I haven't written in a while. I've been avoiding you, Diary, and it's because I don't want to pass along my sour news. When I write things down here, they feel more real. Hank isn't on board with my bakery idea. He actually laughed when I first told him about it, thinking I was only pulling his leg. When he realized I was serious, he grew quite serious. "But Hester, who will watch the children?" he asked me.

Do you know what's silly? Here I thought we'd come up with a plan for that together, somehow. Foolish and naïve.

"You aren't foolish," Sadie murmured, quickly flipping ahead in the diary. Had Grandma owned a pie shop and Sadie had just never known about it? Grandma Hester was so confident, so capable. If the woman had wanted to run a bakery, by God, she must have done it.

She stopped on October 19, 1975. That seemed like a good amount of time for Grandma to have gotten things up and running.

I just adore the children's Halloween costumes this year—Jack is being a cowboy, Brent a scarecrow, and Melissa a puppy dog!

What a funny crew! I've been busy for weeks now sewing their ensembles. They'll make quite the trio.

Sadie's pulse quickened as she turned to a year from that date, and then six months past that. She flipped through the diary, landing at its last page: June 30, 1978.

Made my signature pies for the Fourth of July celebration! Getting to sell my creations is the highlight of my year. It makes me a little melancholy thinking about my own shop, but oh, how I love watching my happy "customers" take their first bites.

So, that was as far as Grandma Hester made it. An annual bake sale.

It wasn't fair.

Echoes of her conversation with Ethan pinged in her brain and her body burned with frustration for her grandmother all these years ago. Grandma Hester had deserved that bakery of her very own. She would have been a badass business owner. No one was as charming or as quick-witted as her grandmother. And her baked goods! They were Cranberry Cove legends.

Grandma Hester had been gone for over a decade now.

But maybe it wasn't too late. Sadie was here now and Renee was here now. Together they could be unstoppable.

Grandma Hester could get her bakery after all.

Chapter Twenty

When others complained of long, tedious workdays, Renee was the type to shrug. She enjoyed her job, especially these past few months with Dan.

Today was not one of those days. After watching Lincoln, she made it to work before Dan and then sat anxiously at her desk waiting for his arrival. Would Essie drop him off, Moe cozy in the backseat wearing a jaunty bandanna and doggy sunglasses?

Et tu, Moe?

Would Dan be wearing designer loafers and suddenly asking her to pencil in tee times at the nearby country club? She imagined the Coastal Kids Medical Group turning into an old boys' club of sorts, with wood paneling, hunter green walls, and cigar smoke wafting through the air. She coughed.

As it turned out, Dan arrived at the office in his own vehicle, having driven himself to work. He was wearing his signature dark slacks and a crisp button-up beneath his white coat, though he did look a little tired, a bit worn. His hair was especially tousled, and he hadn't shaved that morning.

Considering the way Renee had tossed and turned last night, she must also be looking a little lackluster. All the lavender-scented lotion in the world and the hundreds of sheep that needed counting could not summon sleep.

Dan gave her a tight smile as he approached the front desk.

"Good morning," she said, sitting up as straight as she could. She immediately launched into overly enthusiastic questions. "How was your weekend? Did you and Essie have a fun night at the dance? Fern outdid herself with those eucalyptus wreaths— did you see them?"

As if Dan cared to discuss the greenery decor.

He nodded absently. "Essie and I had a nice enough time. She took Myles and me to her condo afterward to show off her latest renovations. I didn't realize what a great view she has of the harbor."

While it was worrisome Essie had invited Dan back to her place after the dance, it was encouraging that Myles had gone with them. Of course, knowing Myles, he had lit the romantic candles and turned on the jazzy music himself before discreetly slipping away.

"Could you see your boat? From Essie's place?"

"I could."

"Cool." She was jealous Essie could admire Dan's sloop from her living room chaise. Maybe he had taken her on the boat that following Sunday, and they'd enjoyed a sunny cruise.

Which he had every right to do.

Even if the thought made her feel vaguely nauseous.

"How's your head?" he asked.

She blinked. "My head?"

"Your migraine. The one you had Saturday night?"

Right. Her migraine. She must sound like such a ditz right now.

207

"I took a long hot bath when I got home," she said, which was the absolute truth. What she didn't add was that she'd also tried to drown her sorrows in half a bottle of merlot and *Sex and the City* reruns. "And, um, I took medicine…Excedrin. And then I went to bed. That seemed to kick it."

He leaned against the doorframe. "You may want to schedule a visit to your doctor. Migraines can be quite debilitating."

He sounded so clinical, like he was speaking to a parent of one of his patients.

"Yes, absolutely," she said. "Thank you."

He nodded before walking away. She waited for him to come back, to bring her their word of the day, but it never came. The next time she saw him was when their first patient, Poppy Mullaney, arrived with strep throat.

The poor girl was curled in her mother's arms and reminded Renee of little Tansy. She'd been plagued with frequent bouts of strep throat before finally having her tonsils removed at age seven. Renee would never forget the sight of her small daughter swimming in the child-sized hospital gown. "Hi Poppy. I know you don't feel very good right now, but guess what one of the cures to a sore throat is?"

Poppy shook her head wordlessly.

"Ice cream!" she said, as Dan rounded the corner. Was she imagining things, or did he just shoot her a disapproving glare? Was he annoyed she'd suggested the sugary treat? Maybe she should have recommended frozen yogurt or something. "Um, you two can go on back with Dr. Hanlon now."

Renee stared down at her keyboard.

So that settled it then.

Whether he was still mourning the death of his wife or was now hooking up with Essie Park, he was no longer interested. She felt as if she'd failed a test. Dan had liked her enough to invite her on his boat. He'd cared for her enough to make her a lobster dinner, to introduce her to his beloved dog. And he had been attracted to her enough to spend the night, to sleep with her. And yet, he wasn't biting now. He'd gotten a taste of what Renee Rhodes was like, and he hadn't gone back for more. He'd spit her into his napkin, uninterested. She had been a flop, a letdown, a disappointment.

You knew this would happen.

This was why it was better to stay in her own head, in her day-dreams. It was a painful reminder why she hadn't dated these past twelve years and instead devoted herself to motherhood. Platonic romances were a lot easier than the real things. And they were certainly gentler on her heart.

I can't take this again. I can't let my heart get broken.

As the day went on, Dan became increasingly distant.

Each time he went into his office, he closed the door behind him. He chose to eat his lunch in town that afternoon—a rarity for him, as he usually ate a turkey sandwich at his desk—and he kept their interactions brief and professional. Usually, they would chat about all sorts of things, mostly the funny stuff kids would say, Moe's latest antics, Tansy's classes, the weather. But today, Dan kept the nature of their conversation practical and painfully formal.

"Did the Smiths' insurance company finally call back?" He was holding a clipboard and leafing through a stack of papers. "Fiona Smith, that is. The little girl who came in with the broken collarbone?"

Renee was insulted, but she hid her annoyance. Of course she knew who Fiona Smith was and remembered her injury. She had a knack for remembering each and every patient as well as the various reasons for their visits. It was something she prided herself on.

"Yes. Let me just check one thing." Renee typed a few things and brought up the child's file on her computer. "That's right. The insurance company is covering the visit. All taken care of."

"Good."

"Yep."

She watched him disappear back into his office. She wondered what he had done with their word of the day. Had he crumpled it into a ball and tossed it in the trash can? Fed it through the shredder?

Renee kept busy that afternoon, first making reminder calls to tomorrow's patients, then recycling old magazines in the waiting room. She even took the time to clean out the little refrigerator in the tiny kitchenette, wiping down each shelf and getting rid of expired mustard and hot sauce that their part-time nurse, Betty, loved to use.

When it was finally time for Renee to pack her things and power down her computer for the evening, her disappointment had turned into frustration.

Maybe even anger.

Whatever the case was with Dan, she deserved closure. She definitely didn't deserve to be iced out like this. Call her old-fashioned, but wasn't it considered poor manners to sleep with one's subordinate and then treat her like a total stranger?

"Well, I'll see you tomorrow," Dan said curtly. He paused in front of her desk. "Before I forget, would you be able to pick up more printer paper? I printed a lengthy article this afternoon, and I'm running low now."

The secretarial ask, though appropriate and normally acceptable, felt demeaning and cruel given the current circumstances.

That was all he had to say to her after such a strangely tense day? She wasn't even deserving of a generic "Have a nice night"? What was next—early morning coffee orders? Taking Moe on noontime walks?

Renee snapped. "What the heck is the matter with you?"

Dan looked taken aback. "I'm sorry? What's the matter with *me*?"

"Yes, you!" She bolted to her feet. "You've been distant all day! I mean, we're both adults here. You can tell me you're interested in Essie Park. It's not like I'm going to break."

He stared at her. "Essie Park? You think I'm interested in Essie Park?"

"Yes, the gorgeous woman you took to the fling two days ago? Ring a bell?" She rolled her eyes, a bad habit of Tansy's she'd evidently picked up. "I understand if you have feelings for her. But that doesn't mean we have to act like this at the office. Please be real with me. I'd rather just know so I can move on with my life. I'm not interested in playing games."

Dan laughed, but it wasn't a cheerful sort of chuckle. No, it was a sarcastic, frustrated laugh.

"*I'm* the one playing games?" He actually stalked across the waiting room and back, clearly rattled. "Renee, I'm crazy about you! The only reason I went to the fling with Essie was because you passed along her invitation and practically forced her on me."

"What?" Renee shook her head. "But...but what was I supposed to think when she came by with that invitation? It wasn't like you even *tried* to ask me. I know you're new to dating and we're too soon to be exclusive or anything, right?"

Dan ran a hand through his hair. "Contrary to what you may think, I'm not looking to sleep with every woman in town."

Speechless, she stared down at the floor, unable to make eye contact with him. The next subject was a tough one to broach, so she tread lightly. "It isn't just Essie. After we spent that night together you seemed a little weird. And then I saw you in your office…staring at a photo of Meggie."

"Oh." Dan folded into one of the chairs. It was a strange sight, seeing him sitting in the waiting room. He bent his head over his knees, intertwining his hands in front of them. "I see."

"I just figured you might not be ready to commit to much yet." Renee crossed her arms over her chest. "I worried you thought of our night together as some sort of mistake. I wondered if you were still mourning Meggie. Or if, I don't know. Maybe I'm not the sort of woman Meggie would have wanted you to be with? I thought maybe that was why you were having reservations. It sounds like she was amazing, caring, altruistic—"

Dan held up his hands, willing her to stop. "She was all of those things and more. But you're wrong about the other points. Meggie would have loved you. And she asked me to move on after her death. She made me pinkie promise."

"Really?"

Dan's voice grew thick and Renee felt her own eyes prickle. "I didn't want to even consider finding someone else after Meggie passed. But it's been a few years now, and I'm ready to try. I wouldn't have asked you out, and I certainly wouldn't have slept with you, if I wasn't."

"And you like me?" The sentiment still felt too good to be true. Renee felt every muscle in her body tense as she waited for his answer.

"More than like," he affirmed after a pause. "I admit it threw me off—how to act around you at work. But maybe we could, you know, figure that out." He coughed into his fist and raked a hand through his hair while studying the ceiling as if the words he wanted to say were printed up by the crown molding. "I want to see where this goes. I want us to be a part of one another's lives and not just here in the office. I want to help you make dinner and take you out on the boat with Moe. I want to bring you coffee in bed and hold you while you fall asleep. I want to experience life, all of it, with you."

Chills ran through Renee's core. She could picture it so clearly, and the images made her heart threaten to burst. Without thinking, she moved toward him. She dropped to her knees, threw her arms around his neck and kissed him, brushing her lips against his.

But he pulled away.

"What?" she murmured, more confused than ever. "What's wrong?"

He held her forearms as he spoke, as if she might leap at him once more should he let go. "We're both too wound up right now. I want to know you're sure about me before we start this, *really* start this."

Every part of her body was shaking with nervous, excited energy. "But I…I think I am sure."

"I don't want you to think. I want you to *know*." He moved his hands down her arms. He interlaced their fingers, squeezing her palms. "A relationship needs to be built on trust, on communication, right? The fact that you questioned my intentions and feelings so early on? I don't think that's the best start for us, babe."

Babe? She stared up at him, still curled in the space between his knees. Oh God, was she a babe?

"I realize that's going to take some time, for you to build up that sort of trust in me. I'm willing to wait for you. I just can't wait forever."

Renee nodded. She understood.

"You are incredible, more incredible than I think you've ever given yourself credit for." He paused, looking into her eyes meaningfully. "But between Tansy being so far away and this prospective new venture, there are a lot of things you still have to figure out. I believe in you, Renee. I just want you to believe in yourself."

With a final nod of his head, he stood and gathered his things. He set a piece of paper on the front desk and walked out the front door.

It was the word of the day.

Meditative.

Spot on, as usual.

Chapter Twenty-One

"Mommy? Look." Lincoln tugged on the sleeve of Sadie's T-shirt. "See dat."

"Hmm?" She'd been only half listening to his chatter. It was hard to focus on anything outside her Weather Channel app. "What's up, sweet stuff?"

Lincoln ran to the other side of the living room. "Watch!" he shouted, trying to contort himself into a somersault but tumbling right into her grandparents' steamer trunk.

Shit. She hadn't gotten around to babyproofing its jagged edges just yet.

She sprinted over. Lincoln howled and there was already a small egg rising in the middle of his forehead. "Shhh...shhh." She held him against her chest, rubbing his back and kissing the side of his neck. "It's okay, baby. You're all right."

She carried him into the kitchen where she used one hand to root through the freezer, finally finding his Boo Boo Buddy ice pack under a half open bag of freezer-burned spinach.

"No touch!" Lincoln flinched when she pressed it against his forehead. "Ouch, Mommy! Too cold. Stop!"

"I'm sorry but it's going to help you feel better." Ugh. His egg was probably going to bruise, a visible testament to her forgetfulness. "How does a strawberry smoothie pouch sound? And some *Daniel Tiger*?"

Lincoln nodded somberly and Sadie gently wiped away his remaining tears. She kissed both cheeks and helped him snuggle up on the sofa surrounded by his favorite stuffed animals with his favorite smoothie variety in hand. She draped their softest throw blanket over his lap, tucking its edges around him.

"Better?" she asked.

"Betta," he said.

She returned to her phone to check the progress of a storm making its way up the East Coast. It seemed impossible for a hurricane to ever hit Maine, much less Cranberry Cove. But when she'd stopped into Shopper's Corner this morning, the nervous chatter had her thinking otherwise.

"Feels an awful lot like the spring of 'eighty-five," Dot Turner had said, hefting a pack of water bottles into her cart. "Remember the lines at the hardware store? It was like a ghost town. Everyone boarding their windows up."

Fred Weber, a man in his eighties who had lived in the Cove his entire life and would yell at Sadie to get off his lawn as she cut across his corner lot in elementary school, agreed. "I hope folks take these warnings seriously. These early season storms can be doozies."

"Sorry, but what?" Sadie had cut in. "We've had a hurricane here in the Cove?"

How had her parents never mentioned this sort of thing before?

"You bet," said Fred. "We even had a big one in June before—

Hurricane Belinda. Significant damage. Everyone thinks of the wind, but it's the flooding, let me tell you. Well, the flooding took out half a dozen farms upriver. They never recovered." Fred had nodded toward Lincoln, who was rearranging the magazine display. Myles would be so pleased. "You make sure to take precautions and stay safe. These storms are no laughing matter."

A little unnerved, Sadie had quickly added a few items to her cart, including batteries, five cans of soup, bottled water, and two bars of dark chocolate. She wasn't exactly a survivalist prepper here.

She'd tried calling Ethan on her drive home.

"The number you are calling is disconnected."

Crap. Maybe the weather was screwing up the lines. She could try again but didn't want to drive off the road at a time like this. Since their talk about her starting work again, they'd been polite around each other but he had never gotten around to reopening their discussion and it made things awkward. They should be celebrating their second child and planning for their new future as a family of four, but despite some happy moments, things felt on edge.

Not to mention the past few weeks he'd been in Boston more than ever.

Now, sitting on the sofa and watching the foreboding radar, Sadie tried sending her husband another message.

Please tell me you'll be home before this storm, she texted. Was just at Shopper's Corner and some old-timers were talking about past storms. I'm starting to freak out a little.

She waited a few minutes. Nothing.

Maybe he was in a meeting and had his phone turned off.

Probably.

Hopefully.

217

Turning to the window, she idly rubbed her lower belly, thinking of their tiny baby floating around in there, safe and snug. Outside was a perfect Maine day, bluebird skies marred only by the occasional fluffy white cloud. It seemed impossible that within twenty-four hours they could be in hell.

She nibbled her thumbnail. This was a time to act. Was she supposed to grab a hammer and start boarding up windows? Ethan might be able to do it, but he wasn't exactly a handy guy. She paced the floor. What good was walking going to do? It was like a dragon menaced them and she was a stupid damsel in distress in her perfect coastal cottage with nothing but some water and a few bars of chocolate.

She sent a text to Renee.

Feeling a little freaked about this storm—how about you?

It took a moment for her friend to respond.

Not SUPER worried yet...Come over here if you get nervous though, ok?

Well, that was a comforting thought anyway. She could always ride the storm out with Renee if things got *really* bad. Sadie set down her phone. At the very least she needed to go search for some flashlights and batteries. But they were in the garage. And the last time she went in there she was chased by a spider.

Okay, maybe it was just scuttling off to make a new web, but it felt like it wanted her blood.

Suppressing a shiver, she took Grandma Hester's worn diary out of her back pocket. She'd been carrying it around with her everywhere, and at this point, she'd read it so many times, she practically had it memorized.

Sinking into the couch, she cradled it on her lap, treating each word, sentence, and paragraph with utter importance, maybe even reverence. She searched the entries for some sort of direction.

Sadie still couldn't get over the fact that Grandma had wanted to open a pie shop and then never seen her dream come to life.

Maybe Sadie's mom, Hester's daughter, would have some answers.

"Hi, sweetheart." Melissa answered on the third ring, slightly breathless. "Just got back from a committee meeting at the Smithsonian. Did I tell you about it yet? It's quite engaging."

"I think you mentioned it." There was so much Sadie wanted to unload, from Ethan, to the storm, to the pie shop venture. But she was on a mission.

"So, I found Grandma's diary. It was in this funky old steamer trunk in the attic that was full of photographs, recipes, that kind of stuff."

"The trunk Mom and Dad always kept in their bedroom? I searched for it after they died but I figured they'd unloaded it at some point."

"Nope, it was in the attic."

"Odd. Wonder how it got up there. That thing must have weighed a ton. But you found Grandma's diary, huh? She was such a character, Mom was. Anything scandalous?"

Sadie smiled. "No, nothing like that. It's mainly just little summaries of her days. But I want to know more about Grandma's bakery idea." She paused, giving her mom a chance to jump in.

But her mom was silent.

"Her what?" she finally asked.

"Grandma wrote about wanting to open a bakery," Sadie said. "It was her dream. She had these adorable logos sketched out and everything. She thought her specialty could be pie."

Melissa sighed, "Well, strange. I don't recall her ever mentioning it."

"She wrote about it quite a bit in her diary," Sadie prompted again.

"I know how much pleasure she got out of baking for the Fourth of July bake sale every year, but no, she never talked about opening up a bakery of her own."

Lincoln abandoned his cartoon and jumped on her lap. She ran her fingers through his curls.

"Well, she did mention that Grandpa Hank was kind of against it."

"I guess that makes sense. Grandpa Hank was a little old-fashioned and they weren't really living in the big city, now were they."

"But Grandpa Hank always told me to follow my dreams, before he died," Sadie ruminated. "Why didn't he encourage his own wife?"

"I'm sure these details are somewhere in her diary, but you know your grandpa loved your grandma beyond measure and always wanted to spoil her to bits. He probably worried about her being overwhelmed, overworked. I know he wanted to give her the best life imaginable."

Sadie thought of her own Ethan's startlingly similar words. She delicately stroked the yellowed diary pages between her fingertips.

Holding someone back was not the same as taking care of them. Grandma Hester knew this, Sadie knew this, and she believed Ethan knew it too.

"Luckily times have changed," her mother declared briskly.

Had they?

"Sadie, how are you really doing? Your dad and I miss you."

Sadie thought about the pregnancy scare, the bakery, the joys and trials of marriage, her friendship with Renee.

"It's been…" she hesitated, settling on, "good." Good felt right. Hard but a good life.

"I dreamed the baby was a girl," Melissa offered.

Sadie sighed. "A girl. I secretly dream that too. Well, I'd love either really."

They chatted for a few more minutes, mostly about Lincoln's new habits and quirks (he'd recently called Sadie by her first name, having heard a cashier use it, and she and Ethan had burst into laughter), before Sadie said, "Mom, I have to go. I don't know if you heard but we're getting a hurricane."

"Has the tropical storm that veered by us made its way all the way up to Maine? Just like 'eighty-five?" Her mom suddenly sounded a wee bit frantic. "How did I not know this? Do you want to catch a train down to D.C. from Boston? You three can stay with us until the storm passes."

"I think it's a little late for that, but thanks. I'm sure we'll be fine. Meteorologists love to blow these things out of proportion."

"Just be careful, okay?" Sadie was surprised to hear the seriousness in Melissa's voice.

She agreed, ending the phone call. Sadie transferred Lincoln, who had fallen asleep on her lap as she talked on the phone with her mom and stroked his head, to the couch. Then, with stiff pregnancy joints, Sadie pushed herself to standing. First she had to tackle the garage and those spiders.

But just you wait, Grandma Hester. You will get your bakery even if it's fifty years too late.

Chapter Twenty-Two

Renee gasped as a screaming gust of wind picked up the cushions from her patio furniture and scattered them around the yard. She tossed her bag of groceries on the countertop and hurried outside. The wind chime's brass pieces crashed against each other, sounding more like warning bells than melodious chords. She rescued one cushion from a tree branch before chasing the others from her tomato plants. One by one, she tossed them into her storage shed. She set the wind chimes gently across the worktable in her garage, pushing aside a pair of pink work gloves and a small succulent she'd been meaning to repot. Then she brought the wrought-iron chairs and table inside, as well, dragging each piece of furniture into the shelter and fastening the latch for extra measure. One last stop to gather the ceramic pieces of Tansy's fairy garden before returning to the safety of her cottage.

She continued putting her emergency provisions away in case the power ran out—bottled water, canned soup, peanut butter, and a loaf of bread—before a special news bulletin running across the TV screen grabbed her attention. Her heart raced at the sound of the alarming beeps so often associated with bad news. With a carton of eggs still in one hand, she made her way to the family room, perching on the edge of the sofa.

For the past few days, the meteorologists had worked themselves into an ever-growing tizzy of speculation. Every hour the projected force of the winds grew, as did the anticipated amount of rain and wave height. They were even interviewing longtime residents along the coast, including a few in Cranberry Cove. She shook her head. Anything for ratings.

"The waves came crashing right through our living room window!" Ninety-two-year-old Alma Wilson swore from the screen, referring to the 1985 hurricane. She gave the Pomeranian sleeping in her lap a loving pat on the head before raising her hands dramatically in the air. "One of the waves took our tabby cat right with it! Never saw that kitty again. Best mouser we ever had."

"Mmm-hmm. Gotta love a feel-good story," Renee muttered, walking to the kitchen table, picking up the phone, and hitting Tansy's contact.

Please answer…

Please answer…

Voicemail. Again.

She dropped the phone to her side with a quiet groan. How long was her kid going to give her the silent treatment? She'd been trying to connect with her for weeks now, but whenever she dialed, Tansy rejected her call after one ring or two. They were getting into an absurd routine. Heartbroken, angry, and completely frustrated, Renee would then leave a terse message, asking her to *please* call her back.

Tansy always followed this up with a cryptic text, usually blaming homework or saying she was about to take a nap.

Predictably, her phone started to buzz.

Studying for a Spanish test. Hablamos luego!

Cute. Real cute.

She punched her fingers into the keys. Just thought you might want to know a hurricane is headed for the Cove.

She paused, debating whether or not to add an extra dramatic touch.

We're being told to take proper precautions—boarding up the house, having a shelter plan, those kinds of things.

Well, that was all technically true. She glanced over at the breathless weather person standing out on some beach making wild gestures. Guess she shouldn't throw stones. Turns out she wasn't above using the storm to boost her ratings.

Her phone buzzed once more. Tansy again.

OMG. WHAT! I JUST LOOKED IT UP!

Guess the dramatic really did capture people's attention.

With a wry smile on her face, Renee neatly typed back, Really. Figured you would want a heads-up, especially if you aren't able to reach me in the next few days. I suspect the electricity will get knocked out.

She laughed, wondering what scenario was more ridiculous: Tansy actually calling her or the power going out from a hurricane.

Will you call me after the storm blows through? Nothing bad is allowed to happen to you!

The sweet glimpse of the old thoughtful Tansy made her heart ache.

So her daughter *was* in there somewhere, beneath the crop tops, secret boyfriends, and too-cool attitude. It had been weeks since they'd talked, and the realization that she hadn't heard her daughter's voice in so long shattered her heart.

Tansy's eighth birthday, *that* had been the last time her daughter was truly angry with her. Renee had thrown Tansy a

1950s-themed party, complete with a jukebox rental and adorable poodle skirts (sewn by Bree) for all the little girls.

"Where's Daddy?" Tansy had asked, giant tears rolling down her pale cheeks. She'd been wearing saddle shoes with white fold-over socks. The saddest, cutest birthday girl the world had ever seen. "Where's my daddy?"

"Honey, I don't know." They were in Renee's bedroom, away from the happy party chatter. Elvis Presley crooned somewhere in the distance. "Maybe he got caught in traffic? Or what if a pack of llamas decided to block his driveway, and he's stuck?"

It wasn't the silliest idea. Russell owned a flock or a pack or whatever of llamas in his awesome new Vermont homesteading life.

"You never invited him!" Tansy accused. "You hate him. You did this."

In fact, she had called her ex two Saturdays prior, carefully dialing each number as if the right combination would yield a magical code for serenity. She'd forced herself to greet his wife as Samantha, and omit the snarky "Ms.," and struggle through a minute of polite chitchat, before asking to speak to Russell. Her conversation with Russ mostly consisted of unintelligible stammering and awkward pauses. Despite the fact that it had been nearly two years since the divorce, her even-keeled personality still went adrift whenever they had to speak.

But Russell had promised he'd be at Tansy's party. He'd insisted he wouldn't miss it for anything, and even had the nerve to ask what Tansy was "into" right now.

The fact that he hardly knew their own daughter made Renee's heart hurt in a whole different way. And now this.

What. A. Cold. Bastard.

Despite this, Renee knew what her daughter needed to hear in that moment. And she'd given it to her.

"Uh-oh. You know what? Maybe I *did* forget to tell him," she said. "I was so busy getting everything together for the party. Shoot. I'm so sorry, baby. This is all on me."

The little girl had instantly stopped crying, her entire demeanor changed.

"Really?" she hiccupped, wiping her nose with the back of her hand.

"Mmmm," Renee murmured in reply, dancing around offering a full-out lie.

Tansy gave her a hug and hopped off the bed. "That's okay, Mommy. I forget things, too, sometimes. I'm going to go play with my friends now."

And that was that. All anger gone. No grudges, no hard feelings. If only a small fib could fix things now.

She just wanted a chance to explain her side of the situation. Let Tansy know why the Colorado announcement had hurt her feelings. And why she was so worried about her schoolwork, her health, her happiness, and her future for crying out loud. Okay, maybe she was a wee bit angry too.

And what about Bree? She longed to talk it all through with her sister about Tansy, Dan, everything.

But her sister had never called to apologize for her outburst at the Spring Fling Gala, and Renee had learned over the years that sometimes Bree went through moods and the best plan was to let her open up in her own time. It was frustrating but she loved Bree and knew how she operated.

Renee racked her memory bank, trying to remember every time her younger sister had acted distant in the past. She'd definitely been moody while waiting for her college acceptance letters to arrive—Renee could remember getting a hairbrush tossed in her direction when she asked if she'd heard from any schools yet. Oh, and then there was that month where Bree was convinced she was going to lose her job. She thought she had overheard her boss talking about downsizing and feared there wouldn't be room for her anymore at the small store. She'd definitely been distant then.

Well, shit.

Maybe this wasn't about a new boyfriend.

"Breaking now from Massachusetts," longtime news anchor, Chip Dierking, said. He was a distinguished-looking man with salt-and-pepper hair and a baritone voice. "There are reports of high winds and flooding, which meteorologists say are only growing in intensity as this storm moves its way up the coast. Joining us now is our own meteorologist, Leslie Daniels, reporting from the Cranberry Cove Harbor."

It gave her a jolt hearing the name of their little town on national news.

"Leslie, what's the latest you can tell us?"

Leslie Daniels's highlighted hair was whipping in the wind, completely shielding her face as she tried to talk into the microphone. "Thanks, Chip. What wild weather we've been having this year, huh? We're closely monitoring the system now. We think it's a real possibility the Maine coast could be hit with a category one hurricane by nightfall. And the small town of Cranberry Cove appears to be ground zero. All residents are encouraged to take precautions—protect your property and, most importantly, yourselves. It's always better to be overprepared than under."

Feeling slightly sick to her stomach, she instinctively picked up her phone and dialed Dan.

"Renee?" Dan answered on the first ring. "Are you watching the news?"

"I am," she sighed. "Unsettling, isn't it?"

"Spoken like an understated Mainer. Listen, Moe and I are

coming over now. I'll help you get prepared." How did he know the right answer before she had to ask? "We'll be there in ten minutes. Sound like a plan?"

"But what about your cabin? And the boat? Are they going to be all right?"

"All good, or as good as I can get them. Time to concentrate on you," he said. "We'll ride this out together."

Renee tried to say thank you, but her voice was caught somewhere between her heart and her mouth. She was too overcome with relief and gratitude. Quickly, she got to work, packing a large cooler with perishables and located long-forgotten flashlights and an inherited storm radio. Thank God Tansy was safe in Southern California. She paused with a rueful smile. This was the first time she was appreciative of the fact that her daughter was thousands of miles away.

Things are picking up. Looks like it'll be a category one, she texted her daughter.

Renee thought of a summer afternoon many years ago, when she and Tansy had gotten caught in a ferocious thunderstorm during a drive home from Portland. She'd pulled her Toyota to the side of the road and dug a battered box of Uno cards from the glove box. They'd played for twenty minutes until the rain eased. And when they spotted a rainbow just as they were pulling onto Seashell Lane, Renee took it as some sort of cosmic sign that she'd done good. She'd been a good mother, staying calm and protecting them both.

Now, with the assurance that Tansy was safe on the West Coast, she could turn her phone off. Smarter to conserve the battery in case the power went out. But first, one last try. She dialed her best friend, her closest confidante. The person who had always made her feel the safest.

"Renee?" Bree answered on the first ring. "Oh my God. This

is so scary! Do you have the cottage all boarded up? Do you need help? Are you freaking out? I keep looking out the window wondering if we're going to end up like SpongeBob, living in some freaking pineapple under the sea."

"Bree." Renee had never felt such pleasure, such relief, in saying her sister's name. "I'm so glad you picked up."

"Why wouldn't I?"

Renee resisted the urge to remind her of how distant and standoffish she'd been.

"Come to my house," Bree said. "It's a lot farther from the ocean and up on a hill. We'll be safer here."

"I'll be there!" Renee paused. "Um, Dan is actually on his way over. He's going to get my cottage all safe and sound. Is it okay if he comes, too?"

"Dan as in Dr. Dan Hanlon?" Bree's voice lifted.

"The one and only."

"I want to tease you so badly right now, but I'll resist since there's a hurricane coming our way and all." They both laughed. God, it felt so freaking good to laugh with Bree again. "Don't spend too much time prepping the cottage, okay? Things can be replaced, people can't."

It was a saying their own mother had said repeatedly, often after a toy had broken or a favorite watch or bauble had gone missing.

"I'll see you soon," she said.

Dan arrived exactly eight minutes later, just as Renee was taking cherished family photos and artwork off the walls, placing them in higher, more level locations.

"I'm so glad to see you," Renee said, as Moe practically jumped in her arms.

"Down, boy." Dan pulled the hound back, but she laughed and scratched him behind the ears.

"Yes, and you too, you big goofball."

Dan pressed his lips to the small spot between her cheek and her ear, a lingering kiss that fell somewhere between innocent and insinuating. "I brought plenty of plywood and caulk. Let's seal your windows. We should take down the front porch swing, too."

"Good idea." She gave her best game face though inside, she was terrified. What if she lost the cottage? Seashell Lane had been her home for forever. This was where she and Russell had taken Tansy home from the hospital. It was where she and her daughter watched Nora Ephron movies every Friday night, chowing through bowls of popcorn. It was where Tansy had tramped up the front steps, her face aglow as she held up the crisp manila envelope from USC. It was where she and Sadie had dreamed up Hester's.

She couldn't imagine living anyplace else.

She took a deep breath. "So, where should we begin?" Instinctively, she added, "Would you like a glass of iced tea?"

"Maybe a rain check." Dan laughed. "Literally. How about you just stick Moe inside and help me hold up these boards as I go?"

Thankfully, he had brought along his drill, which made the process move much faster. She focused on the tasks at hand, while covertly watching the muscles in Dr. Dan's forearms flex and relax as he held up the planks of wood and drilled them into her house. She admired the concentration in his eyes, the determination across his face.

He might break her heart, it was true, but that risk was worth taking. A good man like this was worth risking everything for.

"Dan," she began, her voice shaking, "I—"

"Renee! Dr. Hanlon!" Sadie called, bursting from her own front door and running toward them. She had Lincoln wrapped in her arms and was breathing hard. "I'm so relieved to see you guys."

"Are you okay?" Renee knotted her brows. Sadie was white as a ghost. She thought of the baby. "Take a few deep breaths. What's happening?"

Sadie breathed in and out, before stammering. "I can't get a hold of Ethan. I…I don't know what to do. He's in Boston. I'm so worried about him, and now I'm afraid for our house. I went out in the garage and faced the spiders and got the flashlights, but there aren't enough batteries and the windows aren't covered and—"

"Have you tried calling his work?" Renee interrupted.

Dan stopped his drilling, recognizing the hysteria in Sadie's voice.

"I haven't," she murmured. "I'm afraid of sounding dramatic. Am I being dramatic? I mean, this storm is all probably a bunch of hoopla, right?"

"Actually no," Renee said softly. "It sounds like this storm is most definitely going to be a big deal."

"Dr. Han-don? No shot today!" Lincoln shook his head emphatically. It was utterly adorable, and made all three adults give a small smile.

"No shot today, buddy," he said gently. "I promise."

Every part of Sadie's body seemed to be shaking. She bounced Lincoln against her hip. "I know I need to protect the house as best as I can. I just buckled down and googled what to do."

"Google?" Dan set one of his tanned hands on Sadie's shoulder. "Listen. Why don't you and Renee head inside and try to get ahold of Ethan again? I can handle storm-proofing both of your cottages."

Renee's heart warmed.

"Really?" Sadie said.

"Really." He chuckled in that easy way of his. "I like to feel like my epic tool collection is not in vain."

Still holding Lincoln, Sadie gave Dan a hug with her one free arm. "Thank you. You are a hero. I don't want to sit around like a damsel in distress, but I've never really used power tools."

"No big deal. I happen to love it."

Renee suggested they hurry back to Sadie's house, volunteering to pack a small overnight bag for Lincoln while Sadie called Ethan's office downstairs. "We'll want to be at Bree's," she explained. "Her house is on high ground away from the oceanfront. It will be much safer than Seashell Lane."

"Oh, I don't want to barge in—"

"Nope." Renee held up her hand. "Stop it right there. We're friends, business partners, and neighbors. You and Lincoln are always welcome. And Ethan for that matter."

The relief in Sadie's eyes made her want to scoop up the woman in a hug and assure her it would all be okay.

Chapter Twenty-Three

Sadie stood in front of the bay window staring out at the gray sea, strangely anxious about calling Ethan's office. Renee had taken Lincoln upstairs, asking him if he could help her pack while his mommy made a phone call. Sadie had to smile as she imagined the items her toddler would deem important during the storm, likely his blankie, a favorite book, and his fire truck.

You know, just the essentials.

She took a deep breath before pressing the "call" button. Should she provide some sort of explanation for calling the main line versus his cellphone? Would Patty Hubbard, the IT department's administrative assistant, simply assume Ethan had forgotten his phone at home or that the couple's wires had been innocently crossed in the confusion of toddler parenthood? Only spouses whose calls were being rejected would reach out this way, and Patty would know that better than anybody.

"Hello, how can I help you?" Patty trilled.

"Patty, hi. It's Sadie Landry," she said. Sadie wished she had a better rapport with Patty. Truthfully, she'd been standoffish toward the middle-aged woman at the holiday party out of loyalty to Ethan. Patty was the right-hand woman to Ethan's awful boss, Frank Marlow, and she seemed to have no trouble doing his dirty work, whether that meant canceling important meetings at the last minute or withholding previous company-wide benefits, like early dismissal Fridays.

"Oh. Sadie Landry?" Patty replied, her voice strangely warmer than usual. "How are you doing?"

"Um, okay? I guess?" Sadie fumbled. "And you?"

"Hanging in there," Patty sighed. "As you can imagine, things have been pretty tense around here following the layoffs."

"Layoffs?" It seemed as if the living room tilted, rising and crashing down on one of the choppy waves in the cove.

"Well, sure. It wasn't like Ethan was the only one to get let go." Patty lowered her voice. "There were at least five associates on Marlow's hit list, and they all got the boot. I had to deliver the letters myself. I'm sorry I had to be a part of it, and I'd appreciate it if you passed along those sentiments to Ethan."

Sadie suddenly felt weak. She set a hand against the window to steady herself.

"When did that all…start?" she asked, not wanting to reveal the fact she hadn't known her very own husband was unemployed while simultaneously searching for more answers. "The, um, layoffs."

Patty whistled. "Ethan was the first to go, and that was what? Three weeks ago now? And it's just continued in a steady stream ever since."

"Three weeks ago," Sadie repeated hollowly.

"Time flies," Patty said, which she thought was weird when one considered the remainder of that idiom. "Anyway, what can I do for you, Sadie? Do you have a question about Ethan's severance package?"

A question? Sadie had nothing but questions.

"I, um…I was just curious…" Sadie racked her brain for a plausible reason to telephone the administrative assistant of her husband's former employer. A severance package seemed like safe territory, and it was certainly a topic Sadie was interested in. "Um, Lincoln threw up on the paperwork. Could you email me another copy of the severance package?"

Perfect. No one could argue with a toddler throwing up.

"Oh, dear…yes, yes, of course I can," Patty said. "What's your email address? I have a pen and paper right here."

Sadie rattled it off.

"Is there anything else I can help you with, Sadie?"

Unless Patty Hubbard could track down her husband or prevent a hurricane there certainly was not.

"Thanks for your help," Sadie said. "Have a nice afternoon."

"Uh huh. You, too. I heard that big storm we're having is headed right your way. Getting worse all the time. Take care."

"I will," said Sadie. "You stay safe too."

Click.

Sadie tried to blink, but it was impossible to move.

Things are a little unpredictable right now.

Ethan's words from their pie shop conversation suddenly rang loud and clear. That hooded look she'd seen in his eyes—he had been hiding something from her. It wasn't the baby that he'd been referring to but something else entirely.

How—and why—had Ethan kept this news from her? Where had he been going these past three weeks on the days he claimed to be driving to Boston? Where was he *now* for that matter? He wouldn't, he *couldn't*, possibly be cheating while she was pregnant with their second child, could he? He'd never betray her like that and besides—she forced a small laugh—how would he have the energy? They both could barely manage to brush their teeth at night, right?

Sadie looked around at their beautiful, freshly renovated kitchen. They'd spared no expense, from the custom cabinets to the terrarium window she'd insisted upon despite her black thumb.

The joke was on her, yet again. If Ethan was out of work, how would they possibly afford this home? It wasn't as though she expected to be bringing in the big bucks from Hester's…

Panic built inside her, threatening to cut her mooring, send her adrift on a sea of terror.

Sadie started when she felt Renee's hand on her shoulder. She had Lincoln balanced on her hip, looking as natural in a caregiver role as she did in the kitchen.

"You okay?" she said with a frown. "Were you able to get ahold of someone from Ethan's office?"

Sadie nodded, trying to find the strength to keep her voice even. "I spoke to Patty, the department's admin. She told me Ethan was laid off a few weeks ago."

Her eyes widened. "Oh my God. Are you serious?"

"As a heart attack." Sadie grabbed her chest. "Speaking of which, excuse me if I just go ahead and have one right here."

Renee set Lincoln down and pointed toward a pile of forgotten toys in the family room. "Oh! That cash register of yours looks fun. Why don't you go show me how to use it?"

"It fun." Lincoln barreled off. "I show you, Miss Renee!"

Renee returned her attention to Sadie, her voice now lowered. "Ethan's been without a job for three weeks now?"

"Apparently." Sadie blinked away tears. "What does this all

even mean? Why wouldn't he tell me about losing his job? And where has he been going in Boston if not to his job?"

But for once, Renee didn't have the answer, which made Sadie feel all the worse. It was a silent confirmation to Sadie that this was bad, *really* bad.

Renee pulled Sadie close and promised, "We'll ride this storm out together."

She held back tears and simply nodded against Renee's shoulder, which smelled faintly and delightfully of pie dough.

The front door opened and then slammed shut with a fury, likely having been propelled forward by the angry wind. Renee and Sadie jumped, locking eyes.

"Do you think it's "

"Ethan," Sadie murmured, before rushing for the foyer. "Ethan! Thank God you're—"

But it was Dan Hanlon standing in the hallway with Moe pacing at his feet. Was his dog always this anxious? Or was it some sort of ominous animal sixth sense? Judging by the deep crease in Dr. Hanlon's forehead, Sadie guessed the latter.

"No luck getting in touch with Ethan?" he asked.

Sadie shook her head. "To be honest, I'm more worried than ever."

"So you heard the latest weather bulletin then?" Renee and Sadie shook their heads. "It's officially a category one hurricane, and we're sitting directly in its path. We only have ninety minutes before the storm hits."

Chapter Twenty-Four

"Oh my God." It was actually happening, and the reality socked Renee in the stomach. She'd been anxious and a little scared up until this point, but now she was terrified. "Do you think the cottages are going to be okay?"

"We've done what we can." Dan rubbed Moe's head, trying to console the sweet dog. "It's time to take shelter."

"Let's go to Bree's then. Immediately," Renee said, jumping into action. "I've packed a bag for Lincoln; it's just at the bottom of the steps. Anything the rest of us need, Bree will have it. Sound good?"

Sadie looked pale. "But what about Ethan?"

"Send him a message. Tell him where we've gone." Dan was already moving toward the front door. "We can't waste a single second. Time to roll."

Renee watched as Sadie lifted Lincoln into her arms and kissed his head, rubbing her face against his soft baby skin. She closed her eyes and took a deep breath, inhaling his sweet, innocent smell. Oh, how Renee missed that smell.

Sadie paused there in the living room, now staring at the family portrait they'd taken in the fall. Ethan and Lincoln were wearing matching flannel shirts while Sadie wore a white chambray dress paired with red cowboy boots. With the lush fall foliage behind them and the sun streaming into their squinted eyes, the Landry family looked nothing short of contented.

"Do you know what Annette says about this picture?" Sadie murmured. "She calls it 'The American Dream.'"

Renee touched her back. "Sadie? We have to go."

An awful look spread across Sadie's face. "The pic shop!" she exclaimed. "What if something happens to the Old Red Mill? If that goes down the tubes we can kiss Hester's goodbye before we even get started."

"Does that mean…?" Renee looked questioningly at Sadie.

"Yes," Sadie confirmed. "I want to do it."

Renee burst into a huge smile.

"But I have to do a final check-in with Ethan," Sadie added firmly.

"Of course," Renee agreed. "I'll contact Essie and see if she was able to secure the Old Red Mill."

A quick reply confirmed her fears. Essie wrote back: Me go out in this weather? I just had a blowout. No way am I risking it. You shouldn't either. Whatever will be, will be."

Renee lowered her phone. "Dan? Do you think we have time to stop at the Old Red Mill and board the windows up?"

He sighed, running a hand through his hair as he did some quick mental calculations. "Enough to make a difference. Let's get Lincoln to Bree's first."

Sadie and Renee agreed, and the four of them (plus Moe) hopped into his SUV. Despite his pleas for them to move fast, he knew to linger in Renee's driveway just a few seconds longer.

The women stared at their respective cottages for a long moment before Dan threw the car in reverse.

"Mommy, why you cry?" Lincoln asked, rubbing away the fresh tears on Sadie's cheeks.

"I'm a little sad, baby," she admitted.

"What are you thinking about?" Renee asked.

"My wedding reception," Sadie said quietly. "It was when Ethan gave me the gift of this cottage, this larger-than-life present. It was supposed to be the start of our happily ever after." She paused, tears caught in her throat. "It's where we went from being a couple to a family."

"I know." Renee reached into the backseat and squeezed her hand. "It's hard driving away, isn't it? Like we're abandoning our cottages, leaving them to fend for themselves."

"What if the hurricane destroys our house?" Sadie hiccupped. "What sort of sign of impending doom is that? My marriage might be crumbling. The house getting demolished would just be the cherry on top of our disaster sundae."

"Stop that," she said. "You can't think that way, especially now."

But just as they were pulling out of the driveway, Renee gasped. "Please, stop the car! There's something I forgot." She jumped out of the passenger door and ran for a mosaic stepping-stone in her walkway. She carried it back to the car and held it up. It read *I love you, Mom!* in pieces of multicolored glass. "Okay. I'm ready now."

They sped toward Bree's Victorian on Starboard Court. "You called her first, right?" Dan said. "She knows to expect us?"

"Uh-huh." Sadie and Lincoln would be a bit of a surprise, but Renee knew Bree wouldn't mind.

Sadie and Renee ran Lincoln up to the front door while Dan and Moe waited in the car. Renee rang the doorbell twice and rapped against the woodwork, sounding as desperate as she felt. "Bree?" she said with each knock. "Bree!"

The door flew open.

"I'm so sorry, I was trying to hunt down a spare flashlight and didn't hear the door! You should have just come in." She was wearing a pair of tired sweatpants and an oversized Disney sweatshirt. Her hair was pulled into a messy topknot, and her face looked splotchy. Quickly, she pulled them inside. She gave Lincoln a little tickle on his cheek. "There's the famous Lincoln Landry."

The toddler giggled. "Me Lincoln!"

Renee nodded toward the little boy. "Can you watch Lincoln while we go and storm-proof the mill? We'll be as fast as we can."

"Why do you have to go there?" Bree asked. "Are you going through with the pie shop?"

Sadie and Renee both nodded at the same time. "I can't wait to tell you more about it when we get back. Maybe over a stiff drink as we ride out this storm?"

Bree smiled weakly. "Yeah, sis. Of course."

"Are you sure you're comfortable babysitting Lincoln for just a bit?" Sadie asked.

Bree reached for the boy, taking him into her arms. She was a natural with children. She always had been. "Can you not be longer than a half hour? I just took a Xanax. I should be find but don't want to risk anything being alone with a little one."

"Of course, I'll go quicker than that," she said, giving her sister's arm a gentle squeeze. "I love you."

"Love you too," Bree whispered, making Renee almost cry with relief.

Then Sadie tugged her hand. "Thank you, Bree. I owe you one—big time! Come on, Renee, let's do this."

They sprinted down the front steps and leapt back into Dan's car. Driving twenty miles over the speed limit, Dan kept his eyes on the road ahead while all of their ears were glued to the radio. The warnings were ominous, with phrases that sent goose bumps up Renee's arms: "estimated time of impact"; "take shelter immediately"; "get off the roads *now*."

Renee found herself thinking about Ethan: no matter where he was at this moment, it couldn't be good. Sadie was naturally thinking the same, as she began to babble. "He might be still in Boston, right?"

"Totally."

"Oh my God, what if he's gotten involved with drugs or some seedy pyramid scheme? Maybe he's been swindled into investing all of our family's savings, and he thought he could make it back twofold before I ever realized the money had been gone to begin with."

Renee swiveled in her seat and soothed, "Ethan? Oh, Sadie. He would never."

"Do you know what scares me the most?" Sadie's bottom lip trembled. "Ethan could be in real danger right now."

Renee nodded silently. It was certainly the scariest scenario and it was certainly more likely than any pyramid-scheme fears.

"What if he got to our cottage after we'd left and went out looking for Lincoln and me?"

"We wrote a note, remember? And you texted him." Renee didn't admit it, but no matter where Ethan was, she had a sickening gut feeling that he wasn't safe.

By the time they arrived at the Old Red Mill, the wind was blowing so ferociously, it nearly knocked them to their knees.

"Renee!" Dan shouted, his voice barely discernible through the sound of the thrashing trees. "Branches are going to start falling! This isn't safe!"

She thought of all the moments she'd cowered in the past, when she'd taken the backseat. When Russ left her, she'd quietly accepted her fate. When she read of fun and interesting career paths, she quickly turned the page, reminding herself how lucky she was to have such a stable and supportive job. When she sat in the audience for countless recitals and performances, when she stayed up late to help with homework despite her own tired eyes and woke up early the next morning despite a tension headache. When she smiled bravely and sent the biggest part of her heart off to California.

Renee was always putting others before herself, always quick to conceal her own feelings and stay out of the limelight.

She was not about to let this hurricane destroy her pie shop.

"It took me too damn long to get to here! I am not losing this dream before it even starts!"

Sadie looked at her in amazement. "You go girl!" she shouted through her laughter. "Like hell we're letting this storm steal Hester's from us!"

"You're crazy! You both are!" Dan yelled, but Renee knew he meant it as a compliment. "Start grabbing plywood!"

Using all their strength, the women held the wood against the doors and windows of the Old Red Mill, as one by one, Dr. Dan secured each with his drill. They wouldn't be able to secure the breathtaking glass wall in the back, not by a long shot, and they certainly couldn't begin to protect the second or third stories. But they did manage to board up the historic leaded windows.

The sirens started to blare and just like that they were out of time.

"Come on! We have to go. Now!" Dan motioned toward his SUV, where Moe was barking.

Sadie ran toward the car, but Renee felt locked in place.

What if she lost her cottage and her dream of a pie shop all in one fell swoop? Maybe the universe was gearing up to play another cruel joke on her. Just as her life was finally coming together, here was this painful reminder that it could all so easily fall back apart.

"We've done our best, and that's all we can do. Now we just have to hope this place is going to be all right." Dan grabbed Renee's hand and pulled her to his chest reminding her that some of the things she cared about the most were right there with her. He hugged her tight. "Let's go. We've got to take care of ourselves."

She whispered goodbye to the Old Red Mill and to her dream of a pie shop, just in case this was it. "Good luck, my friend."

The ride back to Bree's was only seven minutes, though it felt like seven hours. The rain had started to come down hard, and the wind was rapidly gaining momentum. They watched in horror as debris flew through the air, narrowly missing the windshield more than once.

Moe was continuing to pant and whine. Dan reached back and scratched him behind one ear. "Dogs can sense the weather. They know when something bad is about to happen."

Renee studied Sadie who was staring down at her phone instead of the trees that were practically bowing in the wind.

When they arrived back at Bree's, her sister was pale.

"If you don't mind, I might sit down for a second," she said, the circles under her eyes a near match for the purple storm clouds outside.

"Of course." Renee immediately busied herself in the kitchen. It was either do or worry about everyone.

"Want me to make us some coffee?" Dan asked, trying to be helpful as usual.

"I was actually going to whip up a quick batch of sangria.

Figured we needed something a little stronger." Renee smiled at him. "Plus, I remember how you make coffee…"

He raised his eyebrows. "Yeah? And how's that?"

"Not well," she said, making him laugh.

Dan had made them a fresh pot the morning after he'd spent the night at Renee's house, and the man clearly was not well versed in the art of coffee-bean grinding. Renee had discreetly spit the gritty sediment into a napkin each time Dan hadn't been looking.

It was the thought that mattered, right?

"Go and keep the others company. Have Moe do tricks," she said, only half kidding. Anything would be better than watching the news reports. "I'll only be a minute."

Renee stood at Bree's kitchen counter, pouring a bottle of tempranillo into a pitcher followed by orange juice and brandy. She also attempted to tidy up. The sink had been full of dishes while the fridge had nothing but expired milk and some sad-looking carrots. There was a stack of unopened mail on the table. Plus, crumbs proliferated on seemingly every available surface.

Bree wasn't a neat freak by any means, but she wasn't a slob either. She maybe went a little too long between regular dustings, and she hated to vacuum, but her house had always been inviting and pleasant.

Renee stared at the photos peppering Bree's fridge. There was one of Bree as maid of honor in Jill's wedding, before her husband died in that terrible motorcycle accident. And one of her working at a booth for Castaway Yarn at the Farm, Fiber, and Craft Festival. And the two of them from a long-ago trip to San Francisco. They had their arms wrapped around one another's necks and were standing cheek to cheek, the epitome of sisterly love.

The photo wasn't a facade, though. Renee and Bree were close. They loved each other like crazy. *What is wrong with my sister?* She spritzed the stove top with disinfectant spray, giving the surface a good rub. Since when had she ever popped Xanax or looked so unwell?

"Mommy, too loud! No more." Lincoln wailed in the living room. He sounded like he was leveling up into hysterical mode, starting to exhale into the sort of sobs that make it hard for a child to breathe. "Want Daddy!"

Renee tossed a handful of frozen berries and a few apple slices into the makeshift sangria and hurried into the living room, the pitcher in one hand and disposable plastic cups stacked in the other.

"Thunderstorms are Ethan's territory." Sadie held Lincoln against her chest, rubbing the little boy's back. "He's the one who goes into Lincoln's room when one rolls through in the middle of the night."

"Want him."

Sadie stared down helplessly. "I know, baby. Trust me, I know."

Renee could only imagine how badly her friend wanted to throw her own temper tantrum.

"Do you know what my mom used to tell me?" Dan knelt beside them.

Lincoln raised his head curiously, hiccupping for breath.

"That scary-sounding thunder? It's only the angels bowling."

"Hey now." Sadie pushed aside his hair, gently wiping the tears below his eyes. "Do you remember what bowling is? It's when we roll those heavy balls like we did at Devon's birthday party while wearing funny shoes. Wasn't that *loud*?"

Recognition flashed across his red face. Lincoln nodded. "So loud!" He paused, sucking his bottom lip. "But why lightning?"

The adults all stared at one another, each trying to piece together some sort of charming anecdote to explain the violent streaks of light.

"That's all the angels' mommies taking pictures," Renee finally blurted out. She imagined the scene in her head, of women with fluffy, white wings snapping photos on their iPhones. It made her smile. "It's the flash of their cameras. Did your mommy take pictures when you went bowling?"

"Yeah!" Lincoln was appeased.

"That's right." Sadie hugged him. "I did."

Everyone sighed in a sort of happy, amused relief.

"Now who's up for a little liquid courage? Sorry, Sade. I brought you a sparkling water." Renee began to distribute the cups, filling each with a generous pour.

Bree shook her head.

"Huh?" Renee paused, frowning. "You love sangria."

"Not in the mood." Bree did a sort of one-shouldered shrug and turned away.

That "something's not right" feeling shuddered around her like a cold blanket. Trying and failing to catch her sister's eyes, she sighed under her breath. "Well, okay then."

She'd get to the bottom of whatever was going on, but prodding in a roomful of neighbors wasn't going to get Bree to open up.

After a failed attempt at Chutes and Ladders, the group resigned themselves to staring forlornly at the screen, where newscasters stood in the driving rain and hollered updates for the camera. The wind howled like some sort of ravenous animal, and the five of them huddled near the center of Bree's living room, away from all the windows should any debris come crashing through.

"Is that a Hoosier?" Sadie asked during a commercial, nodding toward the antique cabinet in the corner. Bree had all sorts of family photos displayed on its surface, including a few taken at Renee's cottage.

"Uh-huh. I found it in Burlington."

"It's lovely."

Bree only nodded blankly, so Renee added, "It needed quite a bit of refinishing, but Bree has the magic touch. Give this woman a sander and some chalk paint, and she's unstoppable."

And then, with a sad sort of sigh, the power went off.

Lincoln began to whimper all over again.

"Surprised that didn't happen sooner," Dan said. "Bree, where did you put the candles? I'll light them."

They all stared at their hostess, who didn't seem to be quite with it.

"Candles?" she repeated, shaking her head a few times. "Right. *Candles.* Um, there are some in the drawers of the china cabinet. The one in the dining room? You should find a few packs of matches in there, too."

Dan thanked her and disappeared through the arched doorway.

Bree took a quick glance at her watch. "It's getting late, and I'm not feeling great. If you'll all excuse me, I'm going to crash. There are guest rooms for everyone, and please feel free to use whatever you find in the bathrooms. Renee? You can have your old room. Also, um, can you make sure everyone gets settled?"

Even though it was only eight o'clock, Renee watched as her sister tossed away the quilt she'd been wrapped in and headed for the stairs. Quickly, she followed after her. She took a shortcut through the kitchen's back stairs—grabbing the stack of unopened mail en route—and caught Bree before she slipped into her bedroom.

"Hey, wait." Renee reached out, grabbing her arm. "Something's wrong, and I know it. You can talk to me! You can tell me absolutely anything. This is and will forever be a zero judgment zone. You know that, right?"

Bree flinched. "I'm fine, okay? I am completely *fine*! Would you stop worrying? It's suffocating, Renee."

Renee shook her head and held her ground. Bree wasn't turning the tables and playing the victim. Not now.

Instead, she held up the stack of mail. "Every time I drop by, you seem like you just woke up from a nap. It's like you're in this eternal stupor, which isn't you. Plus, your house is getting messy. All of this forgotten mail had piled up on the counter and was in danger of spilling into the sink. Are you on more than Xanax?"

Bree swallowed. "I found a lump. In the shower."

"Oh my God. No. Shit. *No.*" Renee felt like she might throw up. Instead, she pulled Bree into her arms, holding her as tight as she could, breathing in the faint lilac of her shampoo. "Why didn't you say anything?"

"Because I didn't want to scare you." Bree began to cry into Renee's shoulder. "Jill said I should but...but...I didn't want to upset you."

"Are you going to the doctor?"

"Yeah," Bree said. "I have a mammogram next week. It was the soonest they could fit me in."

Neither had to ask what the other was thinking.

Fuck cancer.

Their dad had a pack-a-day smoking habit so it wasn't such a shock when his chronic cough eventually got a stage four diagnosis. But when their mom went, it had started just like this—she'd gone in for a routine checkup when her doctor discovered a lump on her left breast. She'd been so brave, assuring her daughters it was probably benign, and yet it hadn't been. And the cancer had already spread.

"She didn't even have a chance," Bree whispered. "It was in her brain when they caught it. Her freaking *brain.*"

Renee was crying now, too. "I still can't wrap my head around it, how one day we were planning a trip to Vermont and then a week later, hospice. It wasn't fair. *This* isn't fair."

"I hate this so much."

"I know, honey. I do too." Renee stroked her sister's hair, the way she used to when they were little girls. "I swear I will be with you every step of this journey. I just wish you would have told me sooner. No one should shoulder that sort of worry alone."

"Jill knows," Bree murmured. "She's been the only one. Until you."

This time Bree's reference to her best friend sunk in. Renee tried to ignore the pang of jealousy. Bree and Renee were close. But what Bree shared with her bestie Jill was something on another level. They finished each other's sentences. They wandered between their two stores—Castaway Yarn and Chickadee Studios—during the day, each sipping chai tea from Morning Joe's.

Renee knew Bree would have sworn Jill to secrecy, but still…it hurt to be left out of something that could literally be life or death. It was also yet another painful reminder of Renee's lack of a friend like Jill. God, she'd perfected the art of evasion, sticking to safe, surface-level friendships most of her adult life.

"Guess my tiny boobs got sick of me complaining about them and decided to try and kill me." Bree tried to joke.

"Stop." Renee wasn't in the mood to smile, much less laugh. "This isn't funny."

"Trust me, I know. But sometimes you have to laugh when all you want to do is cry." She squeezed her sister's hand. "I didn't tell you because your worry would have freaked me out even more."

"What do you mean?"

"That mother hen instinct of yours. Sometimes it can be a little overwhelming. That's all," Bree said quietly. "It was easier to pretend this all wasn't actually happening."

Renee nodded. She got it.

"Listen. I'm going to try and sleep. All of this anxiety is exhausting." She leaned against the oak doorframe. "I was thinking Sadie and Lincoln could sleep in the big room upstairs, the one with the adjoining bath?"

"Good idea." It was the room with mauve wallpaper and a four-poster bed. There was a big armchair in the corner perfect for Sadie to read to Lincoln by candlelight before the two went to bed. "And Dan?"

"Forget your old room. You two could share the honeymoon suite?" Bree waggled her brows.

The honeymoon suite was an inside joke between the sisters. One of the countless items left behind in their parents' house had been the infamous waterbed, something the girls had always teased them about. Bree kept the bed in a guest room now, which they'd nicknamed the honeymoon suite.

"Not too tired to have a dirty mind I see." Renee swatted at her.

After a final hug, Bree retired to her bedroom and Renee returned to the living room.

When she returned to the living room, Lincoln's eyes were dropping and both Sadie and Dan looked a little worse for wear.

"I'd be happy to show you your rooms," she told them. "There are plenty of fresh towels in the hall closet and lots of extra blankets. There's some bottled water in the kitchen if you'd like to wash your faces and whatnot. We should all be very comfortable here tonight."

Dan and Sadie each grabbed a few bottled waters and followed Renee upstairs, Lincoln commenting "spooky" each time the steps creaked.

Dan whispered in her ear, "I am hoping you're with me."

"Shhhh," Renee implored, trying not to blush. "Dan, you can use this restroom, Sadie follow me."

Sadie's eyes widened at the elaborate room where she and Lincoln would be staying. "How many bedrooms does Bree have? How does she keep up with all the housework? I can barely keep the dust bunnies at bay in our little cottage."

"There are five bedrooms in this house, plus the turret. It's our parents' old place." Renee swiped a finger across a dusty piece of cherry furniture. "As for keeping up the housework, I'm not so sure she does."

"How long has she lived here?" Sadie asked.

Renee shrugged. "She has never lived anywhere else. She loves it here as much as I love my cottage."

Sadie's lower lip quivered. "Do you think our homes will be safe?"

"Of course," Renee said, forcing the lie to come out calm and reassuring. She gently shut the door behind them, smiling at the sound of Lincoln already attempting to jump on the bed. Bree would definitely approve.

She took a deep breath and walked down the dark hall to find Dan exiting the bathroom, toothbrush in one hand, flashlight in the other. Outside, rain pelted but the wind seemed to be dying down.

"Okay, looks like we've got the weird room," Renee announced when she walked back to him.

She was rewarded with a megawatt grin. "We?"

"It has a waterbed." She opened the door, to the guest room with lavender walls and a bay window, and sat on the bed's edge. Dan sat beside her, and the water shifted, lifting Renee up in its wave inducing a chuckle out of them both. "What do you think? Ready to transport back into the seventies?"

"Kinky."

"Definitely. But less kinky than getting it on in my old bed. I couldn't handle Mr. Snuffles watching."

Dan arched an amused brow. "Mister…?"

"Snuffles. He's a knit dog that's still perched on my dresser. It's Bree's place now. She can do what she likes. But she's not big on change."

"Well, I did want one of these so bad when I was a kid," he said, pulling her close and planting a long kiss on the top of her head. "But I hope we don't pop it."

"Seriously. The last thing we need around here is more flooding!" Renee suddenly grew quiet, her thoughts once again on Bree's uncertain future.

"Hey." Dan held her tighter. "Where'd you go?"

She stared at the family portrait hanging on the wall across from them. It was taken during the time when they both had insisted on matching plaid outfits and pigtails. Their mother had Renee's same red hair and was standing behind them, and their father's arms were wrapped snugly around their little family.

"Bree found a lump," Renee muttered. She hated saying the words out loud, like speaking the thing made it true. "It's why she's been acting so weird. She didn't want to tell anyone."

"People react in different ways to health scares." His hand twitched. "Has she had it tested yet? Most times a lump ends up being harmless."

"We have PTSD. Our mom was only fifty-five when she found her own lump. It was stage four. The cancer had spread everywhere."

He blew out a quiet breath and reached out to stroke her hair. "That must have been devastating."

"I can't lose Bree that same way," Renee admitted, leaning into his touch, reveling in the warmth and security. "I'm not sure I could survive that."

He took her into his arms, and she finally allowed the tears to come. "It's sort of terrifying how fast your life can change."

Dan, surely thinking of Meggie and her own diagnosis, nodded. "We never know how much time we have. That's why we owe those who have gone before to live every day to the absolute fullest. No regrets."

"You're right." Renee took a deep breath. "I guess now is a good time to tell you a few things."

He raised his eyebrows. "Yeah?"

"The first is that I'm officially resigning from the practice. Sorry, not sorry."

"Hot damn." A smile creased his craggy features. "I've never been so happy to receive a resignation. Now what's the second? You're naming a pie after me? Your sexy and modest-as-hell former boss who happens to be good with his mouth?"

Her cheeks heated. The man didn't lie. "That's still a possibility, but no. It's better than that." She picked up both of his hands and held them in her own as she sucked in a deep breath. "Okay, ready or not. Here it goes. I love you, Dan Hanlon. And I...well, I think I've known it for a while. Because my favorite part of the day is that very first moment I get to see you, when you tumble through the front door all fresh-shaven and smelling like a pine forest. And I hate it when we say goodbye in the evening."

Dan moved his face toward Renee, his lips brushing hers softly before pressing them more urgently. "And I love you, Renee Rhodes. I have since the first time we met. You had just taken a bite of scone, and the way you covered your mouth and brushed off your lap. God, it was just adorable. I was smitten from that very moment."

Renee scrunched up her nose. "You were?"

"It's hard to explain, but in that instant, this relief washed over me, a sort of warmth. I knew everything was going to somehow be okay," he said. "You made me come back to life. I want to be with you. I want us to be a real thing."

"I want that too. So, so, much."

They moved with such natural, fluid movements, it was as though the two had rehearsed this act. Slowly, carefully, they tugged on one another's clothing. They kissed and caressed, tenderly pushing aside any remaining barriers.

There in the soft candlelight, they pressed their bodies together for a second time, hungry and curious. When he entered her with a sharp gasp, it was as if their souls connected. She threw back her head as a sweet pain filled her chest, like a part of his heart entered hers. And together, despite the storm, they found safe harbor in each other's arms.

Chapter Twenty-Five

Sadie sat in the wingback chair, studying Lincoln in the pale early morning light. His hair was matted, and his cheeks were rosy. He ran hot, just like Ethan, and always woke sweaty and groggy. He slept soundly now, just like he had all night long. The angels-bowling theory worked like a charm and each thunderclap and flash of lightning made him giggle until finally, he drifted off. Sadie, on the other hand, hadn't gotten a single wink. She spent the long raging night curled on her side, one arm wrapped around Lincoln and the other clutching her pillow in lieu of her missing husband.

Where was he? No way of knowing with the phone lines down.

Lincoln stirred and she returned to the bed, nestling in beside him, forcing herself to calm down, or at least look as if she was the picture of motherly reassurance.

"Mommy?" He blinked before rubbing the sleep from his eyes. "Where are we?"

"Bree's. We had a sleepover, remember?"

He threw back the covers and cocked his head, listening. "Storm all gone?"

She nodded. "All gone, baby. We're safe."

"Daddy?" Lincoln popped his thumb into his mouth, a bad habit she was usually quick to correct, though right now she was half tempted to suck on her own.

Her hug would have to suffice in lieu of an answer, and she wrapped the blanket around them. A snug cocoon to keep out the world.

There was a knock on the door.

Guess the world didn't enjoy being ignored.

"Come in," Sadie called, sitting up.

Renee poked her head inside. "Morning, you two. Everyone sleep okay?"

"Lincoln loved listening to all of the angels bowling. Wasn't that fun, honey?"

She didn't want to burden Renee with her insomnia. Her friend would somehow find a reason why she herself could have prevented this, maybe by bringing a heavier blanket or choosing a different guest room.

Plus, Sadie didn't feel like explaining the true reason why she'd tossed and turned. She didn't want to share how Ethan was still MIA. It hurt too much just to think the words.

"How did you sleep?" she asked instead.

"Oh, you know." Renee fidgeted, casting her eyes toward the floor. And God—was she blushing?

"Renee! You better dish."

"I can't say I got a lot of sleep." She was glowing. "But the reason why I wasn't sleeping was…um, lovely. Really lovely. Honestly, it was sort of the best *ever*. The best, um, not sleeping ever."

Sadie's eyes widened in understanding. She squealed, jumping to her feet and nearly toppling Renee with a giant hug while Lincoln clapped in amusement.

"I know it's not like it was the first time," Sadie said. "But something is different about you! This was a more important time, wasn't it?"

"Uh-huh," Renee said with a wistful sigh. "We were much more, um, in sync this go-around."

"You mean you both finished at the same time?" Sadie cocked her head to the side. "I have to admit, that has literally *never* happened for us—"

Renee covered her mouth, looking scandalized. "Do you want the whole house to hear?"

Dan appeared behind her. "Good morning, gang! How did you two sleep?"

Not as well as you, Dr. McDreamy! Sadie grinned. "Oh, we got along fine."

Lincoln wiggled off the bed. "Where my daddy?"

Please stop asking, Sadie thought, as Renee and Dan's gazes focused on her. "I still haven't heard from him," she revealed after a long pause.

"Oh, Sadie—"

She held up a hand. "Can we please not talk about it? At least, not yet?"

Renee frowned, looking uncertain. But Dan was quick to move the conversation along. "Let's make breakfast," he said. "I don't know about anyone else, but I'm starving."

"Yeah?" Renee paused, the wheels almost visibly churning in her head as she seemed to debate if she should let the topic go or probe further. "Yeah, okay. I guess I am pretty hungry, too."

"Oh, we are too," Sadie fibbed, as she was decidedly *not* hungry. Thank God Renee had backed off. She was *this* close to cracking. "Just let me make the bed and straighten up a bit, and we'll be right down."

Maybe Ethan would call in the next sixty seconds, explaining everything and sparing her from the pitying eyes at the breakfast table. But even if there wasn't a miracle, she could use these moments to gather her breath, to push away the terrifying thoughts in her head and plaster on a happy face.

Of course, no one called, so after she puttered around for as long as she could, she scooped up Lincoln and trudged down the creaky staircase.

"Have you looked outside?" Renee asked as she slid into an empty chair, bouncing Lincoln in her lap.

"No," she admitted. She'd been too nervous to face it. "Is it bad?"

"Depends on who you ask." Bree was standing at the stove. She flipped a large pancake before giving another pan with sizzling bacon a little shake. Renee had luckily brought supplies when she'd landed on her sister's doorstep with a horde of people. "It doesn't sound good for Castaway's. Luckily the inventory is safe and dry but the roof is mostly off."

"Oh, Bree. I'm so sorry," Sadie said. "How do you feel?"

"It's still sinking in, honestly. Jill came by a half hour ago. Chickadee Studios is in the same boat." Bree stopped cooking, running a dish towel over her damp forehead. "We're not sure what to do."

"That's awful," Sadie breathed, wondering if her own cottage was obliterated or if the mill was damaged beyond repair.

"I'm just glad it sounds like no one was hurt," Bree said.

"I'll drink to that," Dr. Dan agreed, holding up his cup of orange juice. "I can take you guys home after breakfast. And then come back to help with the cleanup, of course." Dan took a bite of his blueberry pancake and chewed thoughtfully. Despite the bad news, the edges of his mouth seemed permanently turned upward, and Sadie wondered if it was the maple syrup or the sex.

Her money was on the sex.

"So far, it only looks like a bunch of downed tree limbs in this neighborhood," Renee said. "At least as far as I can see from the windows."

"Yeah?" Talking felt impossible this morning with the unknown status of her husband looming so darkly over her head. How was she supposed to manage morning small talk during this sort of crisis? "That's good."

Bree set a plate in front of Sadie, and she thanked her, saying she and Lincoln would be fine splitting the meal. In truth, Sadie felt sick to her stomach and knew she wouldn't be able to manage more than a bite or two (and even then, only for the sake of being polite).

She understood that everyone wanted to talk about the storm's damage, but for all she cared, her house could have been swept right off the map and carried into the Atlantic Ocean. Maybe some mermaid family could rehab the cottage next, or a school of clown fish could move in.

It's okay if the cottage is destroyed. Sadie began to bargain with God. *But please bring Ethan home safely.* She rubbed her lower abdomen. *He or she needs to meet their daddy.*

"When are you due?" Bree asked, noticing Sadie's discreet caress.

"Right before Thanksgiving." Sadie blew on a forkful of bacon, recalling an article she'd read just last week about the benefits of maintaining a vegan diet during pregnancy. Oh well. "We could go with Macy for the big parade. Or Peregrine, after the first child born to the pilgrims.

Bree gave a low whistle. "Look at you Ms. History Buff. Maybe you want something with more passion. Because Scorpions? They're intense." Bree stirred a generous spoonful of sugar into her coffee. "A force to be reckoned with."

Sadie laughed, enjoying the welcome distraction from her scary thoughts. "Hopefully not too intense. I had a third-degree tear pushing out Lincoln."

"Damn woman, I don't know what that means but it doesn't sound like anything good."

"I love my kid, but real talk, childbirth is for the birds."

Bree wrinkled her nose. "I'll take your word for it."

They clinked mugs.

After what felt like forever—Dan had asked for seconds on the blueberry pancakes—it was finally time to head back to Seashell Lane. No one spoke during the short drive down the road, as each of them prepared for the worst and prayed for the best.

"Our homes! They're okay!" Renee shouted at the first sight of the two cottages. "Sadie, your cherry tree survived, too! I can't believe it."

"How awesome! Thank God!" Sadie hoped she sounded convincing.

She was thankful, she truly was.

But she was also crestfallen, devastated. Because when Dan pulled in front of her home, the only thing she registered was the empty driveway.

She thanked both of them for all their help before quickly retreating inside her cottage. She set Lincoln down in front of the TV with a sippy cup of juice and some Goldfish crackers. Then, she slipped inside the first-floor powder room, sat on the closed toilet seat, and gave herself over to her tears.

Should she begin calling hospitals? Or was it customary to alert the police first? Something terrible had happened to her husband. She felt it in every cell of her being. But where did she begin? Where should she turn?

She splashed cold water on her face before gulping down

handfuls from the faucet. The mirror reflected a sober sight. Dark bags bruised the delicate skin beneath her eyes, and her complexion looked ashen.

She imagined Ethan in a ditch off the side of the road, his hood flat against a tree. She gasped, stumbling toward the toilet, braced her hands on the cool porcelain and vomited the contents of her stomach.

All this fear wasn't hurting the baby, right? Because she couldn't lose it.

Not now. Not if—

"Mommy! Someone here!" Lincoln was pounding the door. "Answer, Mommy! Answer!"

She wiped her face on her sleeve because naturally, she'd forgotten to replace the hand towel in here the last time she'd done the wash. She took a deep breath before opening the door, picking Lincoln up as she strode into the foyer. "Good boy for getting Mommy. Mommies and Daddies always open the door, right?"

"No Lincolns!"

"That's right. Unless Mommy or Daddy is with you," she confirmed.

Sadie swung open the front door, expecting Renee or maybe even Essie Park reporting on the status of the Old Red Mill, and nearly threw up a second time when she saw their unexpected visitor.

It was Officer Tyler Cox, hat in hand.

The bottom fell out of her world. It was as if the sky itself had started to cave in.

"Oh my God," she gasped. "No! No no no no."

This was it then. She sank to floor still holding Lincoln against her chest and leaned her back against the doorframe. "I can't handle this."

Tyler knelt beside her. "Sadie? Shit. Breathe."

"Lincoln, go and play with your blocks, okay, baby?" she said weakly, setting him on the floor and giving him a gentle nudge.

"Why?"

Thankfully, Tyler stepped in. "I want to see the tallest block tower you can build. Can you do that for me, Link?"

Lincoln looked out at the police car longingly. "Kay. I can. Be right back!"

And off he went, scampering toward the living room.

"W-what's happened?" Sadie asked once Lincoln was out of earshot. "Just say it and be done."

"Ethan was in a car accident yesterday. He was trying to get home to you," Tyler explained. "It was serious, and his car is totaled. But your husband is going to be fine. He's in the hospital now, but it looks like he's coming out of this with a few stitches and a broken foot. He is extremely fortunate that his injuries weren't worse."

Sadie couldn't breathe, much less speak.

"Ethan's okay," he repeated. "The doctors think he'll be released by tomorrow."

"Alive? Okay?" She started to cry all over again.

"I'm sorry as heck to show up here and scare you like this," Tyler said. "But all of the phone lines are down. I'm sure Ethan would have called you himself if he'd been able."

Sadie nodded, but still, she struggled for words.

"Is there someone I can call to come and sit with you for a bit?"

"Renee," she murmured. "Next door."

"Sure thing," he said gently. Tyler started to walk toward Renee's house before he suddenly stopped, turning around. "Sadie?"

"Yeah?"

He gave her a small smile. "Ethan wanted me to tell you that he loves you."

Chapter Twenty-Six

When Renee's cell service was restored later that evening, she was greeted with dozens of texts, missed calls, and voice-mails, all of them from Tansy. She leaned over the kitchen counter reading and listening to each of them. The messages started off concerned and quickly turned hysterical.

WOW! A hurricane in the Cove?! Stay safe!

Mom, you guys OK? Reading the news coverage now...This is super scary!

Where are you? My calls go straight to voicemail.

I just tried calling and texting Aunt Bree. She's not answering either. I am REALLY worried about you both! Please call me back!

Mom??? CALL ME!!!

And so on.

While Renee would never want to stress her daughter out, it was nice to know that she did care. She was still there.

Dan was outside gathering fallen tree limbs and other debris that had blown into Renee's yard. She stood in front of the kitchen window while her kettle boiled, admiring his steady, careful movements. He'd gone home to change and was wearing an old pair of jeans and a fleece zip-up with a sturdy pair of work boots. He looked rugged and masculine, and Renee let out a small squeal when she remembered this gorgeous man was her *boyfriend*. She couldn't wait to show him just how appreciative she was later that night.

The storm had brought in a cold front, and the air felt fresh and brisk. Renee started a fire in the living room, delighting in the sound of each crackle while Moe enjoyed slumbering beside the warmth. She lit a pomegranate-vanilla candle and changed into her softest cashmere sweater and most comfortable pair of jeans. Her cottage felt so warm and safe and full of happiness. She wanted to remember this moment forever.

With her tea mug in hand, she settled into a corner of the sofa and called Tansy.

"Mom?" Tansy answered after a single ring, the relief palpable in her voice. "Oh my God! *Finally!* I've been so worried about you. Are you okay? Is the house okay? What about Aunt Bree? Is *her* house okay? How is the Cove?"

Renee laughed out of sheer happiness.

"I'm okay," she said. "So is Aunt Bree, our house, Aunt Bree's house, and most of Cranberry Cove. Unfortunately, Castaway's and Chickadee were completely destroyed. The roof came clean off."

"Oh my God."

"It's pretty bad, but Bree is taking it okay."

Tansy exhaled. "Oh, Mom. Holy shit, I was so freaked out."

Renee nodded. "Me too."

"Can we FaceTime?" Tansy asked. "Please? I just really need to see you right now."

Who is this and what have you done with my moody, distracted daughter? Renee mused, as she smiled. "Of course we can, honey. I would love that."

Ten seconds later, Renee was seeing her daughter for the first time since Christmas (excluding disturbing social media photos, of course). She was relieved to see Tansy looking like herself once again. She was wearing a USC hoodie and jeans, sitting cross-legged on her dorm room bed. Her hair was still wet from a shower, and since she wasn't wearing any makeup, Renee could make out the freckles across her nose and cheekbones. She was especially pleased to see an open textbook behind Tansy as well as a stainless steel water bottle.

Much better than a blaring speaker system and a can of White Claw.

"It is so good to see you, sweetie," she said. "You look great. What have you been up to this afternoon?"

"Studying for an American studies exam," she said. "And then my roommate and I are going to go to a conservation speaker series tonight. The man speaking? He apparently used to work with Jane Goodall!"

"Yeah? Now that sounds pretty cool."

Tansy paused before taking a deep breath. "Mom? I am *so* sorry. I really messed up this year."

Renee pulled the chenille blanket up over her knees. "Go on," she said, knowing she wasn't going to let Tansy off easy on this one.

"I'm sorry for risking my scholarship," she began. "I got to campus and messed up trying to figure everything out."

Renee nodded. "Finding balance is always a challenge."

"I went out too much and at first it was fun, but then it felt like it was just easier than facing my fears head-on."

"What are you afraid of, sweet pea?"

Tansy's eyes turned glassy. "Letting you down? Turning out to be a fraud?" She laughed ruefully before rubbing her eyes. "Too bad I ended up doing both."

"You aren't a fraud, Tans."

"Coming here and being surrounded by so many insanely talented people, it was wicked intimidating."

Renee looked directly into the camera as she spoke. "I get it but I know you. You'll find your way. And all those big fish better watch out. I know you've got more talent in your little fin than they do total. Got it?"

"Got it," she said, smiling. Tansy looked down at her comforter before raising her eyes back toward the screen. "Mom? Most of all, I'm sorry for what an awful daughter I've been. You've always given me the world, and you're my absolute best friend. I'm sorry I've been an asshole."

Renee felt the tears well up in her eyes, and she swallowed hard. "Don't swear, honey."

"You can send me some soap to wash out my mouth."

"Oh, Hon. I've missed you, too," she said. "But I'm so proud of you. I really am. You've worked so hard to get where you're at. I just need to know you're making smart decisions. And even though I don't want you spending your entire summer with your new boyfriend, I certainly want to meet him. Maybe you can spend a week in Colorado, and then he can come visit the Cove."

Tansy covered her face with her hands. "Ugh, Mom, don't worry about any of that. I broke up with Beckett."

"What happened?" Weirdly, Renee thought of Tansy's nerdy-but-lovable high school boyfriend and how she'd broken up with him. "You didn't use the mouth-breather excuse again, did you?"

Poor Alfie Davidson. He was exactly the sort of boy you hoped your daughter dated—sweet, smart, and slightly timid—but Tansy hadn't kept him around for long, telling Renee she couldn't stand another minute being around his mouth-breathing.

"No, no," Tansy said. "We just had different priorities. Besides, he's dropping out. Can't hack it. School interferes too much with his social life. He actually said that."

"Yowza."

"Plus, why would I want to date a guy who doesn't even know who Nora Ephron is? I don't care if he has a six-pack, I have to have standards, right?"

Renee laughed. "That's my girl."

They chatted a while longer. Tansy talked about her end-of-the-term assignments, including a handful of extra-credit essays she'd taken on to make up for her previous poor performance. She'd taken up a shift at the college radio station and was looking forward to being home this summer. "You'd better have my favorite strawberry pie waiting!" Tansy teased.

"Funny you should mention that…"

Renee filled Tansy in on Hester's, telling her how it had all started with Essie Park telling her about the Old Red Mill and how pleasantly surprised she'd been when Sadie Landry hopped on board. Her daughter was speechless.

"Wait, so you and Sadie are going to run a business together?" she repeated. Sadie had been Tansy's most adored babysitter and she still idolized her. "Is she going to design it? God, I am just obsessed with her style. I love following her on Instagram. You guys are going to be superstars."

"Well, we'll see about that." Renee was a firm believer in cautious optimism. "But I'm really excited. It's fun to wake up each day not quite sure what's going to happen next."

"I'm loving this new free-spirit side. Any other major news you're holding out on?"

Almost on cue, Dan walked in the front door, kicking his boots off and hanging his jacket on a hook.

"Um, Mom. *Who* is that?" Tansy whispered. "Do you have a *boyfriend*?"

Renee widened her eyes mischievously toward the screen. "Dan? I want you to come over here and finally meet Tansy."

He grinned, sitting beside her and waving at the camera. "It's nice to meet you, Tansy! I've been hearing about you since my very first day at the practice. How's the weather out there?"

"Um, sunny," she said, more than a little confused. While Tansy had heard plenty about Dan, she'd never actually met him before. And she certainly didn't know about her mom's gigantic crush on him. "Are you two—"

"Dating? Yep." Renee squeezed his hand. "Tansy, you remember hearing about my soon-to-be-former boss, Dr. Hanlon. Well, he's been promoted to boyfriend."

Dan rolled his eyes, but he was smiling.

If Tansy's mouth opened any wider she'd be able to swallow a volleyball. "I can't keep up with you these days, Mom! A new business, a new boyfriend. Look at you living your best life."

Renee blew the camera a kiss. "Looks like life can be exciting in Cranberry Cove after all."

"Mom, it was amazing. I am amazing. I mean you are. I mean, I'll let you all go. But I'll talk to you very, very soon, okay?"

They both disconnected with smiles.

Renee curled up against Dan's chest, rubbing his shoulder, his arm. "Thanks for cleaning up outside. Are you sore?"

"Ah, just a little bit."

"Let's go run you a hot bath then." Kissing his cheek, Renee stood, heading for the stairs. "I've got the most amazing salts that will help, too."

But Dan pulled her right back down on top of him. "You know what would help more than bath salts?"

She raised an eyebrow.

"You joining me."

"It'll be a tight fit, but I think we can squeeze."

Chapter Twenty-Seven

They were supposed to be here ten minutes ago.

Sadie stood by the door anxiously tapping her foot and checking her watch.

Tyler had volunteered to pick Ethan up from the hospital today in one of the police department's SUVs. Not only was the vehicle better suited for the unpredictable route, it also boasted a comfortable amount of space for his broken foot.

Plus no sticky spots on the door handles or Cheerios buried in the seat cushions.

An upgrade all around, really.

Renee and Dan were babysitting Lincoln for the evening, which would give Sadie time to get Ethan situated. Plus, she wasn't sure how severe his injuries looked, and she thought it was smarter to figure that out first before Lincoln saw him.

Annette was flying in tomorrow to help with things around the house. Tickets were purchased before Sadie could even ask. Even though the woman could overstep off a cliff, Sadie had to admit it was pretty cool that Annette was always willing to drop everything and come.

Finally, a pair of headlights swung down Seashell Lane.

If the last forty-eight hours had taught Sadie anything, it was what mattered the most: Ethan, Lincoln, the new baby.

As for Ethan's frequent trips to Boston, the early mornings and late nights shut away in the home office, their arguments, his lukewarm response to the pie shop idea. Hell, even the fact that Ethan had hidden the fact that he'd been laid off.

All of those things could be figured out, worked through.

Her husband had driven directly into the eye of a category one hurricane in an attempt to reach her and Lincoln in time, and the thought left her a little breathless.

She opened the door and ran down the sidewalk. A warm June wind blew and the sun was just beginning to set in the sky.

Before the car had even come to a complete stop, Sadie was at the passenger-side door. "Ethan!" she breathed. There he was.

She embraced him as gingerly as possible when all she wanted to do was crush him with love. "You're here. You're here!" she sighed with her head buried in his chest.

There were stitches across his forehead, and he had a bad scrape on his left cheek. He was wearing a button-up shirt and slacks, probably an outfit he'd packed for work, so Sadie couldn't be sure how his arms looked. His foot was in a cast though, and Tyler was pulling a pair of crutches from the trunk.

"You look great," she told him.

"You don't mean that." He squeezed her hands. She squeezed back, acutely aware of all the cuts and bruising.

"I do." Sadie nestled her nose in his tousled hair, relieved the scent of her husband was still so present despite the clinical hospital smells. "I thought you were going to look a whole lot scarier."

Ethan kissed her forehead, her cheeks, her mouth. "I love you so much. It is *so* damn good to see your pretty face."

"I love you, too," she murmured into his ear.

Sadie helped Ethan get out of the car and Tyler handed him his crutches. And with Sadie standing beside Ethan and Tyler behind him, they got him up the stairs and into the master bedroom.

"I think I can take it from here," Sadie said, thinking how awkward this all suddenly was. She was grateful for Tyler's help, of course, but it was also pretty darn weird to have the town cop help get your husband situated in your master bedroom. "Thanks for everything, Tyler. We really appreciate it."

Ethan held out his hand. "Thanks, man. We'd love to have you over for dinner soon."

"But only if we're getting takeout. I don't know if one of my home cooked meals is considered a gift," Sadie said with a smirk, making them all laugh.

"Happy to help," said Tyler, "and it also happens to be my job."

Sadie walked him downstairs.

"We owe you," she said. "Seriously."

"It was a wicked accident." His lowered his voice. "It's nothing short of a miracle Ethan is alive. He was about twenty miles south of the Cove when it happened, right off 295. Another motorist lost control of her car after her windshield was struck with debris. She crossed over the double yellow and hit Ethan head-on."

"Oh my God." The image was a sickening one. Sadie leaned against the doorframe for support. She swallowed. "Is the other…other motorist okay?"

He nodded, and Sadie felt overwhelming relieved for this stranger and her own family members and friends. "She was taken to the hospital in serious condition but is expected to make a full recovery."

After a final tearful thank-you, they said their goodbyes.

"Let me know if there's anything else I can do!" Tyler called. "Take care."

Sadie stood in the front yard for a few minutes after Tyler had driven away, trying to catch her breath and wrap her mind around everything that had happened these past few days. Ethan was home safely. Their cottage had been spared.

How much good luck could one person be blessed with?

She looked over at Renee's house. The front curtains were open, and Sadie could see Renee, Dan, and Lincoln doing some sort of goofy dance in the living room. She bet it was one of the *Wiggles* routines from Tansy's childhood. Retro! But Lincoln was giggling and boogying away like it was 2010. To add to her blessings, she had a neighbor, a *friend*, like Renee.

She walked back inside and returned upstairs, where Ethan was sitting on the edge of the bed. "Would you like a sponge bath?" she asked him. "After Lincoln was born, I couldn't wait to rinse all of those weird hospital smells off me."

He was holding out his hands, staring at the abrasions as if they weren't real. "I wish I could go for a hot nurse fantasy right now, but I think you'll need to settle for an exhausted invalid."

"My pleasure." And she meant every word.

She carefully stripped him out of his clothes, tossing them into the hamper, and with slow, steady movements, got him into the tub. With his cast safely propped on the ledge, she wet a loofah and gently massaged it against his skin. His arms looked worse than his face—he had at least five sets of stitches between the two of them and a good amount of bruising—and the sight made her stomach turn. *A wicked accident*, she thought, Tyler's words forever scarred her mind the way these wounds would eternally scar Ethan's skin. *Nothing short of a miracle.*

She ran her fingers through his hair, dampening the curls, and the intense feelings of love, relief, and gratefulness filled her heart.

After toweling him off, Sadie found Ethan's favorite pair of sweatpants and a "Maine Is for Lobsters" T-shirt for him to change into. Both smelled of fabric softener and home. She helped him into their king-sized bed, and pulled the comforter up over his lap.

"Thank you," he said with such sincerity, such tenderness, Sadie almost cried. "The moment of the car crash, all I could think about was you, Lincoln, and the baby. And how our final memories wouldn't be that great. The pie shop argument, and all..." He trailed off.

"I was so worried about you," she stated, sitting on the bed beside him. "If you were dead, I'd have crossed over and killed you."

"You're such a force of nature." He gave her a wry smile. "I was grabbing a late lunch at the diner when the breaking news bulletin came on the TVs. I threw down whatever cash I had in my wallet, and I got on the road as fast as I could. I was so worried about you guys, Sade. I've never been so afraid in my entire life. I just kept thinking how I should be in the Cove already and what a shitty husband and father I must be for not being there to protect you guys."

She rested her head on his shoulder. "Does that hurt?"

"No, feels good."

She nodded, trying to gather her thoughts and words.

No more secrets. Not anymore.

"I actually tried calling your work—you know, after I hadn't heard from you for an entire day—and Patty told me you were let go weeks ago," she said. "Ethan, what's been going on? Why wouldn't you tell me that?"

He ran a hand through his hair. "I guess that's as good a place as any to start."

He tightened his arms around Sadie. "Marlow started on his rampage about a month ago, but I didn't want to worry you, even though I knew it would be my head on the chopping block soon enough. He thought the company was spending too much money on our developers, that our roles could be outsourced. Three weeks ago—when it finally happened—well, we'd just found out about the baby. I couldn't bear to tell you."

"Kind of like I couldn't bear to tell you about the pie shop."

"I'm sorry. I am so sorry about that. Not telling you was totally wrong. I convinced myself it was so I could spare you the stress. But Sadie, you are my life partner. I want—no, I need—we both need to stop keeping secrets."

"Completely agree," confirmed Sadie. "Even if things get shitty, we need to tell each other. Neither one of us is going to break."

"Especially you, my strong beautiful wife. You amaze me every day, but the fact that you kept everyone safe during the storm…I mean, God. You even prepared the cottage, saved our home…I really let you down. My cellphone plan was tied into the company and I had no idea none of my texts were going through. I thought you were busy, or mad, or honestly, I just wasn't thinking. And of course, I didn't get any of yours. I totally suck, I'm sorry."

"You do kind of suck," Sadie agreed, "I was insanely worried."

He groaned.

"I forgive you just this once but don't ever do that again," she said lightly, but meaning it. "But what have you been doing in Boston these past few weeks?" She snuggled closer to his side. "Was it all an elaborate cover-up?"

"No, far from it," he said. "I've actually been laying the groundwork for my own business these past few months. And since

I got let go, I've been meeting with various business partners in Boston."

She bolted upright. "Oh. Oh, *wow*."

"It's also why I'm always on my phone when I'm at home," he said. "And why I've been so secretive about it. I was so afraid the investors weren't going to follow through…that something would get messed up in the process. There were so many moving parts. I didn't want to get your hopes up in case it didn't pan out."

"So tell me about this new business of yours, honey." She gently squeezed his hands, intertwining their fingers. "No more reporting to that rotten Marlow, huh?"

Ethan told her all about his new software development company, how he'd already secured funding, two employees, and a handful of clients.

"What about an office space? Have you scoped out a good spot in Boston yet? Oh, you should choose someplace right by your old company so Marlow has to witness your tremendous success!"

"That's the best part of all," he said, his voice catching in his excitement. "Everyone is set up to work remotely. I'm going to be here in Maine, Sadie. No more trips to Boston."

She couldn't help it—she burst into tears of relief. Her husband was safe, their marriage was safe, his career was safe. Even if she was still just a tiny bit mad. She could let it go and move on to better things.

"Sadie?" Ethan rubbed her back as she cried into his shoulder. "I think you should move forward with Hester's. I *want* you to. You deserve your own new adventure."

She stopped crying. "You really think that?"

"I do," he said. "I'm sorry I wasn't supportive from the moment you told me. I'm embarrassed by how I reacted. I was just so set on this idea that my kids' childhoods had to mirror my own. And, maybe I was a little insecure about not being able to provide for them the way my dad provided for us."

"I love your mom, honey, I do," she said. "But I'm not a carbon copy of her."

"That would be pretty twisted, wouldn't it? Very Freudian." Sadie laughed as Ethan made a grimace. "I think you and Renee make an incredible team, and I know Hester's is going to be wickedly successful. Plus? I'll be right here in Maine, so I can help shoulder the load at home. No more fifty-fifty. We're doing things hundred-hundred from now on."

"Thank you," she said, hugging him all over again. "You have no idea how much this all means to me."

"I think Lincoln is going to love preschool, and I can't wait to see my incredible wife shine." He smiled, tucking a strand a hair behind her ear. "I love you, Sadie. And I'm damn lucky you're mine."

Chapter Twenty-Eight

On the flat-screen, Russell strode into the shot, Tansy on his broad shoulders, with that old cocky smile.

"How old are you today, baby?"

Why was it always so disconcerting to hear the sound of your own voice? Renee cringed. Did she really sound like that, all high-pitched and perky?

"Tansy, sweetie, wave to the camera!"

"I'm five!" she declared happily, holding up the appropriate number of fingers and then waving toward her mother. "And Daddy's teaching me how to ride without training wheels! 'Cause now I'm old enough."

With the camera still rolling, Renee followed her husband and daughter out the front door and into the driveway, where a brand-new bike was waiting in place of Tansy's trike. There were pink streamers fanning from its handlebars and a matching glittery seat. Renee had tied a giant, white bow to the front of the bike and lime-green balloons to its spokes.

"Is this mine?" Tansy asked, her eyes wide. "Is this *my* new bike?"

The camera moved up and down as she nodded. "It sure is, sweetie. What do you think?"

Russell gently lowered Tansy to the ground, and she sprinted for the new toy. He helped her remove the decorations, handing them to Renee's phantom hand.

As Renee continued to film, her ex fastened Tansy's new helmet beneath her chin—it was as pink as her new bike but complete with a Disney princess design—and balanced her over her new set of wheels.

"Don't let go, Daddy! Not yet," she pleaded.

"We'll go slow. I promise," he said. "I'll start off holding on and then slowly let you go. Okay?"

"Ohhh-kay."

Tansy teetered over a handful of times, catching herself before meeting the cement, and then *bam*. She went down hard, scraping her knees and even her tiny button nose. As the little girl began to sob, the camera clattered to the ground, landing in the much more forgiving grass.

"If you weren't so busy filming, you could have caught her," Russell barked off camera, his tone bitter and accusatory. "Jesus Christ. Why weren't you spotting her?"

"I wanted to capture the big moment! I didn't realize she'd get hurt!" Renee frowned, hearing the sob in her long-ago voice. "It was an accident! Plus, you were the one running right along with her. *You* should have caught her!"

"Well, great job there, Spielberg."

Even now, over a decade later, her ears burned in humiliation. All she'd managed to capture on camera was a horrible parenting moment and one of her and Russell's final fights.

Shamefaced, she fast-forwarded to the next scene: Tansy and Renee both running through the Crazy Daisy sprinkler in the backyard. Tansy was wearing a pink-and-white striped suit, and Renee had on her favorite pink bikini. Russell must have filmed this one, and— *Shit*. This must have been mere *days* before he left them. What was he thinking as he recorded this scene? Did the sight of his adorable daughter and beautiful wife running through the yard make him second-guess his decision at all, at least the tiniest bit? Or was he thinking about his girlfriend and counting down the seconds until they could be together?

"Missing Tansy?"

Renee startled, dropping her spoon into the nearly empty bowl of ice cream she'd been enjoying. Taking a deep breath, she set it on the coffee table. "Jeez, Bree. You scared me."

Bree continued down the staircase and settled into the sofa beside Renee. Her biopsy was scheduled for eight o'clock tomorrow morning, and Renee was going with her to Portland. She'd insisted Bree stay at her house the night before, too, thinking the company might help her sleep better. "I don't want you to be alone with your thoughts," she'd said.

"You're the one watching old home movies in the dark. *You* scared *me*," Bree teased. "By the way, check out that stellar bod!"

"Stop it. I was twelve years younger." Renee paused, thinking this over. "And doing aerobics daily."

"Well, I could never wear a bikini like that. Not at any age," Bree said. "So, why the home movies? Isn't Tansy home in a few days?"

Renee nodded. "She's done with finals. She wanted to wrap up a few things at the radio station she's volunteering at first."

"See, she'll be here before you know it."

Renee picked back up her ice cream bowl, resuming her delicious late-night dessert of cookies and cream. "Oh, I know it. I was actually watching these for another reason." She pressed the "stop" button on the remote.

Bree wasn't one to accept vague answers. "And why is that?"

Renee hesitated. "Do you think that I made myself unlovable somehow?"

Before Bree could respond, Renee continued to spill her deepest fears. "Do you think I did something to drive Russell away? It's okay, you can tell me. My feelings might be hurt, but it will help in the long run."

Bree's eyes widened as she moved closer to Renee, nuzzling into her side. "Why...I mean...*How* could you ever think such a thing?"

She sighed. "I've been watching these old videos a lot lately, trying to pinpoint what it was that made Russell leave me. You know, so I can prevent myself from doing those things all over again and losing Dan."

"Russell left you because he was a selfish asshole," Bree said. "If he wasn't boning your kid's kindergarten teacher, it would have been some other woman later."

"That has occurred to me," she admitted.

"You are one of the most lovable people I know."

Renee shook her head. "You're just saying that because you're my sister. You're genetically programmed to love me."

"Even if I wasn't, I know I would," Bree said.

Renee ate the rest of her ice cream in silence, mulling this over. "There are so many wonderful things happening for me right now. Sadie is working on the design plan for the pie shop and we signed the lease. Tansy is almost here. I'm with a man I'm madly in love with. It just feels like maybe my bubble is destined to pop, the way it's always managed to when I feel so happy, so content. Does that sound stupid?"

"Stupid? No." Bree rubbed her back, just like she used to do when they were girls. "But I'm quickly realizing that life is too short to worry about what-ifs. You have to enjoy the present and appreciate the good things as they come. And sis? Don't take this the wrong way, but you've been giving Russell Rhodes way too much power over your life for twelve freaking years now."

"What? I have not." Renee was adamant. "I haven't so much as sent the man a Christmas card. The only times I've ever talked to him were to discuss Tansy's care, and I hardly cried a tear over him."

"You've let him control your life in other ways. You're doing it right now, all over again," said Bree. "You just said it yourself— you're watching these home movies to try and see how you were a bad wife. And you simply weren't. You were an awesome partner, a *wonderful* wife. And as for your life being happy and content before Russell up and left you—do you honestly believe that was true?"

Renee thought of the weeks, the months, really, before Russell left. She remembered the quiet nights after Tansy had gone to bed, when her husband would veg with sports while she read a book or baked. She thought of the awkward twenty minutes they spent at the dinner table each evening, Tansy their sole source of conversation, and the strained arguments about Russell's desire to leave Cranberry Cove. Most of all, she thought of her mother's heartbreaking reaction to their engagement: "Are you sure about this?"

No, her marriage to Russell had been challenging from the start. But she would never regret it because of the beautiful, messy, perfect miracle of Tansy.

"Russell leaving was a blessing," Bree said quietly. "I know it certainly didn't feel like it at the time, but my God, Renee. It showed you how strong you are. You never give yourself enough credit for that. And now that your pie shop is coming together and Dan has entered your life, I think it's the universe's way of rewarding you. You deserve this. You deserve all of this."

Renee hugged her tight. "Thank you," she said. "I needed to hear that."

They found a *Mary Tyler Moore* rerun on TV, and both sisters settled deeper into the couch. They tried to ignore the elephant in the room, that big fat ugly elephant.

"Are you scared for the biopsy?" Renee finally asked.

"Terrified." Bree kept her eyes on the TV, avoiding Renee's stare at all costs.

"But we could find out it's all okay."

Bree swallowed. "We could also find out it's not."

"I know."

"Yeah."

They pretended to watch TV for an hour longer, though both were preoccupied with the impending future.

"What's your happiest memory?" Bree asked Renee, taking her sister's hand.

"Tansy's birth," Renee answered automatically. But inside she was thinking about the night of the hurricane. It was blossoming in her chest as a treasure, a shining gem to hold on to forever. "What about you, sis?"

"Being your sister has been pretty amazing," Bree said and Renee felt tears spring to her eyes.

"You're going to be okay. I just know it," she declared fiercely. "I need to make many happy memories with you for years to come."

"I guess we should go to bed," Bree reluctantly suggested.

"I have melatonin tablets in the medicine cabinet." Renee nodded her head toward the bathroom.

"Those never work for me."

"They don't work for me either." She sighed.

Bree began to gently shut the guest room door behind her. "Goodnight. See you in the morning."

"Stay in my room tonight," she told her sister. "I doubt either of us is going to fall asleep anytime soon. I'd rather lay there in silence with you than be alone."

"Yeah, this sort of distraction is terrible for my knitting," Bree said, smiling. "You should see the hideous sweater I've been working on. If Tansy starts wigging out again, it's going in her Christmas stocking."

After brushing their teeth and washing their faces—just as they had done as girls—they climbed into Renee's bed. She pulled a sheet and the comforter up to her chin, while Bree was content with a knitted blanket.

"You still don't use comforters like the rest of us?"

"Never have, never will," Bree quipped.

They closed their eyes and tried to sleep.

"I've been thinking about what I want to do with my life, if I only have a few months left or so," Bree whispered.

Renee felt her mouth go dry. She swallowed and blinked. "You're going to be fine. Stop talking like that."

"Don't. You know very well neither of us has any idea what's going to happen."

"I'm not letting you go anywhere. Not when there's underwater basket weaving to tackle. And poodle training. Or you could attempt to sail the world!"

Bree let out a sad giggle.

"Or mushroom hunting, or learning the art of southern barbecue."

"Maybe I'll learn Klingon and become a YouTube sensation."

The two sisters laughed and it felt really good.

"Do you know what scares me the most?" Bree confessed when they caught their breath. "I haven't met the love of my life yet, and that isn't something you get to plan. I may very well die and never meet the one."

"Oh, Bree," Renee sighed. "I hope that for you more than anything."

The two sisters grasped hands and finally, finally fell asleep.

Chapter Twenty-Nine

This morning, Sadie had chosen to take her work outside, spreading her various design books and sketchpads across the deck, so she could enjoy a healthy dose of vitamin D as she brainstormed. Things were moving fast. Their business cards with Grandma Hester's own pie logo from her diary were set to be delivered from the printer. In the past weeks, she had convinced Renee to donate some of her more striking antique finds to decorate Hester's and had scored adorable vintage tables and chairs from an estate sale that were being refinished by a local woodworker. And once Dot Turner caught wind of the action, she'd offered up a few candid pictures she'd snapped of Grandma Hester selling pies at the town fair in the early eighties. Sadie was having them touched up and enlarged to adorn the walls alongside some of Grandma Hester's own cooking utensils and pans.

Yes, the plans were well in motion and recently she had started thinking seriously about some ideas for the additional shop space in the Old Red Mill.

The old building had gone head-to-head with a hurricane, and had proved its grit unlike some of those poor storefronts downtown. The mill had come through with a few shattered windows, a dozen missing shingles, and a twisted weather vane, easy fixes in the grand scheme of things. Plans for the riverwalk were definitely the word on the street these days as the town tried to focus on the brighter days to come, words like "revitalization" and "economic development" were getting bandied about in the paper.

The Old Red Mill was opening at the perfect time and Sadie needed to talk to Essie about the idea that had been taking root: relocating some of the displaced businesses like the Castaway Yarn Shop and Chickadee Studios to the mill.

"Hey there." Annette stepped through the sliding doors. With her bright eyes, yellow chinos, and navy striped top, she looked like a Talbots model. "Do you have a second to chat? Lincoln is upstairs with Ethan. They're playing Candy Land."

"Uh-huh. Sure." She stood up. "Oooof. Hang on, I get a little dizzy here and there. Happened with Lincoln too."

"How much weight have you gained so far?" Annette asked, before smacking her forehead. "Sorry! I didn't mean it that way. Sometimes my mouth moves before my brain can catch up. You look terrific. Glowing, actually."

Good lord, Annette might mean well, but she was going to choke on her foot one of these days.

"I don't know about that, but thanks." Sadie was suddenly dreading this conversation. What did she want to discuss? Had she seen the Kid Cuisine box in the recycling bin? Sadie only gave Lincoln the processed chicken tenders and macaroni and cheese when she was *really* desperate, though Annette probably judged anything that wasn't fresh from the local organic farm.

"What's up?"

She reminded herself for the umpteenth time how amazing her mother-in-law had been, pitching in however she could, even if that meant simply lightening the mood with a joke. Her own parents had been calling a lot more lately and sent an enormous gift basket full of French cheeses and mini wines, perfect for a pregnant person, naturally, but it wasn't the same as having someone do the nightly dishes.

Annette had been a *huge* help these past few weeks. Quite frankly, Sadie wasn't sure how she would have managed otherwise, what with Ethan being on crutches as they both worked their butts off to start their new business ventures. It was thanks to Annette that Lester's grand opening was still on schedule, Ethan's company was officially up and running, and Lincoln was happy and well fed.

Honestly, they were *all* feeling happy and well-fed with Annette around.

Annette studied the ground for a few seconds—probably noticing that the deck boards needed replacing; it was the one area she and Ethan hadn't tackled during the renovation—and then sighed. "I believe that I owe you an apology."

Wait—what?

Had the earth stopped spinning?

Was hell flash freezing?

Were pigs flying over the Cove?

"I'm sorry, can you repeat that?" Sadie shook her head a few times, making a pen fall out from behind her ear. "Did you say…an apology?"

"Oh, where to start?" Annette wrung her pearly pink manicured hands together. Sadie was surprised to see how anxious she was. "I'm sorry for overstepping. I've done that a lot since you and Ethan got married, and especially since Lincoln was born—"

"Aren't they one in the same?" Sadie smiled, making a joke at her own expense.

Annette smiled back, visibly less nervous. "I suppose I had a difficult time wrapping my mind around the fact that there are many ways to parent, to *mother*. I am so proud of the man Ethan is today, and I think I gave myself a little too much credit for that."

"No," Sadie said. "You *did* help make him the wonderful person he is today."

"Well, thank you. But that's just it. I helped. I contributed," she said. "A lot of things made my children the adults they are now. And it wasn't like I cracked some sort of secret mothering formula. Yet, I have a bad habit of thinking it's my way or the highway."

"I have to admit, the parenting book you sent?"

Annette interrupted, "One of my sisters suggested it. But that's no excuse. It was stupid. Do you know what Richard used to say? 'It's Annette's world, we just live in it.' It was a joke—sort of. And I had *no* business offering you advice on your marriage. Lord knows I am hardly a paragon of perfection."

Was her mother-in-law demonstrating humility? Sadie was tempted to glance out the window and see if a flock of pigs were taking flight.

Annette cringed while attempting a smile. Impulsively, she pulled out a chair. "Hey, why don't I go and grab us some lemonade and we can have a proper heart-to-heart? You know, sitting down rather than leaning against the rails of this rickety deck." This time Annette's smile reached her eyes as she gratefully sunk into the offered chair.

A few minutes later, the two women were sitting around the wrought-iron table. Sadie had brought out a pitcher of lemonade and a box of Cheez-Its to share.

"I know it sounds like a weird combination, but the salty, sharp cheddar and sweet lemonade is delicious. I'm pretty sure Tansy next door is the one who turned me on to it, when I was babysitting her one night."

"Renee's daughter, right?" Annette asked. "Small world."

"That's Cranberry Cove for you," Sadie said. "But yeah, Tansy is Renee's daughter. She's home from USC for the summer, and Renee couldn't be any happier. Plus, Renee's dating the most amazing man. Her former boss. A doctor."

"Well, well." Annette cocked a well-plucked brow. "Lucky Renee."

"So, tell me more about Richard. I always thought you had a great marriage."

"I've certainly made it sound that way, haven't I?" Annette took a tentative nibble of a Cheez-It, washing it down with a swig of lemonade. "Oh, that *is* good. Anyway, Richard and I were high school sweethearts. He was bound for an undergraduate degree at Vanderbilt and then set on law school."

"Ambitious," Sadie said with a nod, already knowing these bits of information from Ethan. He loved that his parents had met so young—he often said how he wished he'd known Sadie sooner—and he was proud of that fact that not only had his father attended Vanderbilt, but he had also managed to graduate in three years.

"We married young, right after he graduated college, just like a lot of people did at the time. We were only twenty-one, and we had our first child one year later. I spent a year at a junior college but ended up settling into that homemaker role." She drummed her fingers against the tabletop, looking off wistfully. "Being a mom makes you grow up fast, doesn't it? It changes you."

"Um, understatement," Sadie concurred.

"The truth is that we didn't have a perfect marriage. Nobody does," Annette said. "We were happy most of the time, but we also fought a lot. Richard was always telling me I needed to hang out with friends more or pick up some sort of hobby. He worried about me, that I was living in a bubble. I would get upset with him, saying he had no idea what it was like to stay at home with the children. It was as though he didn't have any concept of how demanding that was. I sometimes wonder if he imagined I sat around the house all day, reading magazines and watching soap operas. It was hard and it was rewarding. But he wasn't wrong. Sometimes I wanted—well, I wish I had pursued my own dreams further. I always imagined I'd make an excellent nurse."

"Oh," Sadie fumbled her way through her thoughts, wondering why Annette always made her feel so guilty, so *unappreciative*, of the fact that Ethan worked while she had "the privilege" of staying home with Lincoln.

"You're probably wondering why I've acted the way I have over the past two years," Annette said, reading Sadie's thoughts.

She blinked a few times stifling an only slightly bitter chuckle.

"Oh, it's okay. I deserve it." Annette chuckled herself. "Frankly? I think I made those awful comments because I see so much of myself in you, Sadie. And you having the courage to stand up for yourself and say you wanted more? Well, that was just proof of how cowardly I was during that time in my life. You made me realize I should have done the same. And I guess I resented you for that."

Sadie nodded her head. "I get it," she finally said. "I do. For the record? I think being a stay-at-home parent is incredible and a huge privilege. It just isn't for me. I missed interior design too much. It, well, it feels like as if I don't function properly without it."

"And it's one of the many reasons why I fell in love with you, my creative daughter-in-law."

Sadie's heart was suddenly caught in her throat, moved by Annette's words. While she was always quick to murmur a perfunctory "love ya" at the end of their phone calls, this was the first time she had said it so plainly, so genuinely.

"I'm really excited for you, Sadie," she continued, her own voice a little raspy. "I think this pie shop is going to be such a great addition to your town, and with you and Renee running it, Hester's is sure to be a success. You should be so proud."

Sadie paused, waiting for some sort of caveat, but it never came.

Instead, Annette reached across the table and squeezed Sadie's hands. "I'm sorry I was such a stubborn old bat. It took me so long to realize the true root of my feelings. Ever since I came here to stay after Ethan's accident? Well, I've realized I was wrong about a lot of things." She sighed. "Seeing what a strong team you and Ethan make when the going gets tough...Well, honey, that says a lot about a person. About a couple. And the fact that you two are managing that while raising a toddler and gearing up for the grand opening of a pie shop? You're quite a woman."

Sadie got up from her chair and engulfed her mother-in-law in a warm hug.

"I love you, Annette," she said, meaning every word. "And for the record, you *have* made our lives easier in a whole bunch of ways. And we are very appreciative of all the love and support you've given us."

"Can we start over?"

Sadie rubbed her tiny baby bump. "I think now's the perfect time."

Chapter Thirty

Renee folded the last of the towels, neatly placing the stack in the hall closet. So much had happened since she and Sadie had joined forces to work on Hester's. She'd been working hard perfecting her menu with the help of Grandma Hester's recipe box and her own repertoire. Banana cream pie, chocolate–peanut butter whoopie pies, wild blueberry pie, of course. But also more inventive offerings like sweet potato–rum pie, salted–maple syrup pie, cranberry-pecan pie, and so much more. Specials would change daily.

She peeked inside Tansy's bedroom as she walked by, lingering in the doorway. Who knew an unmade bed and a forgotten, crumb-filled dessert plate on the nightstand could bring such happiness? Ever since Tansy had returned home, Renee could not stop reveling in daily reminders of her daughter's presence. Entering, she smoothed out the comforter and picked up the plate, walking down the steps to the living room.

Tomorrow morning, at ten o'clock sharp, Renee and Sadie would cut a red gingham ribbon and officially be living their dream.

They were ready—Renee was sure of it—yet still, she was constantly reviewing her mental checklist. She was waking up at four o'clock tomorrow morning so she could begin baking before five (as if she'd sleep a wink anyway). She had already dropped off the commemorative tea towels the first one hundred customers would be receiving, and her outfit was hung over her bedroom chair: a green tunic and skinny jeans. It was pretty for photos and practical for baking.

Hester's, the flagship store at the Old Red Mill was ready to shine.

The woodworker had refinished the round tables for Hester's not a second too soon, and Sadie had spent all afternoon putting the final details into place. Along with her other finds, Sadie had gathered eclectic clutter from Renee's house and made it shine. It was fairly mind-boggling how the space had come together. A playlist, including some songs Sadie could remember Grandma Hester playing during their cooking sessions together, was set to go on their streaming account.

It was going to be a *great* opening day. But now she had to chill out a little.

"Oh! Sorry about that, Mom. I couldn't resist a slice of your gooseberry pie before bed last night. It was incredible." Tansy started to move from her cozy corner of the sofa, but Renee shook her head, smiling.

"Don't worry about it. Glad for the positive review. I was considering adding more vanilla." Not only was she happy her daughter was home, Renee was also thrilled she'd replaced her nighttime vodka cranberry with local berry pie. "Whatcha reading tonight?"

"Some cozy murder mystery I picked up from the library."

"When did you go to the library?"

"This afternoon." Tansy padded into the kitchen, hugging her mother from behind. "Are you nervous for tomorrow?"

Nervous was an understatement.

As if the pressure of Hester's grand opening wasn't monumental enough, unbeknownst to Tansy, Bree was going in for a second test next week. The first biopsy had come back inconclusive, an especially evil form of torture. A larger sample needed to be taken and sent to a special lab. "Please don't tell Tans," Bree had pleaded with her. "I want to be her cool, strong aunt for as long as I can."

Renee sighed. "Oh, I'm nervous all right."

"Well, just remember this." Tansy whirled her mother around, her eyes big and teasing. "If you need me to distract people somehow, I can definitely do something dramatic."

"Yeah? Like what?"

"I don't know—give myself a haircut with the giant opening-day scissors? Smash a pie in my face?" Renee shook her head, starting to laugh. "I mean it, Mom! I'm willing to do anything for you."

"And I so appreciate that!"

The doorbell rang just then, and Tansy sprinted toward the front door. "Mom!" she called. "Sadie's here!"

Renee made her way to the foyer. Sadie stood on front porch, a bottle of chilled sparkling apple juice in one hand, champagne and two flutes in the other. "Hey there, business partner."

She had the same sweet smile as the very first time she knocked on this very door, her bike resting against the house. She must have only been fifteen then and had brought markers and crayons instead of champagne. But at this moment, time melted away and she was so grateful to now call Sadie her dear friend and partner.

"Okay, so I realize you probably have crazy romantic plans with Dan tonight, but I was hoping to steal you for just a bit," Sadie said. She held up the bottles of champagne and sparkling cider. "Have a few minutes for a well-deserved toast?"

"Can I join?" Tansy asked, poking her head out from behind her mom.

"Grab an extra flute from the cabinet and get your butt out here."

The three women squeezed into the glider on the front porch, using their feet to propel them forward and backward. Renee did the honors of uncorking the sparkling juice, while Sadie and Tansy cheered. Renee overfilled each flute, causing the fizzy liquid to spill down their hands.

"What do you know? Our cups runneth over," Renee said, smiling.

"Hardy har har." Tansy rolled her eyes but her face was bright. "To my mother, Renee Rhodes, and to my former babysitter, Sadie Landry—may their pie shop be wildly successful! May Hester's be as wonderful and brilliant as they are!"

The three women held their stemware high in the air, the setting sun making the crystal glasses sparkle.

"I have so much to be thankful for," Renee said. "I'm not even sure where to begin my toast."

Sadie nodded, clearly understanding what Renee meant.

"How about we start with your grandmother?" Renee suggested. "To Hester, an extraordinary baker and a truly remarkable woman."

"Yes! To Grandma Hester," Sadie proclaimed, squeezing her friend's hand. "And to Renee Rhodes, Cranberry Cove's incredible pie maker, the world's best neighbor, and the perfect partner in crime."

Renee got a little teary and leaned in, hugging Sadie tight. "And to my business partner, Sadie Landry, a true creative with fantastic vision who also happens to be the world's best neighbor and a truly wonderful friend."

"To the women of Hester's," Sadie said. "Past, present, and future."

The three of them sat there in a happy silence for a bit, the only sounds the creak of the swing and the gentle-but-persistent buzz of the evening's first cicadas.

"What are you most excited about, Mom?" Tansy asked, leaning her head against Renee's shoulder.

She stared out at her front yard, at the flickering gaslights that lined Seashell Lane. "I can't wait to hear about where my pies are served, the moments they'll become a part of," she said at last, hooking her arms around her knees. "I love the idea of someone picking up one and considering it special enough to be enjoyed at a birthday party or to celebrate a promotion or some other cool milestone."

"Aw, I love that. I leek, maybe someday a guy will propose by hiding the ring in one!" Tansy gushed, ever the romantic.

Renee and Sadie both laughed.

"What about you, Sadie?" Renee asked, turning to her business partner. "You must be thrilled with the magazine write-up."

A Boston design magazine had recently visited the Old Red Mill, interviewing Sadie about her work and taking dozens of photographs. The article had been published just this week, and Renee knew Sadie's inbox had already flooded with interior design job offers. But she'd been surprised to learn of her response. "Thank you for the kind words, but I'm happy where I am."

Sadie set a hand over her middle. "I feel like I'm *me* again, and it makes me so happy to know Lincoln and the new baby will know me *this* way." She laughed. "I'm busier than ever, yet not sweating all the small stuff. I don't feel like the sky is going to fall whenever Lincoln has a temper tantrum or throws my flip-flops in the toilet."

"Oh my God—he did that?" Tansy covered her mouth.

"That's like, the least scary thing about parenthood," Sadie said with a smirk, making Renee laugh. "He loves preschool, though, well preschool 'summer camp.' He's already made a few new friends at Little Acorns, and his teachers say he takes naps. I can't even believe it."

"What are you going to do about child care when the new baby arrives?" Renee asked.

"Probably carry him or her around in a sling for a while," she said. "And then I'm going to ask for help, like I should have done with Lincoln. I think Ethan and I will make a much better tag team this time, and hopefully we can find a good sitter to cover our butts when we're both tied up."

"That's a perfect plan. I know I was lucky to have a great sitter of my own when I was a young mother," she said looking meaningfully at Sadie.

Tansy squinted as a pair of headlights made its way down the quiet road, turning into Renee's driveway. "Who's that?"

"By the looks of it? Your mom's cute-as-heck new boyfriend," Sadie said, before nodding her head toward the house. "And probably your cue to go back inside. Unless you want to enjoy a romantic tête-à-tête with them."

Tansy swatted at her but was quickly scrambling toward the front door. "Hi Dan! Bye Dan!" she called.

"Hi Dan! Bye Dan!" Sadie mimicked. As quick as she'd come, she disappeared with her sparkling apple cider, leaving the champagne behind with a wink.

"Well, shoot. I sure know how to empty a room." Dan smiled

shyly, holding out a bouquet of the prettiest pink peonies. "How are you feeling?"

"Oh, wow! These are beautiful." Renee held them to her nose, delighting in their delicate scent. "Thank you! And I'm feeling okay. A little shaky." He swept her to his chest, pressing his lips against hers and slowly working his tongue against her in a rhythm that threatened to make her forget her own name. "Okay, and that? Not helping with the shakiness."

He gave her a wicked grin. Any sign of the gentle small-town doctor was gone as he growled, "Do I make you weak in the knees, Renee Rhodes?"

By way of reply, she nipped his neck, licking the salt from the skin, and making him shudder. "Two can play at that game."

"Take a walk with me?" He squeezed her hand. "Before I do dirty things to you on that porch swing."

"Maybe once the neighborhood goes to bed." She winked as she set the flowers down on the bistro table. "Lead the way."

Once they made it down to the shoreline, they kicked off their shoes and walked in the surf, the water tickling their feet. It amazed Renee how they walked in tandem, their sides brushing, their fingers interlaced. Every movement in sync.

"How's Michelle working out?"

Michelle was the new receptionist at the Coastal Kids Medical Group, a twenty-something, single mother Renee had helped interview. The young woman's story was remarkably similar to her own, except in her case, it had been an oboist rather than a kindergarten teacher.

"She thinks we should start an Instagram account," Dan grumbled—good-naturedly, of course—which made Renee laugh. "It would feature me giving out medical tips and tricks. Who in the world would tune in for such a snooze fest?"

"I sure would," she said, playfully kissing his neck, his cheeks.

They paused and watch the light fade out over the water as the sun dipped into the woods behind them.

"I hate that I don't know what's going to happen with Bree," she whispered at last. "Why is this dragging out?"

"Ah," Dan breathed, sliding an arm around her waist. "So, you have two things weighing on your heart tonight. One happy and one sad."

"Pretty much."

They stared up at the darkening sky.

"Good thing there are a few stars to wish on," he said, pointing out the brightest ones.

Renee closed her eyes, offering both a prayer and a wish for her sister. *Please let Bree be okay. Do not take her from me. I can't bear it.* She reached for Dan's cheek, resting her palm over it. "What did you wish for?"

Dan looked at her curiously.

"I already have my wish. She's standing right beside me."

Chapter Thirty-One

It was impossible to fully take in such a day.

How did you soak up every sound, every taste, every scent? How did you bottle up those sorts of feelings, this sort of wonder, pride, and appreciation? Where did you even begin? Maybe it was impossible, but Sadie was trying.

She had woken up at 4:00 a.m. and crept downstairs to brew a pot of tea. She took her warm mug out to the beach with her, taking comfort in the fact that Renee's kitchen light was also already on for the day. She must not have been the only one who couldn't sleep last night.

Renee was standing in front of the window above her sink, her red hair striking against the periwinkle blue of her robe. Sadie knew she was filling her own teakettle, but wondered what Renee was feeling and thinking.

Was she as excited as Sadie was? Was she as nervous, overwhelmed? Was she this astonishingly happy?

Sadie had taken a seat on the beach, on the edge of the surf, and watched the sun rise.

I want to remember these colors, the pink, orange, and yellow. I want to remember the salty smell, the gentle breeze that sent a chill down my bare legs. I want to remember how wonderful this warm cup of tea felt in my hands, how soft the sand felt between my toes. How perfectly content I felt in this moment.

Not only did Sadie want to remember these details for herself, but she also wanted to tell them to her children someday. She wanted them to know every element of this day, how it felt to have everything come together and create something so amazing, so awesome.

Now, nearly six hours later, Renee and Sadie stood at the front of the pie shop, beaming as cameras flashed and their friends, family, and neighbors applauded. They were here, they'd made it. Not even a hurricane had been able to destroy this dream of theirs.

"How are you feeling?" Sadie whispered, smoothing her light blue dress. She'd paired the J. Crew find with a smart, navy blazer and red kitten heels. "Can you tell I'm sweating? Please say no."

"Stunned. This feels surreal," said Renee. "And no, I swear I can't tell you're sweating."

Practically the entire town had showed up for Hester's grand opening, every citizen wanting to cheer on Renee and Sadie. "I didn't bake enough pies," Renee murmured in a panic.

Sadie grinned. "Just more reason for everyone to visit in the many days to come."

She spotted Ethan, Lincoln, Annette, and her parents by the stairs. With her mother-in-law and Melissa leading the charge, they were edging their way up to the very front.

"Is she always so bossy?" Her mother had whispered this morning, when Annette chastised her for cutting Lincoln's strawberries into halves rather than his preferred quarters. "I didn't realize there was a wrong way to cut fruit."

"Always," Sadie said with a grin. "But you'll grow to love it. I promise."

Melissa and Christopher had made the trip from D.C. and were blessedly staying at a B&B run by old family friends rather than the Landrys' crowded cottage. They'd had a commemorative plaque made for Sadie with "Hester's" engraved in gold, plus the shop's opening date and Sadie and Renee's names. It was stuffy and formal—plus, where in the heck was Sadie supposed to hang such a thing? But Sadie knew her parents meant well, and she appreciated it.

What she appreciated more than their present? Their presence, of course.

"Sadie! I cannot believe you designed this!" Melissa had exclaimed, sticking a well-manicured hand against her chest at her first sight of the newly renovated Old Red Mill. "It's certainly come a long way from that stuffy restaurant that used to be here."

"You did good, sweetheart," Christopher chimed in, clapping her on the back as if she were a banker buddy, "though that place did put out a nice steak."

"I wish your grandma was here to see this." Sadie was surprised to see tears in the ever-composed Melissa's eyes. "She would have loved it. All of it. You are making her dream come true, and I know she's smiling down on you today."

"Thanks." She'd smiled, too pleased to say anything more interesting. "I feel her here today too."

Ethan's bruises were almost faded, but while he'd given up the crutches he still had a limp. Christopher had Lincoln balanced on his broad shoulders and they both smiled, revealing matching sets of dimples. How had Sadie never noticed Lincoln inherited those from her father until this very moment?

Annette and Melissa were having an ever so polite showdown,

in which both women were using their hips to bump the other a little farther back, trying to get the coveted spot closest to Sadie.

"That's my daughter-in-law!" Annette was saying to anyone remotely close to her periphery as Melissa chimed in, "And my *daughter*, of course."

Sadie giggled—seriously, what world was she living in?

From the schoolhouse lighting to the checkered floors, she was so proud of this space, and sensed her grandmother would have loved it, too. The walls were full of old memories and soon so many new, wonderful ones would be created within them.

And her work at the Old Red Mill had only just begun. The notion filled her with such happiness, such *purpose*, she thought her heart might burst. Her next assignments? Designing new spaces for both Castaway Yarns and Chickadee Studios. Her little chat with Essie had turned her brainstorm into a reality. It didn't take much convincing to get the businesses to relocate to the Old Red Mill. The insurance money didn't hurt either.

"The way we see it, we're going to take our lemons and make lemonade," Jill told her over brunch, as Bree's boss, Nina, nodded. "Essie persuaded us the hurricane was simply clearing the path for bigger, better things."

"So, what do you say?" Nina smiled. "Will you help us design our shops?"

"I'd be honored," Sadie replied.

When was the last time she'd felt this excited?

The baby kicked, seemingly in agreement, and Sadie instinctively rubbed her hand over her abdomen.

"When are you due?" Alexis Vogel, a reporter for *The Bog*, walked over. "Has it been difficult juggling parenthood while starting your own business? How are you balancing it all?"

Sadie fought an eye roll. The kid meant well. But seriously, would anyone ever ask Ethan this question?

Not in a million years.

Hester's was much more Renee's business than Sadie's—they'd agreed to split the profits seventy-thirty—but Sadie was certainly working a full-time schedule when she considered all the hours she was putting in on the rest of the Old Red Mill's renovations. She'd been talking about taking over as special event manager once all the stores were up and running. There was so much potential at the mill, from holiday events to catered parties and even weddings.

"I'm due in November," Sadie smiled. "And honestly? Being a working mother suits me pretty damn well. I love my children *and* my job. There's no way to be a perfect mom, but this is my way to be a good one."

And with a full heart, she walked to the front of the crowd, toward her future.

Chapter Thirty-Two

"M om! Look over here! That's it, strike a pose. I love what you're serving here." Tansy put her new Instax camera to her eye and snapped another Polaroid-esque photo. Wearing her knit violet dress and favorite denim jacket, her daughter looked like herself again.

"Dude." One of her high school band friends walked over. "Your mom is the coolest."

"Well, duh," Tansy replied with a wink and Renee couldn't hold back the ear-to-ear grin.

Renee looked around, taking it all in. Sadie was busy chatting with high school friends. Dot Turner was talking Dan's ear off about resting heart rates and Sadie's dad was clapping people on the back right and left. A pretty perfect scene.

"Hey, sorry to stop all the chitchat, but if we could have our families please join us up in the front," Sadie called over the crowd, motioning for Ethan, Lincoln, Annette, and her parents to come forward. Renee did the same with Tansy, Bree, and Dan. *Her* people.

"I always knew you could do it," Dan whispered in Renee's ear, his warm breath sending a delicious shiver down her spine.

"Yeah?" She smiled up at him. "Well, now I believe it myself."

It was mind-boggling how many people had shown up for Hester's grand opening. She'd made at least fifty pies praying that she wouldn't have *too* many left over, and it turned out that she could have baked four times as many and not had nearly enough.

Renee cleared her throat. "If you'll all humor me, I have a few words." The crowd grew quiet. "We would not be here today if it wasn't for the love and support of not only Cranberry Cove, but of those closest to us. They've put up with a lot of long hours and done a lot of the heavy lifting as we embraced this dream, and we will be forever grateful." Renee slung one arm around Bree and the other around Tansy. She caught Essie Park's gaze in the audience. "And we certainly wouldn't be here if a certain real estate agent wasn't so darn persistent."

Everyone laughed, and Essie gave a delicate wave fitting of Queen Elizabeth basking in the attention.

"Thanks to every single one of you for believing in Hester's and the Old Red Mill. And for believing in *us*," Sadie chimed in. "This town is such a special place. Not only do we get to enjoy the best beach in all of New England—not that I'm biased or anything—but the most amazing people in the whole world call this place home. This is a town that looks out for each other and we have each other's backs. I know and appreciate that more than ever."

Tears prickled Renee's eyes as she watched Ethan kiss the top of Sadie's head and heard him whisper a hoarse "I love you." She saw them nod toward Officer Tyler, who tipped his hat in reply.

Her next-door neighbors were going to be okay. Her sister was going to be fine—she had to, there was no other option here.

After offering up a silent prayer, she took a step forward. "We want everyone to feel welcome here, at Hester's in particular, but also at the entire Old Red Mill. This is going to be a space for everyone to gather, whether that's over a slice of pie, while searching for the perfect shade of yarn at Castaway's, exploring their artistic abilities at a pinot-and-painting event at Chickadee, or taking a break on a nature walk. This old mill can teach us new lessons about family, friends, and community. We hope you'll all become regulars."

Everyone clapped and cheered.

"We'd like our children to do the honors of cutting the ribbon," she said as Sadie reached for Lincoln, helping him to the ground.

"Me help! And then I eat!" Lincoln shouted, making everyone laugh.

With a dramatic snip, the ribbon was cut.

Hester's was officially open for business.

Renee's heart was full of love, hope, fear all mixed up together to create this one unique moment. This was her life.

"Now, who wants a piece of pie?" she asked.

About The Author

Sarah Mackenzie lives and writes in New England.